D0425715

THE
YEAR
AFTER
YOU

THE YEAR AFTER YOU

NINA DE PASS

DELACORTE PRESS

Text copyright © 2019 by Nina de Pass
Jacket art copyright © 2020 by Elena Pancorbo

All rights reserved. Published in the United States by Delacorte Press, an imprint of Random House Children's Books, a division of Penguin Random House LLC, New York. Originally published in paperback in the United Kingdom by Ink Road, an imprint of Black & White Publishing, Edinburgh, in 2019.

Delacorte Press is a registered trademark and the colophon is a trademark of Penguin Random House LLC.

Visit us on the Web! GetUnderlined.com

Educators and librarians, for a variety of teaching tools, visit us at RHTeachersLibrarians.com

Library of Congress Cataloging-in-Publication Data
Names: Pass, Nina de, author.
Title: The year after you / Nina de Pass.
Description: First American edition. | New York : Delacorte Press, 2019. | "Originally published in paperback by Black & White Publishing, Edinburgh, in 2019." | Summary: Cara, consumed by survivor's guilt after her best friend is killed in a car accident, is not convinced attending a boarding school in Switzerland will make any difference, but new friends Ren and Hector hope to break down her emotional walls.
Identifiers: LCCN 2019003342 | ISBN 978-0-593-12076-7 (hc) | ISBN 978-0-593-12077-4 (glb) | ISBN 978-0-593-12078-1 (ebook)
Subjects: | CYAC: Emotional problems—Fiction. | Friendship—Fiction. | Boarding schools—Fiction. | Schools—Fiction.
Classification: LCC PZ7.1.P3745 Ye 2019 | DDC [Fic]—dc23

The text of this book is set in 11.5-point Granjon.
Interior design by Michelle Gengaro

Printed in the United States of America
10 9 8 7 6 5 4 3 2 1
First American Edition

Random House Children's Books supports the First Amendment and celebrates the right to read.

To Clem, with love

THE
YEAR
AFTER
YOU

1

If I'd known the temperature in exile would be this low, I'd have found it within me to put up more of a fight. Even if there was anyone to hear me now, the time for protest has come and gone; I'm a very long way from home.

I allow the minutes to pass, watching as the soft, sticky snow is caught in the wind outside the taxi and, on its descent, is forced back high into the air.

The driver my mother arranged to meet me at the airport, perhaps mistaking my silence for fascination, seems to decide it's safe to speak. "Excited for your new school?" he asks, the words barely decipherable through his thick French accent.

I don't reply at once, allowing my finger to slide across the misted glass of the window. When I eventually do, I don't bother to curb the sarcasm in my voice, knowing that the language barrier will mask it anyway. *"Excited?"*

I don't know why I phrase my response as a question. I don't want to invite him to have a conversation with me, or for anything he says to be memorable. I want to forget him, just like I want to forget everything else.

He laughs nervously before continuing. "Is it your first time in Switzerl—"

The end of his question is lost. I watch in horror as he swerves out of the path of an oncoming truck and closer to the edge of the winding, narrow road up the mountainside. There are no barriers to the waiting abyss below, and I feel my body tense as I clutch at the door handle. Every muscle turns to glass as the car, losing its grip on the icy road, coasts to the right. I close my eyes, waiting for impact. Time converts to slow motion, and I wait to hear the screams. For the world to blur out of focus. For the earsplitting pop of the airbags deploying. For the pain.

For a split second, I feel euphoric. Maybe I won't survive this time.

Instead, I feel the car veer back to the left, away from danger, and am drawn into real time as the driver resumes his nervous laugh. He sounds the horn too late, when the truck is a dot in the distance, and I catch him looking at me in the rearview mirror. "Crazy drivers," he says with a repentant smile.

I don't smile back, anxiously tracing my fingers over the frayed edges of the seat belt, and find my most unforgiving stare. "Just keep your eyes on the road," I snap.

—

In the hour that follows, the driver tries again to engage me in conversation, but this time I ignore him, not bothering to disguise my hostility. I keep my eyes off the encircling Swiss mountains, focusing on bringing all my fear-frozen limbs back to life. Trying not to think about what could have happened. Or about the part of me that momentarily welcomed it.

My mind is filled instead with a memory from eight months ago, when I woke up one morning in the hospital back in California to the sound of voices. My mother and one of the nurses were trying—not particularly well—to speak in hushed tones.

"Cara's psychiatrist, Dr. Burns, wants us to keep her in for a few more nights to observe her," the nurse said.

My mother, probably irritated by the inconvenience of my prolonged stay (the hospital was over an hour from where we lived), responded sulkily. "Why on earth would she need to stay? Her injuries are physical and, as the doctor said again this morning, relatively minor. The fact that she escaped with just a broken arm is a miracle in itself. But she did—now that she's healthy enough to go home, that's where she's going."

"That's the thing, though, Mrs. Cooper—"

"Mrs. Blair," my mother interrupted—as she always does when people call her by my father's name. It took her no time at all to remarry after my father left, and even in the interim months, as I like to call them, she reverted to her maiden name.

"Sorry, Mrs. Blair," the nurse continued, "but Dr. Burns isn't convinced that Cara *is* healthy. She's concerned that your daughter is having suicidal thoughts."

I can almost imagine my mother's eyes widening in horror

at this, her glancing around to check no one we knew was in the vicinity. "My daughter is *not* suicidal!"

To her credit, the nurse's voice remained steady. "It wouldn't be surprising if she were suffering from a form of post-traumatic stress disorder. Cara has lived through a very distressing experience."

There was a long pause while my mother digested the nurse's words.

"It's a mental illness—" the nurse continued.

"I know what it is. I just don't want to hear any more," my mother cut in. "I am her legal guardian, so give me whatever forms I need to get her out of this place. Mental illness. *Honestly.* She's in shock, not mentally ill."

"It would be against medical advice," the nurse warned. "You'd have to sign a waiver."

My mother's response was curt, all attempts at whispering put aside. "Then get me that waiver."

In retrospect, two elements of this exchange stand out. Firstly, that my injuries were described as physical. The physical pain of breaking my arm in four places was nothing compared to the other pain I experience daily when I remember what else was broken that night—something metal bolts can't fix. Secondly, that this injury and the endless web of bruises that covered my body were described as minor. Nothing about the accident felt minor, and calling it so felt as though they were belittling it, making it seem as though it, in the grand scheme of things, didn't matter.

My eyes stay glued to the seat in front. I don't want to risk looking out again at the scene whipping past the windows. The fact that I have gotten this far in my journey is a near miracle. Even so, I'm at the limits of my endurance and am relieved when I register the car slowing. As soon as we stop, I fling myself out into the open, hiding my hands behind my back so the driver won't see they're still shaking.

"Your destination," he says, gesturing up to the large building.

It looks more like a Russian palace than a school: a flat-fronted, sky-blue façade of a building at least six stories high, with three golden domes on the roof. There are crumbling touches of the same gold paint around symmetrical, old-fashioned windows, and on the ground-floor level, mint-green and white-striped awnings protrude. I turn around, with the extravagant structure behind me, and look out at the view. There is a cable-car station to my right. I follow the wire supporting the still, suspended carriages until it is swallowed by a small town on a nearby mountainside.

Now that my feet are firmly on solid ground, the descent between the two peaks doesn't feel quite so perilous. The school itself does feel like a slight safety hazard, though; it's dangerously close to the edge of the mountain, with just a waist-high pale blue iron fence to keep everyone penned in. Even then, as I notice the elaborate twists of the metal, it feels more like a decorative feature than a precautionary one.

"Should I bring this in for you?" the driver asks as he unloads my luggage.

"I'm fine," I say quickly, pulling the one duffel bag I brought with me from his grasp and hauling it over my shoulder. At the last minute I look back and murmur a hesitant "Thanks."

He looks startled, so I turn away from him and head toward the entrance. As I get closer, two figures come into focus: a girl and a boy of around my age. The girl has a long stream of dark red hair that falls below her shoulders. Her skin is fair, like mine, but covered with freckles. The boy at her side is at least a head taller and lanky, but with a round, childish face and white-blond hair.

"Let me take that," the boy says, gesturing to my bag. His words sound strange and unfamiliar, tinted with another accent—perhaps something Scandinavian.

"I've got it," I say, then instantly regret it. This is exactly what my mother warned me not to do. *It'll be a clean slate for you,* she reasoned. *Nobody will know you there—you can go back to being yourself again.* Her words had extinguished what was left of my fight. Surely she knows as well as I do that there is no going back. Yet now, despite the fact that I can't fathom how I'll pull it off, I resolve to try to seem normal in front of these strangers. I can't smile, so I adjust my expression to the brightest one I know.

"Welcome to Hope Hall," the girl says.

2

"*Everyone is in the conservatory—that's why it's so quiet,*" *the girl* says with the faintest hint of a French accent. "I'm Ren, by the way, and this is Fred." She gestures to the tall blond boy, who starts to give me an awkward wave, then pulls his hand down to his side as though he's thought better of it.

"Cara," I say, and they nod in unison. They know this, of course: they're my welcome committee. I wonder just how much they know about me.

"As I mentioned, everyone is doing prep, so it's the perfect time for a tour."

"Prep?"

"Oh, sorry! I always forget some of the words we use sound a bit odd," she exclaims with what seems to be genuine enthusiasm. I can't help thinking she's unusually pretty—just not in an obvious way. Her porcelain cheeks are tinged with pink from waiting out in the cold, the only blemish on her otherwise flaw-less skin. She's petite, a few inches shorter than me, with a thin face and round, chocolate-brown eyes that make her look over-eager. "God, sorry, and now I'm making you feel more alienated for being new—"

"Ren, relax," Fred says. He's so tall that he towers over both of us, and when he speaks, he uses swooping hand gestures that teeter on awkward, like he doesn't quite know what to do with such long, spindly arms.

"Sorry," she says. "I always talk at a million kilometers an hour when I'm nervous—"

"Prep means homework," Fred cuts in, suddenly businesslike, relieving Ren of what I imagine would be a wordy explanation. "It's between seven and eight every evening. All year groups do it in the conservatory, so we'll have free run of the place for the next forty-five minutes or so. We should probably get going, actually. Leave your bag here, and we'll come back and get it in a bit."

Ren looks on gratefully as I let my bag slide off my shoulder and follow Fred farther into the school.

Forty-five minutes isn't even close to being enough time to tour the place. We start on the ground floor, making our way across dark-stained floorboards toward the classrooms. Like the school in its totality, nothing is generic about these rooms. Each one is drastically different—a mishmash of odd, old-fashioned furniture and different arrangements of around ten desks per classroom. They seem to all contain a fireplace or log burner, giving out their last dregs of heat at the end of the day.

Everything is at odds with the associations of school that I'm used to—the metal detectors back home, the routine locker searches, the plastic chairs and white hallways. It disorients me, tilting everything I've come to know and making my already fragile composure harder to hold on to.

We eventually walk out into a large, square courtyard, glistening with ice, at the back of the building. The school is built in an extended U shape, with this courtyard marking the center of that U. It's framed on three sides by six floors of building, the fourth side composed of a wall backing up to the ever-darkening grounds, a lit path just visible through a stone arch carved in the center. I instantly realize what they meant by the conservatory. In the middle part of the building, the wall bordering the courtyard has been replaced by a glass one, rising at least five stories, made up of hundreds of individual panes. Every now and then, one of the clear glass panes has been swapped for a colored one. Through the glass, lit up from the inside, I can see into a vast, old-fashioned library that hasn't been split into floors.

"The conservatory," Fred says.

I feel him watching me closely as I nod, turning away from the numerous other stares no doubt directed our way. "How many students are there here?"

"Just over two hundred."

"That few," I say. "There were more than that in just my grade back home."

"You'll find that won't be the only difference here."

"The sports hall is over there," Ren says, leading me to the stone arch at the back of the courtyard and pointing to a modern structure in the distance, only partly visible through thick trees. "And then, through here is the dining hall." She pushes hard against double doors adjacent to the conservatory window, which don't budge. "Damn."

Fred jogs over to the conservatory window to get someone's attention, and I tuck my coat closer around me. There is a gap between my jeans and sneakers, and the biting cold sears my exposed skin.

"It doesn't usually snow at this time of year," Ren says, gesturing to the light dusting of snow that floats lazily around us and is starting to collect on the window ledges. "Normally we get to November with a bit of green still showing."

Fred appears back at our side just as one of the doors gives way.

A dark-haired boy holds it open for us. "Ah, if it's not our new inmate—the U.S. transfer," he says, his voice low and oddly loaded. I slip past him inside to the warmth, only looking up properly at him when we're inside. He's tall, with olive skin, high cheekbones, and swampy green eyes. A flash of something like recognition floods through me, but I cast it aside, as I definitely haven't met him before.

"You're from California, right?" he prompts, holding my gaze.

I tear my eyes from him, nodding once, and Ren is quick to introduce us. "Cara, this is Hector. He's in our year."

I mutter a brief and unenthusiatic "Hi."

"Well, we should get going. We've still got to get to the dorms before prep is over," Ren says. Even though the boy hasn't said anything else, I can feel him assessing me. I briefly consider telling him that he won't like what he finds.

"You're right," says Fred, turning to pat the other boy on the shoulder in a brotherly gesture. "Thanks, Hec."

Hector doesn't turn back as he stalks toward the conservatory, instead holding a hand up in the air in dismissal. He keeps his voice at the same volume, which strikes me as very self-assured, like he doesn't have to question whether his words will reach us as he says, "For you, Fred, anything."

I turn back to the dining room, relieved that Hector's gone. The walls are paneled in thick, dark wood, and dozens of circular tables, covered with blue and gold tablecloths, are already laid out for breakfast. I look around, wondering where the serving area is, expecting to see piles of trays, cash registers . . . anything familiar. I might as well be in a restaurant.

Fred clears his throat. "We eat at eight a.m., twelve-thirty p.m., and six p.m. Oh, and afternoon tea—which, if you ask the headmaster, is nonnegotiable—is in the conservatory."

I raise my eyebrows.

He flashes me his first, brief smile. "You'll see. Anyway, Ren will show you the dorms—I'm not allowed in the girls' wing— but I'll see you around."

"Okay, thanks," I say limply.

When he's out of sight, I feel an empty sort of dread. Now that the tour is almost over, the reality has begun to set in. And the reality of all these new people, places, and rules is unavoidable. Back in the front hall, I grab my bag from inside the door and follow Ren toward an old-fashioned elevator, a gilded cage in the center of a grand staircase, circling up and around it like a spring. At the last minute, I freeze, catching her attention as she calls the elevator.

"Everything okay?" she asks.

"How many floors up are we going?" I keep my eyes fixed on the stairs. "Could we not . . ." I let my words trail off, embarrassed.

She looks confused for a moment, then, in time with the clattering of the elevator's arrival, gestures to my bag and says, "Hand me that and we'll send it up." She pulls the gated doors shut on it, and we watch as it travels above our heads.

She starts trudging up the stairs, and I follow her in admiration and gratitude. How many other people wouldn't have asked why I wouldn't get in the elevator? I decide to try to seem a bit nicer, even just for her, when she doesn't complain as we climb six flights right to the top floor.

"Left side is for boys," she says, her breath heavy as she collects my bag from the elevator. "Right side is for us."

We turn into the girls' corridor, a long, blue-carpeted hallway with doors lining either side. A typed card with the names of the inhabitants is stuck in the center of each door. Ren leads me right to the end of the corridor, where my name has been hastily scribbled underneath a solitary name: *Bérénice de Laure.*

"You're with me," she says, examining my reaction closely. "I hope that's all right?"

"Short straw for you, then," I say flatly. It is a lame, halfhearted attempt at a joke.

She ignores it. "I have to help the younger years get ready for bed. I'll leave you to unpack, but I'll be back in a bit."

I watch her go, deflated. I hadn't considered that I would be sharing a room. I go inside and feel like I've stepped into a chalet. There are two raised single beds across from each other, with wooden ladders leading up to them and desks carved into the hollows underneath. My side is empty except for a neat pile of school uniforms. Ren's side is chaotic—a corkboard over the desk is covered with photographs that branch out past the frame and onto the wall. I trace the faces in the pictures with my finger. Fred is a common feature, as is the other boy, Hector, who let us into the dining room. In the center of the desk is a silver-framed photograph from which two people, presumably Ren's parents, stare out at me. I turn away, realizing how different my side of the room will be when I've unpacked. I've brought only one photograph with me, and it's not one I'm willing to put on display.

I take my time unpacking, feeding my pants through hangers and matching up my shoes so that they sit exactly even with each other in the bottom of the wardrobe. From the loud, unguarded chatter seeping through the cracks in the door, it's clear that prep is over.

About half an hour after Ren leaves, there is a firm knock on the door, which is pushed open before I can answer. A round, elderly woman enters.

"You must be Cara," she says in an Australian accent. Her voice is stern and gravelly. For a second, I wonder whether she's going to be one of those hateful teachers from the books I read as a kid. Then, as we make eye contact, something about her softens. Her eyes are a brilliant periwinkle blue, youthful and conspiratorial despite her lined face and short crop of thick gray hair. "I'm Madame James, your housemother. I'll be in charge of your pastoral care while you're here with us. I'm sorry I wasn't here to welcome you when you arrived—hopefully Ren and Fred did the tour with you."

"Yes."

"Ren's a good one to have around. She'll look after you." Madame James gestures to the pile of clothes on my desk. "I see you've got your uniform—that's good. Ren'll take you through everything else. But if you have any questions or are worried about anything at all, come and find me. My room is directly below this one, on the fifth floor, and my door is always open." She tilts her head, appraising me with something close to pity; I immediately look away. "What I want, above everything, is for you to be happy here. We don't have much time with you, so we'll have to make the most of it."

"I'm here for an entire year," I say, still looking away from her.

"It'll fly by, dear. A year is nothing at all."

I feel my face fall. A year is *everything*. If I think about all the things that have happened in the last year . . . If I think about how long the last few months have felt . . .

Ren pushes open the door, and Madame James takes this as her signal to leave. I sense them having some form of silent exchange, so I turn my back and begin unfolding and refolding my uniforms. There are two navy moleskin skirts that I expect will fall to just above the knee as Ren's does, four white scallop-collared long-sleeved shirts, two round-necked navy sweaters, and several pairs of dark blue tights.

"It's a good look," Ren says with a wry smile, moving up beside me. Her expression softens. "You probably want a bath after such a long trip—come on, I'll show you where the bathroom is."

I follow her back into the corridor. This time it's full of girls, loitering and chatting with their doors propped open. When we pass, their laughter quiets, and I feel the curious gazes trace my steps. Ren pulls open a door halfway down, not paying them any attention. At least ten sinks line one wall opposite a row of baths without any curtains. The lack of privacy unnerves me; I'd expected cubicles, at least.

As we enter, two girls wrap their towels tighter around themselves. "You could have knocked," one of them says in a haughty American accent.

"Sorry," Ren replies, not sounding particularly apologetic. "This is Cara; I'm just showing her around."

The girl who spoke looks between us with an expression I can't quite decipher.

"I'm Joy," she finally says. "This is Hannah." She gestures lazily to the other girl, who looks on unsmilingly.

They both have eerily polished black hair, and I recognize them as the girls you find in every school—the popular ones. Seeing them here, and judging from their stares, it is clear Ren is not one of them. Strangely, I feel an immediate, instinctive loyalty to

Ren, so instead of trying to make friends, as I'm sure would be the thing to do with everyone at this point, I stare back and pointedly say nothing.

I see them for who they are—after all, who'd know them better than me? Up until nine months ago, I was them. It's vaguely reassuring to find that five thousand miles from home some things never change. I was the girl who'd wake up early to blow-dry my hair perfectly before class, who made sure to keep my highlights touched up. My makeup was always flawless, my clothes on trend. I wonder what people back home would think of me now: pale, barefaced with barely blond hair, wearing ripped jeans and a baggy sweatshirt. I wonder what Joy and Hannah are thinking of me.

Back then, I would have cared, but now, something about their sense of superiority—their entitlement—repulses me. Because the truth is, I know how this works: they're about to make their minds up, waiting for me to answer so they can judge where I sit in the pecking order, whether it's worth their time to befriend me. When I don't say anything, Joy's eyes narrow.

I turn to Ren. "Are there no showers?"

She shakes her head. "I could guard the door?"

"Well, the two of you holed up in here will give us all something to talk about," Joy says, beckoning the other girl to follow her into the corridor. As she passes, she puts a hand on my arm in what I guess is supposed to be a gesture of camaraderie. I pull it back, cradling it possessively. She shrugs. "Or maybe you're into that sort of thing . . ."

I turn to Ren, whose chocolate-brown eyes are nervous as the door clicks closed. "Your response to that was a test," she says in a quiet voice, "and you just failed."

I shake my head with indifference. "Don't worry about me."

After a very quick bath during which Ren dutifully sits with her back to me reading, feet pressed against the door to prevent anyone entering, we get into bed. Our light is already off when Madame James comes around for lights-out at eleven.

I press my palms to my face in the darkness, wondering if now is the time I'll finally find tears. Predictably there are none, yet the sadness is so acute it chokes me. I squeeze my eyes shut in another pointless attempt to block it all out, and hear Ren's breaths level and fall into a steady rhythm as she is pulled into the haven of sleep. I'll be there soon, I promise myself. It won't be long until I'm enveloped by painless nothingness. Yet sleep doesn't feel close enough; my mind is whirling. How will I be able to disguise my sadness here? How will I answer their questions about why I'm here for just the final year of school? What happens if we have to go somewhere by car again?

I can't. I can't. *I can't.*

I push myself down the ladder and as silently as possible sift through my toiletry bag. The sleeping pills the doctor gave me back in California aren't here; my mother must have taken them out after I packed them. I fight the urge to scream, before eventually—furiously—finding my way back to bed.

Blurred shapes come to life through the thick cloud of night in the dorm. When I let my eyes adjust, I count ten turquoise glow-in-the-dark stars fixed to the ceiling above Ren's bed. I begin to count them again and again, like I used to count sheep as a child, soothed and bored by the monotony.

After what feels like hours of empty time, the blackness finally swallows me.

3

My sleep is different here: fitful, temporary, but uneventful. Back home, waking up meant one of two things. Some days, there were moments, just after I woke up but before the world came into focus, when I felt almost peaceful. That was before the wave, before the crashing realization of what had happened bore down over me. The other days were worse, when I woke straight from the dreams, the reconstructions of that night.

Those days I woke up screaming.

When I got home from the hospital and had to sleep without any of the pain medication, I quickly decided I couldn't put myself through either outcome, instead losing a whole chunk of my life to never sleeping for fear of remembering, for fear of having to go through it all again. But not sleeping didn't help: being awake for so long distorted everything. There were moments when I was sure I was going mad—mad enough for my mother to take me back to the emergency room, where I was given sleeping pills that were heavy-duty enough to ensure my sleep was dreamless. And, after a while, dreamless sleep became a way to hide. There was infinite beauty in not remembering. Even though my mother took to rationing the pills, sleep was my solace.

But today, as the morning sun begins to seep through the cracks in the curtains, waking up seems easy. Perhaps it's jet lag, or perhaps it's uncertainty? All I know is I can't lie here for much longer.

I look down at my bare arms on top of the white duvet, pinning me inside. In the dimly lit room my scar is all the more noticeable, a jagged burgundy line from wrist to elbow, a reminder that I am here, and I was there. This I will have to cover at all costs. It was dark when Ren and I put our pajamas on last night, but still it was careless of me. I look at Ren's untroubled sleeping form. I mustn't let my guard down with her, or anyone else; otherwise there will be no point at all to this experiment of my mother's.

It's early, but still I dress quickly and head to the bathroom. As I expected, it's empty; yet, even though I'm finally—properly—alone, I feel claustrophobic. I open the window a crack and let the icy air trickle into the room. The radiator beneath the window is on, so I sit with my back to it and turn on my phone for the first time since the flight. It buzzes for at least a minute, filling up with messages. I scroll through them absently; they're all from my mother. Of course they are. I've long given up hope of getting any from anyone else. I delete the voice mails without listening to them and pull up the final text.

> I've spoken to the school. They say you arrived safely.
> A little acknowledgment of my messages would be
> appreciated, Cara. I know you're there xxx

I write a quick reply to sedate her.

> I'm here, as you already know. What more do you
> want me to say?

She knows as well as I do, there is *nothing* left to say.

I press send before I have time to overthink it and go through the earlier messages, shaking my head as they become more and more urgent.

> Are you there yet?
> Send me a message when your plane lands.
> Honey! Where are you?

I delete every one. *Don't forget you sent me here, Mum. You banished your only daughter over five thousand miles away.*

Now that my inbox is clear of my mother's messages, only one thread remains. The last message I received was in December last year.

> I'll pick you up at 8.

I call her. It goes straight to voice mail, her voice trilling out, a mixture of laughter and embarrassment. *Hi! You've reached G.*

I'm not here—obviously—but you know what to do. Beep. I hang up. Then dial again. After the tenth time, my hands shake so much I have to put the phone down on the floor. I let my head rest on my knees and take deep, long breaths as one of my many therapists taught me. I saw a string of them last year. My mother, a firm alumna of the school of self-help, had finally relented at my stepfather's request. I'd heard his pleas: *It's not healthy for her to spend all that time alone in her room. She hasn't even cried since it happened, has she? She needs someone to talk to, seeing as she won't talk to you and me.* So off I went, sent to spend the first of a series of unbearable hours in front of a therapist set on chipping away at my guard, desperate to figure out what was going on inside my head.

The sessions taught me a few things:

1. Therapists want progress, and you can fabricate progress.
2. Therapists are disposable, and since my mother doesn't believe in them anyway, it became easy to get her to give up on one when I'd had enough.

And finally:

3. Sometimes, just sometimes, they say something of note and it works. Like put your head between your knees and breathe deeply until you regain control.

However, to maintain points 1 and 2, it's crucial that point 3 is kept secret from said therapist in order to avoid another wave of psychoanalysis. And psychoanalysis must be avoided at all costs.

There is commotion in the corridor. I glance back at my phone and light up the screen. It's 7:30 a.m.—much later than I thought. I shakily pull myself off the floor, and as I head back to my dorm, I run straight into Madame James.

"You're up early," she says brightly, banging on one of the dorm doors with her fist. "Wakey wakey, girls!" Her eyes flick down to the phone in my hand. "Ah, I'm afraid you'll have to give that to me. I should have got it from you last night. We have a no-phones policy here, but there is a phone box in the common room that you can use if you need to make a call outside school hours."

I hand it over freely. In fact, a part of me feels relieved.

"Do you want to jot down any numbers you might need before I take it?" she asks in surprise. Most people probably put up more of a fight. But then again, most people probably have people they want to stay in touch with. I shake my head. "Okay, then. Have a good first day!"

I try to adjust my expression to replicate her enthusiasm, then go to find Ren.

I've grown up in a household where breakfast is a time for quiet. It is the only time my mother, who will happily chatter her way through the remainder of the day, doesn't utter a word. And so I have always thought of it as a sacred time, when even the smallest notion of conversation is met with a death stare. Here, however, those rules don't apply. The dining room is packed and alive, and as I pass by noisy tables with my head bowed, I can't help but feel out of my element.

Ren and I stop next to an empty table for four, and I choose a seat facing the window, where I'll have my back to the rest of the room. Ren points to the dark paneled walls, which, since last night, have been adorned with bunting made up of miniature French flags.

"I thought the primary language here was English?" I ask, alarmed. This was, after all, my first defense back in California. I told my mother I couldn't possibly go to a school in Switzerland. I'd never been any good at languages—did she really care so little about me that she'd send me somewhere I wouldn't understand anyone?

"It is," Ren says calmly, "but there are students here from thirty-one different countries. Each week is dedicated to one of those cultures. There are special activities, and the kitchen staff theme their menus accordingly. This week it's France." She smiles gleefully at me. "The best."

I stare down at the table, and sure enough, a basket of croissants and mini brioches sits in prime place. A woman wearing a pale blue apron meanders between tables, refilling the emptying baskets from a silver serving platter balanced between her arm and hip.

"We don't have long," Ren says, smothering a croissant with

apricot jam. "We have to be in the auditorium at eight-fifteen, so I'd grab something while you can."

"What's happening at eight-fifteen?" I ask tentatively, pouring myself a glass of juice to give myself something to do.

She takes a large bite of her croissant before speaking. "The Monday meeting. It's like an assembly: the whole school gathers together, and the headmaster runs through anything of note for the week ahead." Another opportunity for the whole school to gawk at the new girl, then. Ren must notice my expression change, because she adds, "Don't worry. We'll keep a low profile."

True to her word, when we leave the dining room and make our way outside, through the stone archway in the courtyard and along the path I glimpsed last night, Ren doesn't do anything to draw attention to us. We advance toward the sports hall, skirting it at the last minute and heading into another modern structure right at the edge of the mountain. Like the sports hall, it's hidden from sight by thick evergreens that look like they've been dusted with powdered sugar. I wonder if these two modern buildings are purposely concealed so they don't ruin the otherwise old-fashioned feel of the school.

My breath catches in my throat when we enter. The auditorium is a semicircular room with a ceiling three times the height of a normal room. Its curved side is made of glass, a vast window to the precipice and mountains beyond. The space is unimaginably bright; the sparkling white mountains reflect the sunlight back through the glass. I have to squint to see the stage in front of the window.

Ren gestures to the top of the tiered seating facing the stage. "Let's find a seat at the back."

I nod and follow her up a set of metal stairs, our footsteps echoing loudly, announcing our presence. I force myself to climb faster, wanting to disappear, to just melt into the background. We sit for a while in silence, watching the rest of the auditorium fill up, until a figure vaults up the stairs toward us.

"Why weren't you at breakfast?" Ren asks the boy I met last night, Hector, when he stops at our row.

"You know what Mondays are like," he replies with an air of resignation, taking the empty seat next to me. "Always tricky to get His Majesty out of bed."

He pokes his thumb in Fred's direction; he is tramping up the stairs toward us at a much slower pace. When he reaches us, he is bleary-eyed, with hair that definitely hasn't seen a brush yet today. He gives us all a silent nod as he slumps down in the seat next to Hector.

Hector casually unwraps three croissants from a paper napkin on his lap. He twists in his seat. I feel his deep green eyes considering me for a moment, then he points between the napkin and me. "Pain au chocolat?" he says in an exaggerated French accent. I shake my head. "One of the only good things about French food, if you ask me."

Ren leans forward in her seat and looks at him with a half-amused, half-exasperated expression. "No one is asking you, thankfully."

He presses his lips together, the corners twitching provocatively, but at that moment, quiet starts to filter up the seating.

A tall, slim man with mousy hair and thick, black-rimmed glasses walks toward the stage.

"That's Mr. King, the headmaster," Ren whispers.

Mr. King moves center stage and starts speaking French that even I can tell is pretty basic. He switches to American English with an apologetic expression and starts to acknowledge the week's events. I hear mention of a boules tournament taking place that evening, a French film screening on Thursday for anyone interested. I glance sideways to where Ren sits very upright, listening politely. On my other side, Hector seems to be paying more attention to the pain au chocolat he's sharing with Fred. I zone out, picking a faraway spot in the distant mountains and projecting all my focus onto it.

"So what's your story?" Hector asks when the headmaster steps down from the stage and the room is filled with chatter again. I sense his eyes boring into me again, trying to work me out.

"My story?" I repeat with engineered indifference, and for a moment I'm distracted by his face. I hadn't realized how good-looking he is—someone who probably would have affected me before. "There's really nothing to say."

I force myself to look at him while I say this, keeping my face blank and unreadable. I underestimate the force of eye contact. I have been mostly alone for so many months, and there is something oddly intimate about the way he holds my gaze.

"Sure," Hector says, his voice a deep drawl, and I know my answer isn't good enough for him. As we start to trudge down the metal steps, he lowers his voice so only I can hear him. "I will get it out of you, you know."

My stomach knots and I suppress the urge to flee.

"You won't," I murmur back with a fierceness that hasn't been around for a while.

He gives me a swift, searching look, but I just shake my head. *Really, you won't.*

4

I somehow manage to get through my first day of lessons, finally finding a reason to be thankful that my mother forced me to do the International Baccalaureate when we first moved to the U.S. She'd said back then it was because I might want to go to an English university and spend time with my dad later on— how could she have predicted that it would come in handy for her a year early? While I am grateful for it today, for the ease of transferring to Hope, it's also the only reason she was able to send me here. If I'd been in the American school system, transferring to Europe for my final year of schooling would have been close to impossible. I'd still be back in California, working from home, submitting assignments and teaching myself from textbooks so I could stay in school without actually having to face everyone. Then again, maybe my teachers' patience for my situation would have wavered by now and they'd have made me come back. I'd have dropped out before I did that, which is probably what my mother was afraid of.

"People's tolerance wears thin," she'd said. I'd always assumed she'd been talking about her own.

Ren spends the day dutifully chaperoning me to classes, and by the time she drops me off in prep, I've started to worry about her own tolerance. I sure as hell wouldn't have been as patient with someone as quiet as me. And yet, when she leaves me outside the conservatory to go to the art room with the promise that she won't be long, she looks almost apologetic.

The conservatory is already full of students dotted around at long, rectangular tables over four different levels. It is even more majestic than it seemed from the outside—wooden spiral staircases lead up to each level on thick bands of balcony. The walls are lined with floor-to-ceiling bookshelves on every floor. The room is warmly lit with yellow freestanding lamps, and I loiter awkwardly next to one with a blue tasseled lampshade that is crooked and dented out of shape, like it has been knocked a few too many times by passersby.

The inquisitive looks this morning, the other students wondering who the girl who arrived a week late to school was, have started to fade. After a while, I recognize familiar faces at nearby tables—an upside to starting at a small school, I suppose. But I'm conscious that the more I linger out in the open, the more curiosity I'll arouse.

"Come and sit over here," a voice calls out.

I search for the source of the voice: the two girls I met in the bathroom last night, Joy and Hannah, are sitting at a table by the window. I move toward them against my better judgment. Better than being stranded.

"Sit down," Joy commands.

I do as she says because I can't think of a good reason not to, but my minute sense of gratitude quickly fades.

"Hannah and I have been talking," she continues before I can think of something to say.

I look over at Hannah, who nods with a fixed, rapturous look on her face.

"We think you deserve to know . . ."

"Deserve to know what?" I ask, a swooping feeling of foreboding in my stomach.

"Well," Joy starts up again, "we realize you didn't have any say over who you shared a dorm with. I mean, no one has wanted to share with Ren for years; it's not your fault she was the only one with a spare bed."

I watch them both, surprised by the flicker of irritation within me.

Joy leans toward me across the table, inviting my confidence, like she's doing me the honor of letting me in on their secret. "Ren . . . well, she doesn't have many friends. . . . None of the girls like her."

I don't miss the implication behind her words. There's truth there, of course. From what I've seen, Ren only seems to hang out with Fred and Hector. So what Joy is saying is that Ren is a boys' girl, right? But that doesn't quite sit right with me either.

I lean back in my chair, annoyed that Hannah is just sitting there, rapping her perfectly manicured fingers on the table between us, letting Joy speak for them both. "Thanks, but I think I'll make up my own mind about Ren."

There's a flash of something behind Joy's eyes, then she attaches a sickly sweet smile to her face. "Oh, of course! We just thought you should know. . . . It's only fair. . . . People will wonder about you, if you know what I mean."

Before I can react, a book slams down between us, and Hector is suddenly there, towering over the table with an expression I can't quite make out.

"Evening, ladies," he says in a voice that is all charm but doesn't quite match his expression.

Joy's smile slips off her face. "What do you want?" she asks in a voice dipped in ice.

He stares indifferently at her. "I've got something of vital importance to discuss with California here, if you can spare her?"

I'm relieved, but I'm also reluctant to follow him. If I go with him now, won't he start where he left off this morning and continue to pry?

"Trust me, it's important."

I decide to risk it, so I stand up.

A nasty hiss escapes Joy's lips, but the other girl, Hannah, is the one who finally speaks, directing her words straight at me. "Don't forget what we said. . . ."

I turn away and follow Hector across the room and up one of the spiral staircases. "And what did they say?" he asks, twisting around to face me.

"Nothing interesting."

He narrows his eyes, then continues to a deserted table on one side of the second floor.

I slide onto the bench across from him, watching him busy himself with a stack of books already laid out. Hannah and Joy's table is perfectly visible from this spot; I wonder how long he waited, watching, before deciding to intervene.

"What's so important?"

He props his elbows on an open textbook and leans toward me. "Oh, nothing. You looked like you needed a hand, that's all."

"Well, thank you," I say through gritted teeth, "but I was doing just fine."

"Didn't want you stuck with the evil twins on your first day . . ."

I study him for a minute. "They don't like you."

"A fine observation," he replies, turning to the math homework we've both been given. When I don't say anything else, he looks back up and surveys me for a moment. "Joy and I had a bit of a thing," he explains. "Didn't end that well."

"You and *her*?" I don't know why my tone is tinged with surprise. The good-looking boy and the pretty, popular girl always find each other, don't they? That's what happens where I come from.

Hector clears his throat. "It was a misjudgment on my part."

I raise my eyebrows. "I'll say."

He starts to flick his pen on the desk, smirking. "Well, California, you are surely elated that you have almost survived your first day. And a full house for you, at that."

"Excuse me?"

"Well, you were in every one of my lessons."

With one last glance down at Joy and Hannah, their heads close together, I pull out my own homework and pretend to read the first question. He's right—he was. And although we haven't spoken since the meeting this morning, I've felt his curiosity across every room.

I feign disinterest. I've had enough practice to nail it down. "And your point is . . ."

He shrugs. "Spectacular first day for you, that's all."

"If you say so," I say, making sure to avoid staring at him, and his smirk, at all costs. I've known boys like him before. Before, he would have been the one to go after, but now he's the kind of person I have to avoid.

After a moment, I push my homework to one side. It's impossible to concentrate with the low echo of voices in the cavernous space. Almost the whole school seems to be here, and for a moment I'm graced with a sense of anonymity. I realize there's a certain advantage to being an unknown, one of the masses— I haven't had that feeling for a while.

"Need help?" Hector asks, gesturing to the homework and pulling my gaze from the room.

"I'm perfectly capable, thank you," I say in a clipped voice. If I could give it my attention, it would make sense to me, as math always has.

My response elicits a low laugh from him. "I'm sure you are."

I resume my attempt to ignore him, looking over at a bookshelf by the wall of glass where Fred is loitering, alternately pulling a book at random from the shelves and sending an occasional glance our way.

Hector follows my line of sight. "Subtlety is not Fred's finest quality," he says, raising a hand to beckon him over. Fred turns his back to us and pulls out another book.

"Am I being sized up?"

"He just doesn't want to get too close in case I don't decide to keep you."

It's a strange thing to say—said for a reaction. I raise my eyebrows, unable to resist responding, "You do know I am a person, not a toy."

There is a mischievous glint in his green eyes. "We'll have to see about that, won't we?"

I clench my teeth, irritated. Did he take me away from Joy and Hannah just to goad me? "Your arrogance isn't endearing you to me, you know?"

"Unequivocally," he says, drawing out the word and maintaining eye contact, as though challenging me to break it. "I'll admit I am surprised you caught on this quickly, though. Much quicker than most."

"If this is a game to you, it's pretty unoriginal."

And yet, as I say the words, I feel something else. For some reason, I find myself compelled to play it with him. For my reaction to surprise him. In fact, my reaction surprises me. There might be some fight in me left.

He laces his fingers together on the table, cracking the knuckles in quick succession. "Call it what you want. Perhaps I'm just trouble. Did you consider that?"

I stare emotionlessly at him. "Of course."

He tilts his head and holds my gaze. With his good looks, I imagine the stream of girls' answers when confronted with the same question. *I'm sure that's not true. . . . You're just pretending to be trouble to cover up who you really are.* I don't give him the satisfaction.

Then, just like that, all amusement drains from his face. "Well, in that case," he says, serious now, "you should watch out."

At that moment, Ren reappears, sinking onto the bench next to me and looking at us with an expression that's somewhere between concern and curiosity.

And all I can think is *No, it's both of you who should watch out.*

5

My first week at middle school in California etched itself into my memory; I expect Hope will be the same. I'm prepared for the worst.

We moved just outside San Francisco in the middle of the school year—friendship groups were already established, routes to classes already navigated, science partners already delegated. My mother sold it to me wrong; she'd watched too many romantic comedies and convinced me that I would be the talk of the school since "Americans love the British accent."

To be clear, this is a stereotype.

Some of them probably like it, just as I like American accents, but in that first week, not one person came up to me because of it. My mother made me think I was going to be some sort of celebrity and everyone would want to be my friend. In reality, I cried myself to sleep; I screamed at her for pulling me away from my friends in England; I swore I'd never make any friends there. The school was huge, no one cared about me, I ate lunch alone. I didn't know things I should have, like that seats were assigned in maths—sorry, math—but not in geography; like that although we didn't have uniforms, we had to wear navy-blue tracksuits in gym.

That was the moment when everything shifted—I remember the muffled laughter in the changing room when I started to pull on the gray clothes Mum had packed me off with.

"Rookie," said one girl to her friend. "Do you think she's trying to make a statement?"

Another girl appeared, and my gut reaction was to stare at the floor, blend into the background, but she came up right beside me, pulled off her navy sweatshirt, and pulled on my gray one. "Half and half," she said, and before I could decide whether she was doing it out of kindness or pity, I felt myself tear up.

She shook her head. "Not here. Never let them see that you care."

The rest of the lesson is a blur, but after that, I never let anyone know they'd thrown me, and I no longer roamed the school corridors alone.

My first week at Hope is nothing like my first week in California. It seems laughable that I wanted celebrity status in California, when here I have it and all I want is to melt into the floor. I'm asked lots of questions about what home's like, about why I'm here, about what it's like to board for the first time. I give one-word answers—*sunny, change, different*—nothing true, nothing to invite conversation. Hector is the only person who doesn't try to talk to me again, but I catch him listening, always listening, as though he thinks I'm going to reveal something by mistake.

After a few days, the questions dry up, but Ren remains at my side. During daylight hours, in the breaks between lessons, she shows me the grounds. We go into the sports hall; the indoor squash courts; the multi-faith chapel, perched perilously close to the cliff. We trek through a wooded area away from the school and reach a clearing where there are three swings, swaying creakily in the frozen air, looking out onto the valley beyond.

I'm struck by how isolated we are here—closed off, at the end of a road to nowhere. The school is on the edge of a mountain, raised and separate, like we're surveying the rest of the world from above.

In the evenings the different grades go to their common rooms—rooms on the landing between the boys' and girls' corridors on each floor. Ren doesn't press me when, for the third night in a row, I claim jet lag and head straight to the dormitory after prep. And for the third night in a row, she joins me there, sitting at her desk with a sketch pad: art homework, or so she says. I want to tell her that the effort she's making hasn't gone unnoticed, but it's also pointless, and yet I say nothing.

I climb up to my bunk, lying fully clothed on top of the duvet. If I tilt my head and open my eyes a crack, I can watch her sitting side-on, making slow, vague pencil marks on the page, almost as if she's pretending to draw while trying to think of something to say to me. Every so often her mouth opens, a determined expression taking over her face, but she closes it again, the silence persisting like it has done every evening so far. I close my eyes and pretend to sleep, listening to the pencil strokes and the occasional rustle of paper.

Then there is a loud crash, and I bolt upright just as the door bursts open to reveal Hector. He is dressed for outdoors; a black beanie hat pulls his dark hair back from his face, and he wears a fur-trimmed puffer jacket, zipped up to the top. He briefly looks around at my side of the dorm, the lack of decoration, then strides forward and makes eye contact.

"What are you doing here? This is the girls' corridor." My voice is accusatory—an unmistakable mixture of annoyance that he's interrupted the silent farce Ren and I are taking part in and genuine surprise.

He ignores me. "Get your coat, California."

Ren twists around in her chair, alarmed. "Hector, wh—"

He cuts her off. "You too, Ren. Come on, it's Wednesday— you can't stay cooped up in here. We're going out—Fred's going to meet us downstairs." He heads over to her wardrobe, pulls out a coat, and chucks it at her.

"Hec—" she starts.

"No, Ren, no excuses. I know you don't have anything better to do."

She looks questioningly at me, but I shake my head. "You go."

She stands up, scrunching the collar of her coat into a ball, but doesn't leave. "The older students are allowed into town for a few hours on Tuesdays and Wednesdays and at weekends," she explains, looking oddly relieved, presumably because she's finally found something to say to me. "It's just for a few hours. . . ."

She must realize she's not getting through to me, as her words peter out. I see her looking around at my side of the room just like Hector did. Suddenly, I feel embarrassed by the lack of life. I'm sure she expected that I'd have decorated by now, when instead I've kept it blank. Unable to contemplate that my place here might not be temporary.

Hector taps his knuckles against my bunk.

"Come with us," Ren says, and there is something about the way she says it that's almost pleading. I fully realize how much her kindness is costing her. She has put her life here on hold, showing me around, sitting with me in the dining room, partnering with me in every lesson. Since I arrived, she has voluntarily isolated herself to make my life easier.

As they wait for my answer, I can't seem to shake my mother's voice in my head. *People won't keep making an effort forever, Cara. After a while they'll decide it's not worth trying anymore.* I should at least act like I'm trying with Ren, like she's trying with me.

So even though the effort it takes is enormous, I turn myself around and climb down the ladder.

Ren and I change out of our uniforms, having told Hector we'd meet him and Fred outside the front doors. I look at the clothes I've brought, realizing how unsuitable they are. What use are skirts and T-shirts in minus temperatures? Eventually I settle on a dark red cable-knit sweater and one of the two pairs of jeans I have. They are black with custom-made rips in the knees that I'm sure I'll regret later. I pull on the coat my mother bought for me before I came here and quickly glance in the mirror. I stand paralyzed by my reflection; I'd never have gone out like this back home. My skin looks almost bleached, all remnants of the fake tan I carefully applied every few days for school in California washed away. My hair, before a bright, shiny blond, looks dull and lank. I don't bother to put on any makeup since Ren isn't wearing any, but I pull my hair back into a ponytail, which is about all I can bring myself to do.

Halfway down the six flights of stairs, I have a realization. "Ren?"

"Yes?" she says, stopping and turning back to face me.

"How do we get to the town?"

"Cable car," she replies breezily. "It opens at eight p.m. Is that okay?"

I'm filled with a building sense of dread and watch as her face freezes, knowing she's thinking the same as me. The girl who won't take the elevator most certainly won't like cable cars.

I clasp the stair rail and watch my knuckles whiten. "Umm..."

"It takes only a few minutes to get there, and it's really safe. They wouldn't let us use it otherwise."

"My issue isn't really about the length of the ride. It's ..."

"About confined spaces," she finishes my sentence.

"Something like that," I say, wishing I could explain it to her. Wishing I could make her see that I'm not just looking for attention.

She screws up her face, searching for a solution. "Does it help that it has windows? We could keep them open the whole way. Or we could order a taxi, if you'd prefer. The trip will be much longer, though. It's probably not worth it, actually, since we have to be back by ten."

I think of my journey up the mountain—how I vowed I couldn't do it again. I mean, I know I'll have to eventually, but . . . I can't think about that now.

"No taxi," I manage to say.

"Okay," she says, still pensive, shifting her weight from one leg to the other. "I know, why don't you come down and see it? Then you can make a decision, and if you don't want to go, we won't."

We won't. I feel a surge of guilt. The last thing I need is for Ren to stay at school because *I* won't get in the cable car. This whole excursion could have been avoided if she wasn't being so nice. I have to try to do this. If I don't, I really will make a scene.

The cable car looms in front of us, and my confidence wavers. The distance between us and the town seems much larger the closer I get to the edge. I sort out the pros and cons in my head. Pros: We're able to coast seamlessly over the dip between the two peaks, cutting out the treacherous route down the mountain and the inevitable fear that would bring. And I can pretend to be normal, which might just be convincing. Cons: Trapped, no way out, never again. Not ever again.

Hector stands in the way of the doors and ushers us through. "Ladies first."

I look back at Ren, but she's too busy scribbling our names

on a sign-out sheet. There is nothing to do but enter the stationary carriage. Fred swiftly follows. I push open the far window as wide as it will go. The four inches of crystallized air don't do much to slow my breathing.

I need to get out of here.

"Wait, Hec," Ren says, alarmed, as she pushes past him into the metal and glass bubble, just as I start to head back toward the doors. "Cara, are you—"

Whatever she was going to say is cut off by a series of beeps. Hector has stepped forward, unblocking the doors, and I feel the carriage shudder and swing as it sets off, across the open black expanse below, the reverberations flooding through my feet and up my entire body.

"What?" Hector asks, his easy expression transitioning into a guarded one. Perhaps he can see my fear, perhaps not. Either way, he knows something isn't right when Ren pulls the other window down in a fluster. He says something else that I don't catch—his mouth is moving, but someone has pressed the mute button.

I look left, right, up, and down. We're floating, soaring, suspended, then falling.

This is it. We're all going to die.

6

A series of things happens. Ren drops down to sitting and scoots over on the bench to pull me down next to her. Fred takes the seat opposite us. I slip my hands under my thighs so they don't notice the tremors.

"Cable cars are really just trains or trams," Ren says, "but in the air. I've never actually been on a tram, but I'm told it's much the same as this."

Even though my vision has started to blur, I see her give Fred a meaningful look.

"It is," Fred says, following Ren's prompt to distract me, but I hear the confusion in his voice.

"Have you been on one, Cara?" Ren asks.

I close my eyes, trying to hold on to reality. I am not trapped. I am not hanging upside down.

"I doubt it. Most Americans are so lazy they can't be bothered

45

to get out of their cars to get to a Starbucks. To get on a tram you'd actually have to walk to the station." Hector's low drawl makes my eyes snap open. He's still standing, watching us with an indifferent expression.

The look I give him makes him laugh, and the atmosphere changes. All the air closing in on me disperses, pinging back to the darker dimension it came from. My body relaxes, and when I go to wipe my palms on the front of my jeans, they are still.

The doors open. We get out. I check myself—I'm still here. They're still here. Nobody is broken.

I am amazed.

"What part of California are you from?" Fred walks beside me as we delve deeper into the village, my episode tactfully forgotten. There's something different, somthing warier, about the way he talks to me, I realize. If friendships were on my agenda, he's the one I'd need to win over.

"My mother lives outside San Francisco," I say, scanning our surroundings with a sense of trepidation. Like at the school, life seems to bustle everywhere here. People mingle outside bars and restaurants despite the freezing temperatures on the streets.

"You were born there?"

I shake my head. "I was born in London. My mother re-married an American. I've lived there since I was twelve."

"Ah, that explains it."

"Explains what?"

"Your dodgy accent," Hector interjects, turning around from where he and Ren are walking in front of us.

"*I* do not have a dodgy accent!" I exclaim, and look to Ren for reassurance. Bar Hector's British accent, pretty much every voice speaking English I've heard at the school has some kind of strange lilt to it—there is no reason why mine should be singled out.

She grimaces apologetically, walking backward to face us, and raises her hand to create an inch of air between her thumb and forefinger. "It is *a little* dodgy."

Something about all of their expressions makes me laugh. The feeling is so unfamiliar that I stop myself short, my hand rising to cover my mouth. Hector's face erupts into a wide, genuine smile, and he stretches his hand in Fred's direction. After a few moments fumbling around in his pockets, Fred places a note in his palm.

"No need to look so sulky, Fred," Hector says. "I think we can both agree that was a clear win, fair and square."

I look from one to the other. "You *bet* you could make me laugh?"

"Could make you smile, California. The laughing was definitely a bonus. But . . . good point. Perhaps you could throw in a little extra for that, Fred?"

Ren directs me into a nearby restaurant. "Ignore them. I can't even begin to tell you how much money has changed hands at my expense."

I barely hear her through the cacophony of voices that fill the bar area. In the corner, a band's warming up to play a live set. Suddenly I feel like an imposter in someone else's life. Who do I think I am, going out with these three people as though nothing has happened? Accomplishing the cable-car ride doesn't change anything. I don't belong here; I belong somewhere separate from everyone else. This room is crowded, full of colorful posters and joyful people—people I have nothing in common with.

I should never have come here.

Hector presses his hands against my shoulders and leans in close enough for me to hear him. "Follow me."

I flinch at his touch but let him point me through the crowd to the back of the bar, through a swinging door, and up a stairwell, all the while trying to think of a legitimate excuse to leave. There is a locked glass door at the top of the stairs, through which the world outside is visible.

"Hang on a sec," he says, pushing past me with a key and unlocking the door to an empty roof terrace. He crouches down next to a metal pillar just as Ren and Fred emerge onto the rooftop laden with bottles.

"Hurry, Hec, it's freezing," Ren says.

I look over in time to see the metal pillar he's been fiddling with burst into life. The orange glow casts a welcome beam of warmth in our direction. I count five outdoor heaters in total; I watch as Fred and Hector proceed to light up the whole terrace.

"What is this place?" I ask.

The terrace is level with the rooftops of other buildings in the town. On one side, there are picnic tables with snow-covered umbrellas shading them. On the other, a miniature golf course is set up, the multicolored structures and damp flags faded under the dark sky.

"In high season, this area is open to the public," Ren says, switching on a string of outdoor fairy lights. "You know, when all the skiers descend."

I look around at the deserted space. The light dusting of snow is untouched—probably has been for a while. "Are we allowed here now?"

"The key, remember," Hector says, dangling it in my face. "I worked here last Easter break. The best dishwasher they've ever had, I'm told."

"Hardly an appropriate occupation for someone from such a respectable family," Fred says, mimicking someone.

"Well, exactly," Hector replies with a wicked grin.

Ren starts handing out bottles of beer.

"Thanks," I say, taking one. "Are they cool about underage drinking here, then?"

"Ah, but that's the beauty of it," Hector says, scraping the snow off one of the picnic benches with his sleeve. "We're not underage. The drinking age is sixteen—for beer and wine, at least."

"One of the perks of being packed off to boarding school here," Fred says.

Hector smiles wryly at me. "You're a bit of a stickler for the rules, aren't you?"

There was a time—after my father left but before the accident—when I tried to be someone who didn't care about rules. When I intentionally didn't go to classes where attendance was mandatory; when I stayed out after curfew; when I smoked cigarettes even though I hated the taste; when I pretended to love the forbidden. I can't pretend to be someone I'm not anymore. Not when I can barely hold on to the person I really am.

I shrug, noncommittal. "You're not?"

"I've found that most rules don't really apply if you play the situation right."

"I'm not sure I believe that. . . ."

He looks directly at me. "Stick around long enough and you'll see."

His words are revealing. He's telling me that he knows I haven't committed to staying here yet. And I suddenly wonder whether, by keeping myself so shut off, I have actually revealed more about myself than if I'd just tried to involve myself.

His eyes search my face, a faint question hanging in the air between us.

I consider telling him that, whatever I might like, I *have* to stick around. I have nowhere else to go.

Ren thrusts a rusty golf club between us and asks, "Who's playing?"

Fred glances over at me; I shake my head. "You go ahead."

Out of the corner of my eye, I see Hector get up to climb a ladder fixed to the wall next to the door we came through. Ren and Fred start chatting animatedly to each other, and I feel that twinge of guilt again—spending time with me has kept her away from her friends.

Hector calls down for me to join him, so I climb the ladder to a small section of flat roof with two folding chairs. He brushes the snow off both and sits down in one, gesturing for me to take the other.

I try to think of something light to say. "Do the three of you normally hang out together?"

"Most of the time," he says, leaning back and tucking his hands into his pockets.

"You haven't these past few days."

"Yeah, well, Ren asked us to keep our distance."

"Why?"

"So as not to put you off, I think." He tilts his head, surveying me with amusement. "How am I doing?"

"I'm undecided," I say, ignoring his smile and the warning pang in the pit of my stomach.

We pass a moment in silence, then I turn to him out of a curiosity I can't suppress. "Earlier, when Fred mentioned your family . . ."

"Ah, you caught that, did you? That was Fred's eerily accurate impression of my father. He works for the British government and considers himself a bit of a big shot."

"Oh." I stare out at the sky. Without the heaters up here, I feel the air bite through my clothes. My knees sting from the cold, so I pull my legs up onto the chair, sticking my hands through the gaps. "So how come you're here?"

"And where exactly should I be?"

"Oh, I don't know. . . . If your father's high profile back home, I'd have thought you'd be at a school nearby."

"What? To share in the fame?" He laughs, but it's different from before. Brittle, somehow. "Us both being in London full-time would be a bit too close for comfort for my father. The public story is that I'm here to learn other languages, it being an international school and all that."

I decide not to probe about the real, private story in the hope he'll stop asking me about mine. "And have you?" I ask instead.

"Well . . . I'm fluent in English, Spanish, and French. But then, my mother is Spanish, my father is English, and I had a series of French au pairs growing up, so it's not that impressive."

"I'd love to be fluent in another language."

"Well, rumor has it you're a bit of an academic, so I imagine there are lots of other things you're good at."

"Where did you hear that?" I snap, and sit up taller in my chair. It's true there was a time when I was known for my good grades. That was before the accident, before I stopped turning up at school. True, I continued to work from home. In fact, I probably worked harder, and more manically, than before—not for good grades but as a way to survive. Which me is Hector talking about, the Before me or the After? Just the fact that he knows this tiny detail about me makes me question what else he knows.

He rolls his eyes. "I saw your maths homework. You got an A. Congratulations."

I sink back into the chair, relaxing slightly. "The results are out already?"

"No, but I like to be prepared so I know what reaction to pull when the paper lands on my desk."

"That can't be allowed."

"There you go with the rules thing again. I wouldn't worry too much—I'm convinced Madame Draper knows I check. She's even started leaving her desk drawer open so I don't have to pick the lock anymore. Very accommodating of her."

"Are you sure neither of you wants a go?" Ren calls up from the terrace. For a second, I'd forgotten they were here with us.

Hector glances sideways at me.

"I'm fine here, but you go ahead," I say sharply.

"No thanks," he calls back, then turns to face me properly. His eyes narrow in assessment. "Something wrong?"

Everything's wrong, I want to say, *because you're pulling me in, and I should be pulling away.* And everything's wrong, because for the first time in almost a year I don't feel like I'm drowning.

I settle on "I can't work out why you're all making such an effort with me. It's pretty . . . unusual."

"I don't know where you've come from, Cara"—it is, I realize, the first time he's called me by my real name—"but here, there's nothing unusual about being nice to someone who's new. Well, Fred and Ren do the nice part, at least. I try not to get too involved."

I raise my eyebrows. "So what's your role in all of this?"

"I'm here to keep you on your toes."

My expression makes him laugh, a quiet, musical sound that manages to penetrate the dark coat of sky all around us.

7

The following morning, I wake up with a single thought.

G.

I slip silently down the ladder and along the deserted corridor to the common room, braving it for the first time. Even though it's early—too early for a normal person to be awake—the phone box is occupied. When I see it, I realize that box is just a descriptive term. There is no containment, just two sides of misted glass to give the caller the illusion of privacy. There is no way to hide what's being said, though, not that it matters now since the one side of conversation available to me is in rapid Spanish. Even so, when Hector sees me enter the common room, he quickly hangs up.

"I didn't mean to interrupt," I say, considering backing out of the room. There's something about this early-morning conversation that I know I'm not meant to be a part of. Just like I don't want him to be a part of mine.

Hector steps into the light. He's dressed in navy sweats and has deep indigo circles under his eyes. He gestures to the phone box. "It's all yours; I'm done."

"If you're sure," I say, waiting for him to leave. Instead, he goes over to a large bay window and hoists himself up onto a window seat adorned with blue and white striped cushions.

"Oh, do you want me to go?"

Yes, I think. *You can't be here for this. If you hear me dial a number and not speak, you'll think I'm crazy.*

"I've just realized you probably need a calling card or something, so I'll have to do it another time."

He pulls one out of his pocket. "Here. Use mine."

I shake my head. "Oh, no, I'm sure calls to the U.S. are expensive, but thank you."

"It's one of those special international ones. Don't worry about it," he says, stretching his arm farther in my direction. I take it from him reluctantly. "Who are you going to call this early in the morning anyway?"

"I could ask the same of you," I say defensively. Too defensively.

"I was just speaking to my little sister," he answers. "It's the best time to catch her."

My defense snaps back in on itself. There is nothing shady about that; I feel like an idiot for projecting onto him.

"I was only asking because of the time difference," he says. "Isn't it the middle of the night where you come from?"

He's probably right, or thereabouts. It must be at least eleven at night in San Francisco. But I can't tell him that I wasn't planning on calling home like he expects me to.

"You're right," I say, realizing he has just handed me the perfect escape. "I don't know what I was thinking. This jet lag is still messing with my head."

"Another time, then," he says. "Keep the card until you get your own; I've got a couple of them." He raises his arms to the ceiling, tilting backward into a graceful stretch. I briefly wonder whether his fingertips will skim the ceiling. He and Fred are probably the tallest boys in the school; I can't help noticing that where Fred's height speaks of gangly arms and clumsiness, Hector's becomes him. When he pulls himself straight again, he looks down at himself, following my eyeline, and smiles. "Right. Uniform time."

I look away, embarrassed to be caught staring. "You sound almost excited."

His eyes light up. "Well, California, where else would you get to wear such a sexy outfit?"

Just like that, his own guard, as quickly as it came down, is back up.

Hector is sitting opposite me in history. I avoid looking at him, just like I did when he joined Ren and me at both breakfast and lunch, but I can't stop my mind from wandering back to our run-in this morning. I'll have to be more careful if I'm going to make early phone calls. Just as I'm starting to regret handing in my phone, I feel the class turn to look at me. I've been asked a question—the first direct one since I've arrived.

"Cara?" the teacher, Monsieur Thauvin, prompts me.

Blood rushes to my cheeks as I think of a million excuses, and disappointment clouds his face. So much for staying under the radar.

Joy raises her hand to answer instead. She delivers her answer with a hideously smug look directed straight at me. I hold her stare, noting that she is prettier than I recall. Her eyes are a rich brown, and in daylight, her black hair gleams. Her sidekick, Hannah, sits next to her, an equally annoying closed-lip smile on her face. Hannah has clearly styled her hair to replicate Joy's; it's lighter but just as straight. There are faint ripples of heat burn on the surface from overstraightening.

They bother me more than they should—irritation floods my body, fizzing ominously just below the skin. I wonder why; then it hits me. I was right about them when we first met—I used to be just like them. I was the brainy one, the popular one, the one people tried to copy. The one I thought people revered. Now that I see it from the other side, when nothing matters more to me than making it through the day unnoticed, I see how ugly it was. People didn't respect me; they were afraid of me. Afraid that I'd call them out on something that I and my closest friends, G, Poppy, and Lennon, would think was stupid or uncool.

I hate to admit that a part of me liked the power I had to define what was acceptable and not. The other part now wants to tell Joy and Hannah that power is fragile. It's painfully easy to cross over into the unacceptable like I did, and then it all falls apart. That's something I learned when my friends didn't visit me in the hospital. They messaged to tell me their parents thought it was too early in my recovery to visit, but I knew their real reasons. They didn't want to associate themselves with me. They didn't know what to say to me after my fall from grace, and they blamed me for it. For leaving the party when I did.

For everything that came after.

At afternoon break, Ren stays behind to talk to Monsieur Thauvin about an assignment. I hang back, too, pressing myself against the wall outside the classroom door.

"Come on, California," Hector says, ushering me away from the stream of people making their way to the conservatory.

"I was just going to wait here for . . . ," I start weakly.

He gives me a knowing look. "Ren could be ages."

He holds open the door to an empty classroom, and I reluctantly follow him inside, mostly just to get away from the crowds. There is a side door that leads to another corridor I haven't been in before. We cross through two more classrooms, an office, then a small sitting room that feels very out of place. He presses his hand against wooden paneling that swings open at his touch, allowing passage into the conservatory.

I twist around to see him close the door, which from this side is a bookcase. "How—"

"A year might seem like a long time to you, California, but you forget I've been here for four."

I look around at the scene being set up. Our shortcut means that we have arrived before everyone else. Four large tables at the far end, normally used for studying, now have sparkly tablecloths on them. I watch from afar as the kitchen staff arrange huge mountains of éclairs for afternoon tea.

"Ren tells me you've avoided this delight thus far."

"I . . ." I try to think of a good excuse.

"Don't tell me." He puts on a terrible American accent. *"Carbs are the devil."*

I raise my eyebrows. "Do you always say things just to get a reaction?"

"Follow me. There's someone I'd like you to meet," he says with a smile, beckoning me over to the table nearest the door to the courtyard, where a stout, red-haired woman wearing a Hope Hall apron is folding paper napkins.

Hector clears his throat. "Mary, allow me to introduce you to Cara. She's come to see us all the way from the USA."

The woman, Mary, looks a little flustered by Hector's sudden appearance. "Oh, hello, dear. I didn't hear you come in. And welcome, Cara. From America?" Her expression turns slightly sour. "Ah, well, I suppose we can't hold that against you."

Hector stifles a laugh as she passes us both a plate. She turns her attention back to him. "Hungry?"

"Always hungry when you've been baking," he says.

"Charm doesn't work on me, Mr. Sanderson—you know that," she says, putting an extra éclair on his plate.

My urge to laugh is quickly replaced with irritation when Joy and Hannah appear at the end of our table. Their voices are audible above the chatter and footfalls that have now filled the room—and I am sure they are meant to be.

"I suppose she thinks if she throws herself at him, he'll eventually be into her," Joy says. "It's pretty embarrassing to watch. I mean, look at her. . . ."

"It's probably why she's spending so much time with Ren," Hannah adds. "I mean, they do everything together. It's like she thinks he'll like her more because of it. Doesn't she even want other friends?"

"Or maybe she just doesn't need anyone else," Joy says. "Don't you think it's kind of gross that she stays in the dorm after school? I mean, she and Ren are basically locked in there together every evening."

They exchange a horrified, malicious look that riles me up so much that, for a moment, I consider confronting them. I glance sideways at Hector to see whether he has heard them, but he's still talking to Mary. He turns to me; his gaze drifts along to the end of the table. He must see something on my face, because he takes a step toward the conservatory door, clutching a plate that now has four éclairs on it, and addresses Mary. "We're going to take these—"

"Just bring the plates back to the kitchen later, will you, dear?" She turns away, not waiting for his answer.

He guides me outside into the courtyard, where a series of benches I hadn't noticed before are nestled into the surrounding walls, set back from the open space under arches carved into the stone. He picks the one farthest from the door, half hidden by a curtain of ivy, and drops his haul in the spot between us.

"Saying delightful things, were they?"

Instead of having to tell him what they did actually say, I ask, "How did you ever date her?"

"Ah, you see, that was the problem. We didn't ever really get to the dating part—"

"Wow," I interrupt, holding up a hand.

"Don't judge me for that," he says in a tone that's suddenly serious. "The timing was . . . let's just say it wasn't my best time." His eyes lose focus for a moment; then he picks up the plate of éclairs. "You need to try one of these. Mary is a total genius, trust me."

I take one, suppressing the urge to push the subject further. "What was all that in there with Mary?"

He rolls his eyes dramatically. "What have I done now?"

"Nothing. It's just . . . well, you've got a real problem with the U.S., don't you?"

He gives me a very bored look. "Not at all. In fact, I have family there."

"So why always such fanfare about it?"

His eyes narrow. "It gets under your skin."

"And you enjoy that?"

"Of course," he says. "That, and this time in particular I knew I'd have a good audience. Mary is going through an anti-American phase. She believes in conspiracy theories, and her latest is that the Americans sank the *Titanic* because they didn't want the British to be known for building a stronger ship than them."

"You're joking." I laugh at the absurdity of it.

"I'm not. That woman is not to be doubted; she used to bake for the Queen of England. Besides, I agree with Mary: it's a real possibility."

He looks at me in a strange, triumphant sort of way.

I glance down at myself, trying to figure out what he's looking at. "What?"

"You do realize what just happened? You laughed without stopping yourself."

"I did not," I say quickly.

"No need to get defensive, California. It was just an observation."

The ivy curtain rustles as it's pulled back to unveil Ren. "Here you are," she says brightly, budging Hector along to sit between us. He offers her the plate and starts to relay Mary's latest conspiracy theory to her.

I sit back, distant, wondering how I could have been so careless as to drop my guard with him. The thought is swiftly followed by another: *Shouldn't I want to laugh?*

I shouldn't be dropping my guard with anyone, but somehow it feels like that will be impossible at this school; there are too many people in one enclosed space. I can't escape from them at the end of the day by going home; during term time, this is my home. And, truthfully, with people like Joy and Hannah roaming the corridors, I'm going to need allies.

Even at home, during my darkest days, there were the twins. Well, at three years old, my brothers weren't exactly a huge comfort, but they were still young enough not to hate me for what happened. And then there was my mother, who, for all her faults, didn't give up on me. Yes, her way of facing the aftermath of the accident was to pretend it hadn't happened, then finally—reluctantly—to call every psychologist and every therapy group in the state of California at my stepfather's request. But I suppose that shows commitment in some strange, detached, I-can't-talk-to-you-about-this-myself and we-need-help-as-long-as-the-sessions-are-anonymous-and-no-one-will-find-out-my-daughter-has-lost-it way.

From my position on the bench, I can see through the glass wall of the conservatory to where Joy and Hannah sit with two other girls I don't know. As long as I keep Ren, Hector, and Fred at arm's length, maybe it's okay. They don't need to know everything.

As soon as I think of Fred, I see him. Like at lunch, he's sitting with a group of boys at a table by the window. When there is a lull in conversation, I ask Ren and Hector who they are.

Hector pulls back the ivy and peers through the glass. "Some of the guys from the basketball team." There is something odd about the way he says it, then I realize he won't meet my eyes.

"Does he do that often?"

"Yep," Ren answers cheerily. "Sometimes he sits with us, sometimes with them. Not a big deal."

Hector and Ren share a look that I pretend I don't notice, and I have a sneaking suspicion that him being over there is, in fact, a very big deal.

8

Fred doesn't sit with us at dinner, or at all the following day. When the weekend arrives, I realize I have barely seen him at all. Hector and Ren persevere with trying to integrate me into their activities, making me brave the common room with them after prep, forcing me into evening trips to the swings before the sun sets, but every time we're in a space where Fred is present, he finds a reason to disappear.

I wake on Saturday to an inch of snowfall on the window ledge. The weather deteriorates, the grounds quickly painted white, and we elect to stay indoors, where the entertainment is old-school, including the flickering television that sits in the corner of the common room. It's rarely on, but when it is, all that's watchable are U.S. crime dramas dubbed in French. There is also a towering pile of board games and puzzles in one corner that people actually play, stacks of outdated magazines on a table, and

64

groups of people playing cards. Without phones, without any-where to go besides the town, I begin to feel stir-crazy.

Me. The girl who barely left the house for nine months.

During my second week, Mexican flags replace the French Tri-colore in the dining room, and as we get deeper into the term, the work steps up a notch and reality sets in. We stay in the conserva-tory later and later each evening with the rest of our grade. The teachers pile on the homework, and trips to the town are swapped for sheets and sheets of math problems, English and history es-says, and reams of French vocab. I throw myself into it all, thank-ful for a genuine reason to keep my head down. I stay even later in the conservatory than Ren and Hector, citing our increased workload but actually seeking the few moments of quiet I can claim for myself.

One such evening, I climb the spiral stairs to the dorm after everyone else. I push myself up the six flights, grateful that no one is around. I barely draw breath, my legs and lungs conditioned to the journey by now, but close to the top I catch the end of a heated conversation taking place on the sixth-floor landing that makes me hang back. The voices are hushed, charged and familiar. I loiter in the shadows of the stairway, but Fred and Ren's conver-sation finds me anyway.

Fred is angry. "... you could just talk to her, Ren? Don't you think it's worth finding out?"

"It won't change anything," she hisses back at him.

"You don't know that! You have no idea what it will change."

"You're making a big deal out of *nothing,* Fred. Hector told me what you said to him, and we both think you're being ridiculous."

"Fine, you and Hector won't take me seriously," Fred says, and I hear the anger in his voice convert to hurt. "I guess it doesn't matter how long we've been friends, huh? A hell of a lot longer than—"

A door slams, and I hear the shuffle of feet on the landing above.

Ren clears her throat. "I'm done talking about this, Fred," she says, and her words are uncharacteristically weighted with a French accent. "I'm going to bed."

I wait for at least five minutes, listening to make sure they've gone before I climb the last flight of stairs to the dorm, much slower than I did the previous five. I finally feel as though I understand. The only thing that has changed for them is my arrival— Fred's hostility has to be directed at me, doesn't it? Wasn't this kind of drama exactly what I was trying to avoid? The last thing I want is to be responsible for breaking up their friendship, which, as Fred was presumably about to say, has existed a hell of a lot longer than my presence here.

Ren, already in her pajamas when I enter the dorm, is crouched on the floor aggressively sorting her clothes into piles. "I'm going to send these to the laundry," she says, and her voice is still thick with irritation. "Do you have anything?"

I scoop up a set of uniforms from the back of my chair and add it to one of the piles. "Is everything okay?"

"Fine," she says, sounding anything but. "Why would I not be okay?"

"You seem a bit upset, that's all," I say, and then risk adding, "Is it to do with Fred? He hasn't been around much recently."

"That's nothing, Cara," she says with rare impatience. "Fred and Hector have had a small falling-out. They're just being boys, and Fred's stubborn as hell. He'll get over it eventually—we just have to wait these things out."

I climb up to my bunk. She's lying, of course. "What did they fall out over?" I ask innocently.

"Nothing important," she says through what I'd wager is a fake yawn. "I'm so tired. Do you mind if we turn the lights out early?"

"Sure," I say, thinking that I'll have to try a different tack tomorrow if I'm going to get to the bottom of this. Hector is much more likely to crack than Ren. At least, I'm less bothered about pushing my limit with him. He does it enough with me. It's time for a little payback.

I find my moment during PE while we help assemble a makeshift exercise circuit in the sports hall. There has been so much snow over the last week that the girls' running club had to be combined with the boys' basketball session. The PE teacher, Madame Monelle, looks considerably stressed by the sheer number of students in the hall and keeps walking around barking orders in French.

"I was wondering when you were going to ask," Hector says offhandedly. He waits for me to pass him a bar to put on top of a metal hurdle frame we're positioning. He's wearing a plain white T-shirt, and I find myself staring at his right forearm, which is wrapped in bandages. I think, briefly, of the scar under the sweatshirt I refuse to take off. I hesitate before passing him a pole.

He gestures for me to get on with it.

I hand it over. "What happened to your arm?"

He glances down at the bandage. "Tattoo."

"Does it hurt?"

"Nah, it's old. I'm just not allowed to, how was it put, uh, 'display it for all to see.' Wouldn't want to encourage the younger years to ink themselves up." He smiles provocatively, stopping when we both notice Fred watching us. "So . . . Fred . . . What do you want to know?"

"What's up with him?"

"Fred's finding your arrival harder than he'll admit."

"Why? I haven't done anything."

"Your mere presence is something. You see, before you arrived, it was just the three of us. Now you're here, it changes things for him."

"Changes things how?"

"Well, it's been a long time since Ren's had anyone to share a room with," he says, moving on to the next frame. "You and she have been spending a lot of time together, which naturally means she has had less time to spend with him."

"She's just being nice because I'm new. I'm sure the novelty will wear off soon."

"I'm not so sure," he says, thoughtful now. "Ren has never had a proper girlfriend here. I think she's secretly hoping you won't get bored of her."

At the word *friend,* I feel a spike of fear. "B-but . . . ," I stammer, "why does any of this matter to Fred?"

Hector gives me the kind of look you'd give someone you thought was being incredibly dim. "Fred's been in love with Ren since we first arrived."

All at once, it makes sense. "Has he ever told her how he feels?"

"No, but I doubt that would help much."

"Why not? She might feel the same way. They're close—even I can tell. That's why she's upset he's being so distant."

He pauses, considering whether to continue. "I know for a fact she doesn't feel that way about him."

"How? Have you ever asked her?" Hector doesn't respond immediately, so I press on. "I don't understand. What am I missing?"

He lets go of the frame, turns to face me, and says, "Ren's gay."

"Oh," I say stupidly.

Hector watches my reaction. I wonder how he's expecting me to respond. Whether he's expecting me to have a problem with her sexuality. Presumably that was what Fred was worried about when he confronted Ren last night. Is he wary of me because he thinks I'll have an issue with it? Is that what he wanted her to talk to me about? Gauge my reaction, see if I'm going to follow the pack?

I mean, Joy and Hannah have alluded to it enough. If I were

more observant and could have stepped out of my own world for even a second and asked Ren about herself, maybe I'd have put two and two together.

"That's why Joy and Hannah have been making those comments."

"Ren doesn't help herself," he says, still staring at me with a cautious expression on his face. "Until you came, she kept to herself, never showed anyone but Fred and me how great she is. For a while, I think they just thought she was only interested in boys, you know." He gives me a look, and I read between the lines. "She got a bit of a bad rep, so last year she set them straight. I mean, I'm sure you know what it's like—there must have been girls like Joy and Hannah at your last school?"

Yes, I think, feeling a little sick, *but there were four of us in charge.*

"You weren't bullied for being gay there," I say, clinging to my only defense. It was about clothes, weight, what car you drove, what parties you were going to, who liked you—everything that now doesn't seem important at all.

"Yeah, well, she's not bullied for being gay here either. It's not that. She stood up to them. They didn't like that. She didn't worship Joy and Hannah like they wanted her to, and she still doesn't. They're threatened by that, so they target her. It didn't help that I wasn't Joy's favorite person at the time, and Fred and I stood up for Ren. That just pissed them off more. The other girls avoid her because they're worried about being targeted too."

I suddenly wonder whether this is why Ren has been so patient with me. I'd put it down to her feeling sorry for me, because

I'm new and because of my inability to help myself socially. I should have realized that she's just as happy to distance herself from everyone else as I am—she hasn't been isolating herself for me; she does it anyway. Now that I think about it, the board of pictures in our room says it all. There are only photos of her parents, Hector, and Fred. When I first arrived—when I had nobody—that felt like an army to me. I suppose I should have questioned why she hasn't tried to integrate me further than them. I've been grateful for it, not wanting to branch out, but I never considered that involving me with the three of them was as far as she wanted—or was able—to go.

Hector clears his throat. "Anyway, it puts a wrench in Ren and Fred's great love story, doesn't it?"

I pull myself back into the present. "It's problematic, that's for sure."

"It doesn't bother you that, in most of the girls' eyes, you'll be damned by association for spending so much time with Ren?"

"Don't insult me," I say, and I find some of my old intensity somewhere inside me.

He looks at me strangely then and shakes his head with a smile.

"What?"

"I wonder about you, that's all. Your reactions always surprise me."

I quote his earlier words back at him. "I'm here to keep you on your toes."

He laughs. "Perhaps you are, California. Perhaps you are."

Madame Monelle blows on her whistle, attempting to gain

control of the sports hall. Some people look up and start to shuffle toward her, but progress is slow.

"Well, enjoy," Hector says as we make our way over.

"You're not staying?"

"For hurdles?" He gives me an affronted look, and for a second he's so good-looking it's almost indecent. *"Seriously?"*

He laughs at my expression, and the sound lingers in the air long after he's gone.

9

If Ren only has a few people she spends time with, I don't want to be the reason she loses one of them. That evening I prep myself to talk to Fred.

He's not in the common room, so I wait until I see Madame James going downstairs before I slip through the door to the boys' corridor and search for his room. It is right at the end; the name card stands out since they're the only names I recognize: Hector Sanderson and Fredrik Lindström.

I knock once but don't wait for an answer. A door slams farther along the corridor, and I slip hastily inside before I'm caught. Both Fred and Hector are there: Fred sitting at his desk cleaning the lens of a professional-looking camera, Hector crouched on the floor over a suitcase, which he hastily pulls closed as I enter.

"Oh, it's just you," he says, relaxing when he sees me. He opens the case again and starts to reorganize whatever is inside.

"You could have announced yourself. I'm going to have to start counting all over again."

I look into the case, where at least fifty cigarette packets are stacked side by side. "What are those?"

"Selling these here is a great little earner. . . . As I'm sure you can imagine, the margins are high in our isolated corner of the world. Can I interest you in an excellent deal?"

"I'll pass."

"This is a social visit, then." He rubs his hands together. "How delightful."

I give him a withering look. "I'm here for a word with Fred, actually."

Fred looks up in surprise when I address him, and my confidence immediately starts to waver.

"If you have a minute?" I add, speaking directly to him.

"Um . . ." He looks uncomfortable, like he hasn't expected me to actually confront him.

Hector springs up from the floor, kicking the suitcase under the desk and making his way toward me and the door with a mischievous stride. "Well, I'll make myself scarce, then. Try not to be too long. You really shouldn't be here in the boys' dorms, California. What if you were caught?"

I roll my eyes at him as he walks past me out of the room, looking especially pleased with himself.

"Yes?" Fred asks as soon as we're alone. There is an edge to his voice now that it's just us. He fixes the lens to the camera, rests it gently on his desk, and twists his chair to face me. He doesn't invite me to sit, instead letting me linger among piles of dirty clothes and books.

"I just, um, wanted to clear the air." I suddenly wish I had prepared what I was going to say. I'd thought if I could just get him to see I'm not here to cause trouble, or take Ren away from him, it would be fine, but I see he's not going to make it easy for me. I clear my throat and try to be sincere with my words. "I'm not trying to cause trouble between you three, and I realize my arrival here has maybe upset the balance."

He blinks repeatedly. "Is that what you've come here to say?"

I feel myself bristle. "I don't know what to say, really. I don't understand what happened. Have I done something to offend you? You were happy enough to include me when I first got here, but now . . ." As I say the word *happy,* I know it's not entirely true. He was never as warm toward me as the other two, but he put up with me, at least.

"Ren and I were meant to show you around, that's all. I wasn't expecting you to become part of our group." He pauses, as though wondering how to phrase his next words. "You know what other schools call us?"

I shake my head.

He leans back in his chair, crossing his arms over his chest. "No-Hope Hall, for lost causes."

"What do you mean?"

"Why do you think you were given a place after term had started with no exams to sit and no entrance interview? The head has a reputation for taking in strays."

I can see the truth in what he's saying. I never questioned how my mother managed to get me a place here after I refused to go back to school. All she told me was that the headmaster was one of my stepfather Mike's clients and that she'd heard it was an amazing place. Blue skies in exchange for blue days, or so she'd put it. Somewhere new, somewhere I wouldn't have a past. Somewhere I'd actually have a chance. She believed that—I saw it in her eyes, and I guess a part of me wanted to believe it too. At least, that part of me won out over the part that fought her on it.

Now it's clear why I am here. *No-Hope Hall for lost causes.* I can just imagine the brochure. *A last resort for hopeless cases.*

I take a few sharp breaths but force myself to hold Fred's gaze. Hector was wrong; Fred's hostility doesn't stem from Ren not spending as much time with him. It's about her choice of substitute—his issue is with me.

"We were told you had problems before you arrived," he says, breaking the weighty silence.

We were told you had problems. The words circle round and round in my head. "What kind of problems?" I ask weakly.

"The headmaster didn't expand, but it's pretty obvious. You're claustrophobic; you're nervous around people; most of the time you look so miserable that I wonder how you've managed to get by at all."

"And yet I have," I say forcefully, and the insistence in my voice takes me by surprise again.

"By propping yourself up with *my* friends," he says, and I don't miss the possessiveness in his tone.

I look past him to the wall behind his desk. Like Ren's, it is full of photographs that spread out past the board. His cover the whole wall; a collection of photos of their life here. Their life before me. In the center is a full-page photo of Ren, caught mid-laugh. It is grainy, matte, and looks from another time—when digital cameras didn't give everyone red eyes and lackluster skin.

"I haven't done anything to you, Fred," I say. "You haven't even given me a chance."

"Growing up, my mum had this old saying," he says, as though he hasn't heard me. *"En ulv i fårakläder."*

I swallow nervously. "What does it mean?"

"A wolf in sheep's clothes."

I take a sharp breath in. "And you think I'm a wolf?"

"I think you're hiding something. Something that the others are refusing to see."

"Fred . . ." I search hastily for something to say, something to defend myself with.

"Okay, Cara," he cuts in. "I'll give you a chance. But before I do, answer me this: Why are you here?"

"Well, it's a school, isn't it?"

Fred shakes his head and stares expectantly at me, waiting for the truth. Finally asking the question that, by some miracle, I've managed to avoid thus far.

I take a step back toward the door.

"I'm sorry, Cara," he says with a sense of validation in his voice now. "It's not that I don't like you. We don't even really know each other. But the thing is, until you decide to be more honest with everyone, I just can't trust you, and I just can't trust you near my friends."

10

I don't utter a word for the rest of the evening, finding an empty, reassuring calm from staring at the blank wall beside my bed. As I lie there, Fred's words circle in my head.

A wolf in sheep's clothes.

How has Fred made this assumption about me already? And is he right? Is that what I am?

When I'm positive Ren is asleep, I creep out and head for the phone box. The common room is empty, but that's not surprising since it's past midnight. I doubt I'm allowed to be up this late, but I don't give it much thought; I've broken the rules already today and nothing happened—I *need* to make this call.

I pick up the phone; I type in Hector's calling-card number and follow the instructions. I dial G's number: *Hi! You've reached G. I'm not here—obviously—but you know what to do. Beep . . .*

I breathe out. This time, I don't hang up.

There is an almighty pause while I let her phone carrier record the silence. I say my next words so quietly that even if she were able to listen to them, I doubt she'd hear them. "But I don't, G. I don't know what to do without you here. I don't know anything anymore."

And then I hang up. *What am I doing?* I have never left a message for her before. Not once. My hands fly up to my cheeks—still no tears. I press them against the clear walls of the phone box and feel a bizarre urge to smash something like people do in films. Sure, it's messy, but you get the sense that it helps them somehow.

I stare at the calling card; it has a generic sunny scene on it that makes me think of California. For a second I let myself feel so profoundly homesick that I might pass out. I wish I were back there, where I could stay in my room and hide the vast black hole in my chest, away from people trying to figure me out.

I pick up the phone again.

"Hello," my mother's voice rings out brightly. In the background I hear a child laugh. I imagine her in our local park with the twins, looking immaculate with celebrity-sized sunglasses while she chats to other mothers in her fabricated American accent.

"Mum, it's me."

"Cara, is that you?" she shouts down the phone. "Speak up, I can barely hear you. I was wondering when you were going to call; it's been almost two weeks."

I don't speak any louder. "Mum, I need to come home."

"You can't come home now. I've spoken to your house mistress and she says you've settled in well."

Hardly. It's typical that she'd cling to an exaggerated version of the truth, unable to acknowledge the real version. I feel a surge of irritation—why did I call her?

"It sounds like you're feeling a bit better, darling," she continues. "It's good for you to be out of the city."

"Why?" I ask coldly, staring at the buttons on the phone. "Because no one knows me here?"

"All I meant was that, well . . . you needed to get away from it all."

"I never get away from *it all,*" I hiss. What a stupid thing for her to say. Does she still honestly think that sending me halfway around the world is going to solve everything?

I hear her labored breaths against the phone. In. Out. In. After a few moments, she seems to decide it's safe to resume speaking. "All I'm saying is that being with new people is a good thing."

"I don't want to be with *new* people."

"I know you don't, Cara." Her voice is suddenly sharp, businesslike. "But you're better there with them than you were—"

"Mum!" I cut her off, that familiar force—infuriation—building in my chest. "Nothing has changed. I'm not magically better. None of this is going to go away."

And then, before I can stop them, more words burst out of me—overpowering, electric words hidden so deep inside that they actually burn as I say them: "It's still my fault."

At first there is a silence so acute I wonder whether there will ever be sound again; then at last she says in a very quiet voice, "Why would you say that? You've never said that before."

I don't answer; I don't know how to answer. All I know is that I feel physically sick, with what happened, with what is happening now—with myself.

A child starts crying on the other end of the phone. "Oh, Cara, that's Kyle," she says, and I hear the relief in her voice, grateful for the disruption. "Don't go away—I'll call you back in two minutes."

"Don't bother," I say, and hang up. I imagine her fussing over the twins. Her perfect little American boys. I wonder whether if I cried, her messed-up British daughter from a marriage she spends every day trying to forget, she'd drop everything for me. I pick up a cushion from one of the sofas and chuck it across the room. I feel nothing; there is no crash as it lands with a quiet thump on another sofa. It almost looks like it was supposed to be there in the first place. I pick up more and hurl them away from me. It brings no satisfaction at all. Eventually I fall to my knees.

The door creaks open behind me. "Go away!" I shout, no longer caring who hears me, and the door closes before I can see who it is.

A few minutes later it opens again and Ren slips in. She crouches next to me on the floor and places her hand lightly on my shoulder. "Come on, Cara," she says, her voice sleepy. "It's late; let's go back to the dorm."

I consider shrugging her off, but my hostility dissolves into desperation. "I can't do this, Ren," I whisper. "I can't pretend to be normal."

I hear Fred's words again, possessing me, taunting me. *A wolf in sheep's clothes.* And I realize I feel so shaken by them because they're true. I *am* a wolf, and nobody has called me out on it until now.

Ren makes an irritated clicking sound. "*Normal?* What does that even mean, Cara?"

I breathe out and force myself to hold her gaze. "Straightforward, then. Like you. I mean, here you are, in the middle of the night, looking out for me."

"It's really not a big deal."

"It is, Ren. Why can't I be like you? You just keep being so nice to me, when I've done nothing nice for you. I mean, why are you even here? I have barely asked you anything about yourself."

She pulls herself to sitting, her back against one of the armchairs. "Well, let's level the playing field, then. What do you want to know that will make you feel 'normal'?"

I smile weakly. "All the things I should have asked you before now. Your family. Where home is. How you are."

"*Should,*" she repeats, giving me a bored look. "You don't *need* to ask me any of those things. Really, I don't mind that you haven't."

"I know you don't," I say. It is the only explanation for why she hasn't given up on me already. "But still . . ."

"Okay," she says in a businesslike manner. "Here you go: I love my parents, but sometimes they make me so mad I could scream. I am an only child, and there are moments I wish I wasn't. Home is just outside Lyon, which is not so far away from here but sometimes feels like a million miles. And I am fine. Absolutely fine. As are you."

I give her a meaningful look, gesturing to myself slumped in the center of the common room floor.

"We all have baggage, Cara. I know that as well as anyone."

The door opens again. This time, Hector steps inside and surveys us both on the floor with a curious expression. "Everything all right down there?"

"We're just clearing a few things up," Ren says. The way she says it—impatient, no-nonsense—makes my chest contract. It's the way G would say it.

I glance between her and Hector, both of whom, for some crazy, misguided reason, are still sticking by me. If I think about it, it really is amazing that they want to be here with me when I've given nothing away. I should feel something more than anger, I think, something more than shame.

Hector nods curtly at Ren, then without drawing breath says, "Well, in that case, now's a good time to let you know that I told Cara you're gay."

"Hector!" She freezes, all color bleaching from her face. I see her mind working furiously behind her circular brown eyes, deciding how to respond. Terrified by my possible reaction.

"It doesn't change anything, Ren," I say. She looks shell-shocked, so I repeat myself for emphasis. "Really it doesn't."

"You see, Ren?" Hector says triumphantly. "Didn't I tell you?"

"What are you doing here?" I ask Hector, mostly to pull his attention away from Ren. She looks how I feel: like she wants to catch her breath separate from everyone else.

"Just checking you'd calmed down," he says conversationally.

"I see you have, so I can go back to bed. All I'll say is that it's lucky I'm not a sensitive soul or your earlier banishment of me could have been quite hurtful."

Embarrassment floods through me as I realize it must have been Hector I told to go away earlier. Presumably he was also the person who went to wake up Ren.

"I didn't realize that was you."

"I think he'll survive," Ren says, standing up and brushing herself off. Her face still looks a little haunted in the moonlight, but there is not a tear in sight. "Come on, it's late. We really should go; if we're all caught in here together, we'll be in serious trouble."

It's an unfortunate prophecy. As Hector pulls open the door to the sixth-floor landing, Madame James is waiting for us.

"What are you three doing up together at this hour?" she hisses with a murderous expression. I take back my first impression of her. She's standing in pale-pink flannel pajamas covered in little penguins, but there is nothing gentle or conspiratorial about her in this moment. I'll tell her that I've lost it, and Ren and Hector were simply there to comfort me. She might then be lenient with them at least.

Hector beats me to it. "I know what it looks like, Madame James, but I promise you there is a very simple—if unbelievable—explanation."

She raises her eyebrows at him as if to say, *I can't wait to hear this.*

"Ren, Cara, and I all came to get a glass of water at the same time. None of us could sleep. It must be because there's a full moon," Hector says, as though it's the most natural explanation. "Don't they say people always have trouble sleeping when there's a full moon?"

"You were all being very loud," she says cynically, her eyebrows still raised to her hairline.

"I gave them a fright. As it's so late, they weren't expecting to see me. And, without daylight, they mistook my good looks for something a little more sinister." He follows this with his most winning smile.

She sighs, slowly letting her eyes close in defeat. "Of course they did," she says tiredly. Then she moves toward the stairs, lightly slapping Hector around the head in an affectionate gesture. "Go to bed, all of you!"

We don't need to be told twice.

When I climb back up the ladder to bed, I'm still trying to work out what has just happened. "Is there actually a full moon tonight?"

Ren pulls back the curtains, searching the sky. We both spot it at the same time: a tiny sliver of white.

"He's untouchable," I say, wishing my voice would sound less amazed.

She doesn't say anything for a long moment, climbing up to her bunk and tucking the duvet around her. "The thing about Hector . . . well, you must have seen, he does a hell of a lot of things that are against the rules, but they're always carefully considered. He doesn't ask for leniency in situations that don't require it. And, more than anything, the teachers adore him. Madame James in particular."

"Because he knows when to turn on the charm?"

"Well, I don't think he's ever got less than ninety percent on an assignment so, as far as the teachers are concerned, as long as he shows up for class, he can do what he likes."

I lie back, wondering why, if he's so smart, he hasn't seen what Fred sees in me. Do they both know, deep down, but don't want to admit it to themselves? Or can I really have deceived them that well?

"You'll see, Cara," Ren says, turning out the light. "Hector can be pretty savage sometimes. . . . He doesn't have much time for other people's secrets"—her voice breaks slightly—"and can be direct to a fault, but he looks after his friends. When he's around, everything is easier."

I want to tell her she's made everything easier, too, and whatever Fred might think, she can trust me, but I can't seem to find my voice.

"Having him in your corner," she continues, "well . . . it's helped me get by these past few years."

I scrunch my eyes shut, and when I speak, my voice has a lackluster quality to it. "Don't you want to do more than get by?"

I hear her yawn from across the room. "The time for that will come."

11

Over the next week, I fold even further into myself, watching from the sidelines as the school is transformed in preparation for its birthday celebration. We wake to clear skies on Friday, and as we descend the stairs, silver balloons in the shape of the number 25 are attached to the banisters, guiding our path.

"Big day today," Hector declares as we approach our usual table in the dining room.

"We can see that," Ren says, looking down to his plate, which is piled high with at least six sausages. Since the unveiling of the Union Jack in the dining room that Monday, he has managed to get there before us each day.

"You should follow my lead and stock up while you can. School Birthday is a grand celebration."

"I don't really see how it will be different from any other day," I say, sitting down and pulling a piece of toast from the china toast rack in the center of the table. It's kitschy, with two figurines of skiers at each end and the words *Welcome to Switzerland* painted on its base.

"There's a big dinner later," Ren says, "followed by the Birthday Performance."

"The what?"

"The younger years put on performances in the auditorium," she explains. "Singing, dancing, plays, that sort of thing. They've been practicing since the beginning of term. It's normally very fun."

"And," Hector adds, "this afternoon's dismal laps around the sports hall will be exchanged for laps on a majestic ice rink. Sport has never been quite like it."

I shake my head in disbelief. "Ice-skating is not a sport."

"It is," he says fervently, replacing his knife and fork on the table. "Or variations of it are. Figure skating, ice hockey . . . they're Olympic sports, I'll have you know. Next term, skating is actually a choice on the PE curriculum."

"That's ridiculous," I say, looking to Ren for confirmation, but she's out of her seat, retrieving a butter dish from the next table.

All around us the room is bright with chatter; the kitchen staff wear party hats as they move between tables, filling up the tureens of cooked breakfast.

Hector leans back in his chair. "A penny for the chip on your shoulder, California."

"I'm not sure that's the expression."

He rolls his eyes at me.

"Fine," I say stubbornly, focusing on a collection of party poppers that have been placed in the center of our table. "There are moments, like today, when this place just seems a bit nuts. It's like we're not part of the real world here."

He tuts disapprovingly. "What you're saying is that it's not part of the world you've come from, not that it's not part of the real world. The real world combines all sorts of irregularities. Don't write things off because you haven't experienced them before."

"That's not it," I say. Although I suppose a part of it is. I have never been ice-skating, and the idea of doing it for the first time with the whole school watching fills me with a certain form of dread. "You have to admit that we're in a bubble here."

"Nothing in the world is excluding if you let yourself be a part of it."

I shake my head. "You're just saying that because of your background; you've been brought up to feel anything is possible."

He clicks his jaw in irritation. "Everything *is* possible, Cara."

"For someone who's grown up how you did, sure," I say defiantly.

"What do your parents do, Cara?" Ren asks, retaking her seat next to me. Even though she tries to hide it, her interest is visible. I realize she's mostly kept her questions in the present thus far, about school, homework, things we've done since I've been here. I've been floating in a false sense of security created by her lack of pressure on me to divulge anything about my past. She must have other questions about me; I'm sure she assumed that, with time,

I would share a bit more of myself. I suppose I'll have to if I'm going to keep other questions at bay.

"My mother had a job in HR when we lived in London, but she gave that up when she met Mike and we moved to the U.S."

"And your father?" Hector prompts.

"My father's a journalist," I say sharply—the sharpness gives away that he's hit a sore spot. "My stepfather's the reason I'm here."

"So what does Mike do that has enabled you to be hanging out with the elite, then?"

"He works in real estate." I pause, debating whether to elaborate.

"And . . . ," he prompts.

"You know in American sitcoms when the real estate agent has a really smug image of their face on posters and billboards in the city?"

He smiles. "Yes . . ."

"Mike is actually that guy."

His smile widens. "You don't like him?"

"Mike's fine," I say honestly. "He's just pretty unremarkable. He sold a house to the head—that's how he and my mother found out about the school."

Something about his expression makes me think he already knows this, or at least he seems slightly too disinterested by the information.

"Do you have brothers and sisters?" Ren asks.

"Brothers," I say, "Connor and Kyle. They're twins, just turned three."

Hector looks at me intensely, something flickering behind his green eyes. "And you've been packed off here while they play happy families back in the Golden State," he says, his tone changing instantly. "One sympathizes."

I swallow. "Don't feel sorry for me; it's more complicated than that."

He knots and unknots his fingers together on the table. "I don't feel sorry for you at all. I'm in a similar situation myself."

"I very much doubt our situations are the same," I say, thinking of the real reason I'm here. I doubt even he would be able to talk himself out of that. "But I appreciate the attempt to empathize."

"You're very welcome," he says with a hint of annoyance. He stands up to clear his plate, hunches down so he's close enough that I can feel his breath on my face as he adds in a low voice, "A word from the wise: Don't be so judgmental, Cara. It's not a good color on you."

I watch him disappear to the other side of the dining room, momentarily stunned by his proximity.

Ren clears her throat. "He's in a strange mood this morning. . . ."

"Mmm," I mumble back, feigning disinterest and busying myself with buttering more toast. I feel ashamed. My criticism of Hector, and how he grew up, says more about me than it does him. I can't help feeling that our conversation has lowered me in his estimations. And that bothers me.

This disjointed feeling stays with me for the rest of the morning. And, more than everything, I realize—too late—that even though I knew from the very beginning that he was someone I should avoid, he's found his way under my skin.

I've let Hector become someone who is able to bother me.

After lunch, we gather outside the front door. The sky is a promising electric blue, and under the dazzling glare of the afternoon sun finally emerging from the clutches of a wall of clouds, the snow-covered mountains sparkle. In the distance, tall, spiky evergreens climb up the edges of the mountainside, dark against the bright white snow.

"The buses will be here in a minute," Madame Monelle announces through a megaphone. "Everyone get into lines so we can check attendance."

I glance sideways at Ren and feel myself unhinge. "We're getting on buses?"

"The ice rink is in a nearby resort," she says. "Come on, our year is gathering over there."

I let her go; I let her think I'm following her, but in reality I'm frozen. At least a dozen buses arrive in the courtyard. I watch them stop in a long line, the tires of a few of them struggling to grip the icy cobblestones. Looking around at the lines of people waiting to board the buses, I feel like I'm underwater. All sound is muted, my vision unfocused.

My survival instinct kicks in.

"It's too dangerous," I say aloud. A group of younger students look my way and laugh. I ignore them. There is no time for this—I must warn them. I need to make sure they don't get on the buses. I need to make the decision I should have made nine months ago.

I weave through the crowds, pushing past the people who stand in my way. My heart beats furiously, rebounding off my ribs, forcing my breath up from my lungs into my throat. I no longer care if I make a scene—as long as everyone is safe, nothing else matters.

"It's too dangerous," I repeat to Madame Monelle, who is by the door of the first bus.

"What is?" she says, looking up from the clipboard she's holding and tapping her pen against the side of it impatiently.

"The road is too icy," I say, my voice growing fervent with urgency. "The buses were skidding as they parked. You can't let everyone get on; the journey down the mountain will be worse. It's not worth the risk."

"You're new here, aren't you?" she says. "Cara, isn't it?"

I nod and keep my words level when really I want to scream at her. "Listen, people are already getting on the buses; you need to stop them. You need to stop them *right now*."

Why is she being so unresponsive? Why can't she see?

"No, you listen, Cara," she says calmly. "These bus drivers are used to these conditions. You have my word that it is totally safe."

"You can't give your word." I hear my voice rise, but I don't care. I need her to understand. "Who knows what's going to happen? You can't ensure that something won't happen. You can't!" I hear an echo of someone shouting and feel spurred on by it. They must see the danger for what it is too.

"Cara, you need to calm down," Madame Monelle says. "We're on a tight schedule; we do really need everyone to get on the buses—"

I cut her off, my fury rising up like a tide. "It's too risky! What if something happens? Do you want that on your conscience? *Do you?*"

Another shout echoes around the now-silent courtyard. I spin around and find at least a hundred faces staring at me. Then it hits me: the shouting is coming from me.

A small, slim woman pushes her way through the crowd. "What's going on here?" she says in a perfectly clipped British accent.

Madame Monelle gestures impatiently at me. "She's concerned about the safety of the students. She thinks the roads are too icy for the buses. Don't worry, everything is under control."

The woman looks at me fully for the first time, and I will her to take me seriously. Eventually she waves me forward. "Why don't you come with me and we'll discuss it?"

I breathe a heavy sigh of relief and hurry after her into the school.

12

The woman guides me along a corridor on the ground floor that I've never been down before. It is carpeted in a thick emerald pile that gives way beneath my feet. We continue to the end of the corridor, and every step we take reminds me of our increasing distance from the courtyard. This is all going to take too long. The buses will leave before we even get wherever we're going.

"Wait, Madame—"

"Mrs. King," she corrects me. She stops outside a paneled wooden door. "Come in here and we'll have a cup of tea."

I shake my head. "Mrs. King, I don't think you understand. The buses. The students. They're in danger."

Why am I the only one who realizes this?

"I do understand, Cara. I promise you that. Just come in here and sit for a minute," she says, her tone leaving no room for argument.

I do as she says, sitting down on the edge of a high-backed armchair in front of an immaculate fire. I feel myself fidgeting, desperate for her to do something about the situation. "Are you going to stop the buses?"

"I'm not," she replies levelly. "The drivers are used to being in these conditions, Cara. It's as safe to get in a vehicle here as it is anywhere else."

"Which isn't safe at all," I say angrily, standing up. "Especially not here. I was almost involved in a crash on my trip here. The drivers are insane. You need to stop—"

"Cara," she interrupts, unfolding a pair of green-rimmed glasses and putting them on slowly. Too slowly. "It's too late. The buses will have already left by now."

"Because you let them."

She goes over to the door to an adjoining room and sticks her head through to mutter something to someone I can't see. She turns back to me. "Yes, Cara, I let them leave. I had to. Plans for School Birthday have been organized for weeks. Everyone was expecting to go. We do this every year."

In this room, with the fire spitting methodically beside us, the tips of the flames stretching up the chimney, my defense starts to fizzle out.

"Please sit down." She looks at me kindly as I hover, unsure, next to the armchair. She nods, gesturing for me to sit. When I eventually do, she resumes her place in the chair opposite. "I should have introduced myself by now, really. I'm sorry I didn't, but you were settling in so well I didn't want to disrupt you. My husband is the headmaster here at Hope. We run the school together. I met your parents—I don't know whether you know, but your stepfather actually sold my husband and me a house not far from where you live. He's from America—like you."

"I was born in London," I say. I recognize that she's trying to find common ground with me—a tactic employed by all of the therapists I've seen in the last year. But this is not a therapy session, and I don't feel like playing along this time.

"Like me," she says with a smile. Another attempt to make me feel more comfortable. "Listen, Cara, I don't want there to be any secrets between us. Your mother told me all about your accident when we talked about you coming here, so I understand why you would worry about the buses today."

I tilt my body away from her and stare into the fire. When I don't say anything, she continues. "We are happy to welcome you to Hope, and contrary to the spiteful things some people say, we don't consider ourselves a last resort. We're picky about who we select to welcome into our ranks; you are a bright girl with lots of potential. I know, once you feel more settled, you'll understand that here you've been offered a chance."

I grit my teeth in irritation. "I get it. I know I'm lucky—"

She holds a hand up to stop me. "You're privileged, Cara. Don't confuse luck with circumstance—they are not the same thing."

My eyes snap back to hers, and I expect to see the pity that all adults who know what happened seem to look at me with. It's there, as I knew it would be, but there's something else mingled in, too, something like determination.

"I want you to get the most out of your time here," she says sincerely. "And I want you to enjoy it."

"I don't know whether I would enjoy anywhere at the moment," I reply. But that's not an entirely true statement. The past three weeks have had their ups and downs, but they haven't been completely horrible.

The door opens and a woman enters with a tray. Mrs. King pours out two cups of tea from a gleaming silver teapot and passes one to me. I take it shakily, droplets of tea slipping from the rim into the saucer.

"The way I see it," she says, "is that your happiness here all comes down to what matters to you. Do you want to make friends here? Do you want to do well enough that you get into university? Do you just want to be away from home? What do *you* want?"

"It doesn't matter what I want," I say angrily. I gave up the right to want things for myself nine months ago.

She leans back in her armchair and surveys me over the top of her glasses. "Okay, let's try this from a different angle. What did you want before your accident?"

I place the teacup, contents undrunk, back on the tray with more force than I planned. The china clinks ominously. "A lot of useless things. To be thinner, for my hair to be blonder, to be less self-conscious . . . the list goes on. None of those things matters now." I pause and feel the anger drain out of me, replaced with a cold, unflinching misery. "The worst thing is, I felt like my life was horribly unfair."

I look up to find her smiling, closed-lipped. "Well, life *can* be horribly unfair."

Her smile reignites my anger. "But life wasn't unfair for me then. All my wants were ridiculous and shallow."

"I wouldn't be overly critical of yourself. What you wanted then was demonstrative of where you were at that particular time."

"And look how far I've come," I say. I clutch sections of my hair, now a mousy blond, the ends bright and coarse from where the dye has grown out. I'm already thinner than I'd ever imagined I could be, but I feel no pleasure from any of it. The time when I cared about my appearance is long gone; I don't have the energy to be self-conscious.

She pushes her glasses farther up her nose and fixes me with a stare so knowing it might pierce me. "Things are different for you now," she says, nodding. Her eyes drift away from me, focusing on a few stray snowflakes floating past the window. "It always astounds me how blind we all are to how much say we have in our own stories. Regardless of what you wanted before—those things that no longer matter to you—there must be *something* now that you want more than anything else?"

The words escape my lips without me really thinking about them. "I want to live without having to force myself through each day."

My whole body stings at my answer. What I should have said: *I want to be able to talk to G again.*

She nods, satisfied. "You'll find that time is a great healer—"

"Time gives you distance, that's all," I say sharply. "It helps you to forget, but I am never going to forget what happened, so how on earth is time supposed to heal me?"

"Of course you're not going to forget the accident; it's part of your history. It's part of who you are. But I promise you this about how you feel right now: it gets better. This setback only feels insurmountable now because you're so young."

I'm hit by a sharp, immediate pain, like someone plunging a knife into my stomach and knocking the air out of me. "*Setback?* You call killing your best friend a setback?"

"Cara, wait—"

I let the door slam behind me.

13

I collect my books from upstairs, then find an empty classroom and set up camp for the afternoon. No one bothers me, but then again there's hardly anyone here. Outside the window, the teachers who are left put the finishing touches on the school for the evening's festivities. They set out lanterns and procession torches, and every now and then I watch one draped in fairy lights disappear out of sight.

Without the other students, an eerie silence takes over. At first, I find a certain degree of comfort in the isolation, like I did after I got out of the hospital, but after about an hour, the panic starts to set in. I didn't just lose it in front of one of my classes— I lost it in front of the whole school.

I distract myself with homework. I start with an English essay, then my math homework, then biology, then French and German grammar exercises. I've finished all of it by the time

I hear the buses pull up, and quickly turn off the lights in the classroom at the sound of the engines. The sun has long set, but the flames from torches wedged into the ground around the courtyard light up the school and beam into the room. I stand at the edge of the window, out of sight, and watch everyone disembark.

Three figures stand out from the crowd. Ren, Hector, and Fred walk together toward the front doors. The action feels natural—an insight into what life was like before I arrived—and I can't help but think I've royally screwed this one up. Hector and Ren must have seen my outburst and realized Fred was right all this time—I can just imagine them making up over me losing it, Fred forgiving them for their mistake.

I'm hit by how different my life is now from what it was a year ago. I would never have been alone like this. I took for granted how easy I had it then—it was the beginning of a new school year and I had my best friends around me. G, Poppy, Lennon, and I did everything together: every party, every lunch, every . . . everything.

We had even created our own code over the summer. It was Poppy and G's idea; they called it the PG Pocket Dictionary. There was something so exclusive about the whole thing: the four of us were the only people who knew the language, and that was exactly how we wanted it. The rule was we were allowed to add one word each a week. I remember that first week of the semester when Lennon added the word *tennis* to the lexicon. We were at Poppy's house, pretending to do homework around her kitchen table while her mum made us brownies. The PG Pocket

Dictionary was open on the table in front of us, disguised by the surrounding textbooks, and she wrote:

tennis—*noun*
To play tennis: to flirt outrageously.

"So, Poppy," Lennon asked nonchalantly. "Did you play tennis with Ben after lunch like you said you were going to?"

Her mum looked between us all, confused, which was one of the reasons we loved the dictionary so much. "Tennis?" she said. "You can't play tennis at school, can you?"

"Oh, you can, Mom," Poppy said. "And I've actually gotten quite good. These girls need a bit of practice, so it's lucky I'm on hand to help out when needed."

"So kind of you," G said.

"My pleasure."

G raised her eyebrows. "So how was the tennis? Do you think you'll play again?"

"I actually didn't play today," Poppy said. "We played golf instead."

She pulled the dictionary toward her and wrote:

golf—*noun*
To play golf: to make out, with tongue.

G suddenly seemed to find the textbook she was pretending to read more interesting than ever; Lennon had put her hand in her mouth to stop herself from giggling; I was trying to choke down a large gulp of water. It was like we were all holding our breath, not daring to be the first to break.

"Oh, now you're just showing off, Poppy," her mum said, beginning to sound annoyed. "You've never played golf in your life."

"Of course I have!" Poppy said indignantly. "I play golf all the time!"

I don't remember who lost it first, but we laughed—God, we laughed. Until our sides burned, and we were bent over, gasping for air with tears streaming down our faces. Until her mum completely lost her temper and demanded we explain what was so funny.

We didn't have a care in the world. We were young, unstoppable, so used to everything going our way—with no knowledge whatsoever of everything yet to come.

An hour later, when my whole body is stiff from sitting on the hard wooden floor, my mind is made up. Everyone will be at dinner, and it finally feels safe to go upstairs and start packing. I stop in the front hall, drawn toward the lights outside the open double doors. It's freezing—too cold to not be wearing a coat. Even so, I push myself onto the sleek, snow-coated cobbles outside. The surrounding mountains are faded and gray, with just a faint hiss of wind coloring the silence, and for a split second I wish I could stay here.

"There you are," says a familiar drawl. A figure hurries down the steps toward me. "California, it's bloody freezing out here. Get inside, you maniac."

"Go back to dinner," I say. I didn't want to run into anyone, particularly Hector. I'll have to explain myself, and it's not worth it. If I am going to get my mother to pull me out of here, I don't want anything that could be difficult to leave behind.

"Dinner just finished," he says, getting closer by the second. "I've come to take you to the performance."

"How did you find me?"

"I have my sources. Come on—let's just slip into the auditorium. No one will notice."

"After what happened this afternoon, everybody will notice."

"Okay, fine, they'll notice. But you'll have to face everyone eventually, so you might as well do it with me."

I push my hair back from my face and hold it there, suspended in the air. He makes everything sound easy; he makes me want to do what he says. I tear my eyes from his. "I can't stay here, Hector. Going to the performance isn't going to make everything better."

"Listen, Cara, what happened this afternoon—"

"This afternoon gave you a real taste of who I am," I cut in. "I'm not the girl who hops on a bus to go ice-skating or who goes to a bar on a Wednesday night with her friends. I don't deserve to have any friends at all."

"That's a ridiculous thing to say."

"Look, Hector, I'm grateful to you for trying to make me feel normal, but I haven't been normal for a while now, and nothing you do is going to change that."

"Why are you doing this?"

"Doing what?"

"Making life so difficult for yourself. It doesn't have to be this hard."

"It should be . . . after what I did."

"And what exactly did you do?"

I pause. I can't bring myself to tell him.

"The way I see it," he continues, "you haven't done anything except be unfortunate enough to be involved in a nasty car accident."

"What do you know about that?" I snap as a cold wave washes through me. My muscles turn to stone, weighty anchors rooting me to the spot.

"I know everything about that."

My self-preservation instinct kicks in. "Who told you?"

"No one told me."

"Don't mess with me, Hector."

"I'm not lying, Cara. No one told me. I read about it in your application file."

"You shouldn't have seen that—who showed it to you?"

"Does it matter?"

"Of course it matters," I say, although I don't know why. If he knows about the crash, he knows some of the worst parts of me. For some reason, he's still here.

"Look, Mrs. King told me that you might like to see a friendly face, so I came to find you. I might have just taken a trip via the registrar's office to see what I was up against first."

I am filled with an empty sort of dread. "You shouldn't have done that."

"Well, it's too late, Cara. I know about your accident. Get over it."

I want to scream at him. How can he say something like that? I turn my back, facing out into the blackness. "I don't expect you to understand anything from just reading the file."

"So explain it," he says softly, and I feel myself flinch from him. "You were driving back from a New Year's Eve party with your best friend. It was after midnight, but you hadn't been drinking. A truck took the slip road wrong, and you were in his blind spot. Your car flipped."

"She died," I say, because above everything I want to make him stop. The words are hollow, too simple to convey something that means so much. As I say them, grief rips through me. There is nothing emotional about this pain; it is purely physical and makes me feel—as close as is possible for a living, breathing person to feel—like I am dying.

I watch him wince. "But you lived, Cara."

I feel my anger flare up again. "You're saying that she died so I could live? A life for a life? Well, when she died, my life ended too."

"No, it didn't," he says in a very quiet voice. "Maybe a part of you wishes that were true. When Georgina died, your life changed course, that's all."

"Don't say her name," I say harshly. "You didn't know her."

"But I know you."

I press my face into my hands. Trying to block it all out. Trying to forget. "I'm not who you think I am," I say at last.

He stares intently back at me. "I've got a good idea of who you are."

I wait for him to take the words back, to walk away from me and never come back.

"You don't know the full story."

"So tell me," he says, hooking an arm around my shoulders, turning me to face the front doors. "But tell me inside."

"I can't," I say, pulling myself out from under his arm. I don't actually know whether it would be possible for me to articulate what happened out loud.

"Try me," he says seriously. "What's the worst that's going to happen? If you regret it afterward, we never have to see each other again. You can leave here, like you want, and it will all be forgotten. It's not like we'll run into each other again."

He ushers me inside, but the cold doesn't leave me.

"You don't need to know," I eventually say. "Really, Hector, you don't."

"But I do, Cara." He stares at me without pity. "You know I do."

I'm struck by a sense of inevitability. All I know is that if I was going to tell anyone, it was always going to be him.

14

New Year's Eve, San Francisco

The doorbell rings in the distance. I check my reflection one last time in the mirror—I bought a new dress especially for tonight: a short, long-sleeved dress covered in green sequins. I saw it first in a magazine ad. The model wearing it had bright blond hair, like mine, pulled back into a wavy ponytail; I'd do that part in the car. Tonight I wanted to be noticed, and this was the dress to do it. I make myself smile, but my reflection looks forced—nothing like the girl in the picture.

Mum calls up from downstairs. "Cara! Georgina's here." When G is around, and because she knows her so well, Mum mostly forgets to use her silly, over-the-top American accent.

"Coming," I call back, throwing one last glance around the

room to check I haven't forgotten anything. On a last-minute whim, I put on the opaquest black tights I own to get past her with the least probability of questions, then pull on a long duffel coat, grab my overnight bag, and head downstairs.

"I thought it was just girls going tonight, Cara," Mum says.

I don't even blink before I lie. "It is."

She frowns. "That's quite a lot of makeup you're wearing."

"Yeah, well, I've been trying out some of the stuff you got me for Christmas," I say, looking to G for backup. Typically, since her parents are strict on makeup, she is barefaced, waiting for me to hand mine over in the car.

One of my twin brothers waddles out into the hall in tears, and Mum is instantly distracted, scooping him up from the floor.

"See you tomorrow," I say, dodging around her and heading for the door.

"Have fun, girls," Mum says, not looking away from Connor, who, despite his tear-streaked cheeks, seems to have gotten over his tantrum as soon as it arrived. "And Happy New Year!" she calls after us as we're getting into G's car. We wave back, over-enthusiastically, then quickly shut the doors.

G pulls away from the house. "God, your mom is chill."

"Well, she doesn't actually know we're not going to Poppy's. . . ." I don't bother to put my seat belt on as I wriggle out of my tights and drop them into the footwell.

"Yeah, you're right; I think she bought it," G says with a wry smile. "Okay, I'm going to stop here and do my makeup." She pulls into a deserted parking lot on the side of the road and grabs the bag.

We both told our parents a well-crafted lie: we were going to stay at our friend Poppy's house for the night. Poppy's parents would be present to supervise. Her father is a pastor; therefore, they presumed there wouldn't be any alcohol. Her house was the safest bet—it always was. Poppy told her parents that she would be staying with G, so we were covered on all sides. In fact, we were going to Lennon's house. Her parents were going to a friend's house out of town and wouldn't be back until 2:00 a.m.— her house was off the beaten track, so there wouldn't be any noise complaints.

"James told me he wants to talk to me about something important," G says midway through applying her mascara. "I think tonight's the night."

"He's going to make it official?"

She crosses her fingers on her lap. "Let's not jinx it, okay?"

"Okay," I say, smiling. Secretly, though, I hope we do jinx it. If I told her that I was worried about her and James, I'd just sound like a jealous friend. James was nice enough, good-looking and popular. To be honest, I didn't really know him. But if they did start going out, wouldn't our friendship have to take a backseat? Wasn't that what always happened?

"Don't forget he's bringing Scott tonight too," she says, poking me in the shoulder. I kissed Scott at the beginning of Christmas break, and G hasn't been able to let it go since. I think, in her head, she has this romantic vision of us both having boyfriends who are best friends.

I smooth out a smeary fake-tan line on my leg. "I haven't forgotten."

She puts on lip gloss and, as she meshes her lips together, a thoughtful expression takes over her face. "How are you going to play it?"

"I haven't decided yet," I say, and start rummaging in my bag for a quarter. "Do you want to do the honors?"

She takes the coin from me and turns it between her fingers, poised to decide who will be the designated driver tonight. The stakes feel like they're higher than usual; if G is going to have a chat with James, I know she'll want some liquid courage. Then again, I wouldn't mind some of that for tonight too.

"Call when it's in the air."

I smile mischievously. "Yes, G, I know how it works."

Her eyes narrow as she launches the coin into the air; we watch as it twists and turns, deciding our fate.

"Tails," I call at the last minute.

She captures the coin between her palms, slowly revealing the president's head. A smile erupts on her face. "Bad luck, C. Looks like you're on the soda."

By the time we arrive, the party is in full swing. There are already fifty or so people there, with more pulling up as we enter the house.

"Thank God you're here," Lennon says as we enter the kitchen area. Her cheeks are flushed from drinking, which makes me wonder when the first people arrived. She gestures to large bags of Doritos splayed across the kitchen island. "Will you help put some of these into bowls, Cara?"

"Sure," I say, spinning around to find G has already disappeared, presumably to see if James is here yet. I take off my coat and put it on a nearby chair.

"Whoa," Lennon says, looking at me properly. "You've really gone all out." From her tone, I can tell she thinks my dress is too much.

"Well," I reply in a bored voice, "it *is* a party. What did you expect?" Then I make a point of looking her up and down, taking in her plain navy dress. She shifts, uncomfortable.

"Oh, good," she says, distracted by something behind me. "The boys are here."

I grab one of the bags of Doritos and busy myself with emptying it into a plastic bowl. I sneak a look in their direction when I'm sure she's not watching me. Sure enough, Scott is here, looking gorgeous as always: blond and somehow naturally tan even though it's winter and the weather has been appalling for weeks. They start to pull out trays of beer and bottles of liquor and stack them on the island next to me, where there is already a mountain of alcohol.

Poppy moves up next to me and starts refilling her vodka Coke. "Just was talking to G. Big night for her and James, apparently?"

"Yeah, she said."

Poppy glances over her shoulder, then lowers her voice. "Don't say anything, but I think she's got it wrong. James told me last week that he didn't want to be tied down."

I twist around just as James strides through the door to the kitchen. G reappears as if on cue and bounds up to him.

A part of me wonders if, as usual, Poppy is just trying to stir things up or if there's any truth in what she said. I want to warn G to be careful, but then they kiss, and I tear my eyes away. It will be all right. This is G we're talking about.

Someone moves up next to me, and Poppy's mouth curls into a huge, winning smile. "Hi, Scott!"

She looks expectantly at me, waiting for me to say something. Before I do, Lennon rushes up and pulls her off to help with the speakers, leaving Scott and me side by side. I glance around and consider what my night is going to look like. Lennon is already hammered, Poppy is well on her way there, and G is clearly planning to spend her whole night with James.

Scott starts to pour himself a drink. "Want one?"

"Can't. I'm the driver."

"Shame." He gives me a lingering look and takes a long sip from his plastic cup. "Nice dress, by the way."

I make up my mind, holding eye contact with him, and think fleetingly of Lennon's definition of tennis. I know if I'm going to play, I'll bring my A game.

I lean back against the counter, tilt my head to one side, and say, "I wore it especially for you."

"Did you?" He looks taken aback—exactly as I intended. I mean, I don't have a reputation for nothing.

I laugh, in a teasing sort of way. "Of course not."

I walk away and, like I knew he would, he follows.

———

G appears after an hour or so and throws herself down next to Scott and me on the sofa.

"James and I are official," she announces. My first thought is that she's on the brink of being really quite drunk, my second is that she's happy—really happy. The happiness is pouring out of her, tinting her words, her body language, and making her oblivious to the look that Scott gives James. One of confusion.

"That's exciting, G!" I say, beaming, and throw my arms around her.

Over her shoulder, James shrugs at Scott and mouths, "I don't know how . . ."

I hold on to G for longer than normal, my eyes swiveling between the two, a tight feeling in my throat.

G pulls herself free of me and rushes over to tell Lennon and Poppy. I grab Scott's arm and pull him up to standing with me. "I need to talk to you."

"Sure," he says, giving me a quizzical look.

"In private," I say, and head toward the stairs. I hear his footsteps behind me, and I go into the nearest empty bedroom I can find.

"What's up?" he says, taking a step closer to me.

I take a step back. "It's James . . . Poppy told me he's been saying he doesn't want to be tied down."

"James has always been a bit of an enigma." Scott smiles, but it doesn't quite ring true.

"Look, Scott, if . . . if . . ." I don't know how to word it. I end up just asking, "Is he serious about her? Because if she goes around shouting about how they're going out and then tomorrow he changes his mind . . ." I sit down on the edge of the bed, and he takes the spot next to me.

"Stop stressing, Cara. You can't do anything about it."

"I know . . . it's just she really likes him."

"And he likes her," he says as if that settles things. I can't help thinking that he and I have a different version of what liking someone means. "You girls are always so literal about everything."

I jerk my head back. "What's that supposed to mean?"

He never answers, because at that moment someone shouts, "Is this a joke?" directly outside the door. I recognize G's voice before I see her, and I rush out to find her. She is glowering through the doorway of the bedroom directly across from where we are.

"You just asked me out. . . . What are you doing with *her*?"

I look through the doorway and am horrified—as horrified as G sounds—to see James and Poppy standing there. I look between them both, but even as I start to question what's going on, I know.

Poppy moves toward her, arm outstretched. "G, I can explain—"

G bats her away, her eyes brimming with tears. She teeters slightly, and I'm reminded of how much she's had to drink. It hits me that if I don't do something now, this is going to blow up, and there are too many people around for the fallout.

"We're going," I say sharply, putting an arm around her and pushing her toward the stairs. She stumbles on them, grabbing me by the arm for balance.

"Let's get out of here," I say with a sense of urgency. "Come on—I'll drive you home."

She fumbles in her bag outside her car, and I take the keys from her. I open the passenger door and help her inside, putting her seat belt on for her. She slumps down and stares out the window, silent tears pouring down her cheeks.

As if in solidarity, it starts to rain as we get onto the highway— thick diagonal streams of water hit the windshield. Inside the car, the clock on the dashboard changes to 12:00. A voice on the radio wishes us a happy new year. We'd talked about this moment for weeks. A new year, a new us. G would be going out with James; I'd be starting something properly with Scott. This year would be different.

Everything next happens in slow motion. I don't register the truck—only the impact. The car spinning first, then flipping.

15

*Hector and I sit at either end of my bunk, facing each other. Some-*where in the story his hands covered mine, pressing them down into the mattress.

"We should have stayed at the party," I say desperately.

He raises his eyebrows. "Stay when she'd just caught one of her best friends with her boyfriend? I don't think so. It was right to leave when you did, Cara. You were just looking out for her."

I hear my sharp intake of breath; if guilt could kill, I'd already be dead, like I'm supposed to be. "I should never have suggested it; I should have just let her confront them properly. Maybe then they'd have been the ones to leave. I hadn't even worked out how I was going to explain to my parents why we came home— why G was blind drunk and why I was driving her car. I hadn't thought it through. We left on impulse. An impulse that cost G her life."

Hector's hands contract over mine. "What about your friends Poppy and Lennon? What was their explanation for the night?"

I close my eyes. "Neither of them visited me at the hospital, then I never went back to school. I saw them only once after it happened, and there was so much blame there, I couldn't face either of them again."

"And they couldn't face you."

I open my eyes. "What do you mean?"

"Come on, Cara, you must see it? Your friend Lennon hosted the party that ended with the accident. There's some responsibility there. And then Poppy and James, well, that's pretty self-explanatory, wouldn't you say?"

"I was the driver, Hector," I cut in sharply. "I'm the one responsible."

He ignores me. "What happened to the driver of the truck?"

"He died on the way to the hospital."

"Do you think you'd feel differently about the accident if he'd survived?"

I pull my hands out of his grasp. "What are you saying?"

"I'm just finding it a little odd that this is the first time the other driver has come up. I mean, if you really felt you were responsible for the accident, you'd be responsible for not one but two deaths. But this truck driver you feel nothing for—"

"That's not fair—"

"It's not a criticism, Cara. All I'm saying is that if he'd lived, I'd put money on him being the one punished for this. The fact that he died means that you have to bear the weight of it. There were three of you there and you're the only one who survived."

"I wish I hadn't survived."

He sits up taller on the bed. "Don't ever say that."

"Hector, didn't you listen to the story? Didn't I make it clear what I'm like? I was vile; if anyone should have died, it should have been me. Not her."

"Cara, it sounded like you were pretty normal. . . ."

"Yeah, well, I must have glossed myself up, then. I should have made myself sound like more of a bitch, because that's what I was. I spent most of my time being horrible to Poppy and Lennon, making them feel insecure because I felt insecure. Scott . . . well, I didn't even like him. I just didn't want to be seen on my own at the party. Hector, I was—I *am*—awful. G was innocent—she was the one who made me even the tiniest bit likeable."

"Cara, you're forgetting how protective you were of her. How you were the one who questioned James's motive, how you were the one who stepped in to take her home—"

"That's what killed her!" I exclaim, the words catching in my throat. "*I* made us leave. *I'm* the reason she was in that car."

We stare at each other for a long moment, and in the silence that follows I regain control of my breathing. *In, out. In, out. In, out.* His green eyes flicker with intent, and without breaking eye contact, he says, "You've got another chance here."

"What's the point in all this? It's the final year. We're here for, what? Nine months max? And then everyone goes back to where they came from. Nothing is going to change in that time."

"Hasn't everything changed already?"

"Hector, you're not hearing me."

"I am, Cara," he says. "Trust me, I am. What I'm trying to say to you, not very eloquently I'll admit, is that you've got a second chance here. And frankly, you've been using it already. I mean, you say you were awful then, but well, you've been fine company here—"

I give him a scathing look, and the corners of his mouth turn up slightly.

"I think you've misjudged me."

He shakes his head. "I disagree."

His sincerity terrifies me; it also makes me want to apologize for a million things.

I only seem to give voice to one: "I'm sorry about how judgmental I was of you earlier. You seem to be giving me all these free passes. Fred is right about me, Hector. I've been hiding stuff, and for some reason you seem to be persevering with me. I wish I could convince you not to."

"Forget Fred," he says, annoyed now. "He hasn't even given you a chance."

But Fred's words are never far from my mind. I want to tell him that Fred is the only one who is seeing me clearly. *I am a wolf, Hector, and you can't see it.*

"I can't stay here."

"You have to stay here, Cara. Don't you see? You've just admitted the hugest thing to me, and nothing terrible has happened."

The slamming of doors and the sound of voices starts to travel toward us as everyone makes their way back from the performance.

"I should go," he says, slipping down the ladder and heading for the door. He hesitates before pulling it open, turning back to face me. "Look, Cara, I'm not saying it's going to be easy, and I'm most certainly not going to sugarcoat it for you. Tomorrow morning people are going to be whispering about what happened today—you've given Joy and Hannah enough ammo for months—and I doubt Fred's hostility is going anywhere. There's also Ren. . . ."

My stomach knots itself into a ball. "What about Ren?"

"You're going to have to tell her eventually, you know. She might be more patient about being in the dark than I am, but she's still human. If you're going to spend so much time with her, you have to let her in."

The voices in the corridor get louder and I will him to go before Ren gets back so that I can pretend to be asleep and don't have to face her tonight.

"I'm sorry," he continues as he opens the door, "but I'm being honest with you, like you've been with me. I'm telling you a horrible truth, because that's what you and I need to do. No filters."

But that's the thing, Hector, I think when he's gone. *I haven't been honest with you at all.*

16

As Hector said it would be, the aftermath of my outburst on School Birthday is brutal. The few people who missed it have quickly been brought up to speed by the whispering and pointed looks that become my shadows over the next week. Joy and Hannah make a point of discussing the ice-skating whenever I am nearby, and I hear the word *unhinged* muttered more times than I can count. Ren loyally skirts the subject, but there's a void of unsaid things between us. How can we pretend that there isn't? Even the evenings, which used to be a time of sanctuary, start to feel like a battlefield.

Because the dreams have started again.

She's there almost every night, the rain battering against the windshield, the tears pouring down her face. . . . The car splinters shortly afterward and I wake up breathless, horrified at how real it is, at all the aspects of that night I can't normally bear to think about. Telling Hector about what happened on New Year's Eve has awakened the night in my mind—in high definition.

I'm on thin ice—someday soon it's going to break, and this time I'll fall right through. Still, I don't call my mother and get her to pull me out of here. I can't say why.

I am reminded why I want to call her during PE the following Friday afternoon. We're inside once again, for a mixed game of basketball. I'm instructed to mark a boy named Drew, who Fred now spends all his time with.

"Should I be concerned that you're my partner?" he asks, smirking. "I mean, it's icy outside." He does an impression. "It might not be safe."

The impression, of course, is of me. But instead of the surrounding people falling into peals of laughter, instead of the looks that I'm used to, Fred appears out of nowhere. "Leave her alone, Drew," he says.

"What?" Drew says. "I wasn't saying anything that the whole school hasn't already heard."

I wait for Fred to agree, but he surprises me by saying, "Just drop it, man."

Drew, annoyed by this dismissal, calls back over his shoulder, "Jesus, Fred, what's up with you? You into her or something?" It's said in a way that underlines how he would be crazy if he was.

I don't move, still shocked by Fred's moment of gallantry. I glance gratefully at him; he remains stony-faced. He turns back to the game and says in a low voice, "To be clear, I categorically am *not* into you."

I take a step forward, so we're side by side, and reply in a low voice, "Thank God for that."

And there it is, a signal that I might actually break through to the other side. It's only there for a second—an involuntary twitch that he tries to hide—but it was there all the same: a tiny smile.

I trudge through swirling sleet to the deserted art building after prep. A half-finished, meticulously put-together wooden miniature of the school sits in the center. It is a perfect imitation, with the exact amount of windows and the three golden domes faultlessly sized on top.

Ren steps out of the shadows. "What do you think?"

"This is yours?"

She nods nervously. "My final piece for the diploma."

"It's extraordinary."

"Extraordinary good or extraordinary weird?"

I roll my eyes. "I've been wondering what you've been doing here all this time. Wow—you're really talented, Ren."

She shakes her head, walking around it in a circle. "I'm trying to get bits together to apply for an art foundation course in London for next year. It's not finished. I need to do the cable-car station somehow . . . and the outbuildings. Have you applied for anything yet? I know Hector's planning on taking a year off, getting a job for a bit back home. It will be nice to know I have one familiar person in the same city as me—if I get in, that is."

"You'll get in," I say, ignoring her question. I am barely considering tomorrow, let alone next year.

"You could apply for something in London too? Didn't you say your dad lives there?"

"Listen," I say abruptly, "I need to talk to you about Fred."

"What has he done now?"

"Well, he—sort of—stood up for me today in PE."

"He did?" Her reaction lacks surprise. "That's good, isn't it?"

"Did you say something to him?" The only explanation is that she told him to back off, that she's had words with him after watching me lose my mind every night.

She shifts uncomfortably. "Half-term is coming up: he's probably just realized you're here to stay. I told you he'd get over it." She passes me a piece of the design. "Will you just hold this while I glue it?"

We don't talk about Fred again, but I can't help feeling that Ren's just as good at dodging questions as I am.

Whatever untruths Ren fed to me about Fred, she was right about the approach of half-term. I log in on one of the computers in the conservatory after Saturday morning prep to download some old French exam papers, and my school email account pops up. Among the dozen emails with photos of the twins from my mother, there's a lone one from my father:

From: thomascooper.freelance@virginmail.co.uk
To: ccooper@hopehall.com
Subject: Half-term

Hi Cara,

How are you getting on? Your mum says it's all going well at Hope. Sounds like it's a pretty fantastic spot.

Been thinking . . . Half-term is coming up, isn't it?

London's only a short flight from Switzerland if you wanted to come here for the week?

I'd love to see you.

Dad

I shut down the computer immediately and head back upstairs to change out of my uniform before lunch.

A noticeboard has been set up outside the corridor with a list of where everyone is going for half-term. There is a note underneath to say that if you're going home, you'll need written permission from parents and a detailed travel itinerary. As the school houses students from all over the world, many have put their names down to stay at school. There is another note to say that if you're staying, a strict activity regime has to be adhered to, along with extra review sessions. It sounds dire, but I add my name to the list all the same—even if I felt I could go home to San Francisco, it's too far, and I'd have to be pretty desperate to take my father's email seriously. Anyway, if I've learned anything from School Birthday, it's that I'm not ready to travel quite yet.

On Sunday evening, I head to the phone room to tell my mother my plans. I look over the list once again before I do. Over the weekend, Hector and Ren have filled in where they are going. Hector, home to London; Ren, home to Lyon. It makes sense that they would go home, their homes not being on the other side of the Atlantic, but it fills me with dread all the same.

On my way to make the call, another name catches my eye. The ink looks wet, like it's just been inscribed: Fredrik Lindström, Lyon with Ren. I feel a dead sort of weight in my stomach. Why has Ren invited Fred to her home for half-term?

It's my fault, really. I need to remember that she is not a surrogate for G. We don't do everything together; we don't make plans with the other in mind. It is not a betrayal for her to ask Fred home and not me. As I am coming to terms with this, a voice in my head says, *What do you expect, Cara? Can you blame her for not wanting to invite you? Remember what you did to your last friend.*

I suddenly feel a rush that has nothing to do with Ren's lack of invitation. The calling card slips from my fingers and onto the floor. When I bend down to pick it up, my hands shake so furiously that I don't know whether I will be able to. I leave it be, turning on the spot and heading back to the dorm before anyone can ask me what's wrong. The voice keeps chiming, circling around in my head, as I climb the ladder to my bunk and press my face into my pillow, willing it to stop.

But it's there, reminding me of the part of what happened that night that I *have* to forget, until I fall straight into the dream.

17

I'm upside down in a car, no knowledge whatsoever as to how I got here. The seat belt is too tight; my chest is too tight. Piece by piece, my sight starts to glue itself back together. Then the panic comes, soaring skyward with every breath I take. Threatening to over-come me, threatening to tear me apart. I have just one thought: *I need to get out of this car.*

I try to pull at the seat belt that's pinning me in my seat. Even with every inch of my strength, the strap doesn't budge. I thrash against it, twisting, trying to gain myself some freedom. That's when I see her. Her body is limp against her seat belt, but there is something I don't recognize. Like a déjà vu that can't be ex-plained. I look away; I have to look away.

There are sequins everywhere: on the dashboard, on the roof of the car, mixed in haphazardly with the shattered glass. I start to recall a dress. A green sequined dress for a party. The radio is on in the background. A song comes to its end, the music fading into speech. I hear three words: *Happy New Year.*

And I remember.

I twist to look at G. Her eyes are open this time. Alive, but something's not right. My sight is suddenly too clear, every movement in high definition. I lift my arms to reach for her, but, no longer lifeless, she pulls away from me. That's when I see it. One of her arms is bleeding, long trails pouring from a deep, jagged bone-baring cut from wrist to elbow. I look down at myself, expecting to see an identical one—the one I know so well—but it's not there.

The sequins lose their shine, coated with even more blood. I can't work out where it's all coming from. My gaze travels to my hands, which are mangled, bent out of shape. In an instant I feel everything shift, my legs twist at funny angles, I start to taste blood, whole mouthfuls of it. I look desperately at her for help.

Her lips start to move and her words—dark, unforgiving— hit me loud and clear: "You did this . . ."

Then the world starts to rewind all around us. The car flips back onto its wheels, seating us upright. The glass starts to repair itself before my eyes. The sequins reattach themselves—to *her* dress. My body starts to straighten again. The door next to me starts to smooth itself out, removing all trace of impact from its surface. There is a terrible crunching noise, like metal contracting. Headlights draw away into the distance. Time stops. The road is still.

I hear the echo, over and over again. A warning, a declaration, an admonishment. *You did this. You did this. You did this.*

And then we press play. The headlights bear down upon us again, and I look at her one last time, before everything shatters.

I open my eyes and sit up, gasping for air. In one instinctive movement, I check my hands. They are whole, unmarked. They are mine, not hers. I jolt out of bed, down the ladder.

I can't go back to sleep.

But mostly, I just can't breathe.

18

I press my face into a basin of freezing cold water in the bathroom, hoping to burn away any inclination to sleep. I can't risk reentering the same dream, not when it's so unfamiliar. When I resurface, my cheeks are flush and raw, and I feel the closest I've felt these past months to tears. Above everything, I don't understand why I'm so upset by this new dream. Isn't this what I've wanted all along? Haven't I always said that it should have been me? Why is the reality of that so horrific?

The person I see in my reflection above the basin disgusts me: she is terrified. Terrified to find herself in G's place. The place she deserved to be in that night. I can't bear to look at her any longer.

Even though it's the middle of the night, Hector is in the common room, dressed for outdoors. He balances forward on his toes by the fire-escape door next to the bay window, fiddling with something there. He snaps down to normal height on hearing me enter. "Oh, it's you," he says, face relaxing as he turns back to the task at hand. He continues over the low rumble of scraping metal. "It's a pleasure to see you, as always, but I have to ask: Why are you here at this late hour?"

"Can't sleep," I answer with a poor attempt to make my voice emotionless.

His arm, stretched up above the door frame, freezes. Eventually he says, "Join the club."

The sleeves of his jacket fall back toward his elbows, revealing part of a black line inked on his forearm. I study him for a few moments, considering whether to turn back. My curiosity gets the better of me. "What are you doing?"

"Trying not to set off the fire alarm," he answers, and there's a loud click. "Disabled," he adds by way of explanation as he pulls open the door.

A gust of freezing air blows into the room. He gestures through the door to where a small metal balcony is visible. "Care to join me? I'd grab your coat if I were you."

"It's in the dorm," I say, looking down at my leggings and sweatshirt and shivering from the cold that has already filled the room.

"Just use one of those," he says, pointing to the line of pegs by the door where branded Hope Hall coats hang. "They're communal."

I choose the fleeciest one I can and follow him onto the balcony, which turns out not to be a balcony at all but a landing area for an outdoor metal staircase that leads up to the roof. Hector props the door open with a slim textbook and we creep up the stairs, taking care not to make our footsteps heard.

Huge snowflakes swirl all around us and settle on my cheeks. It feels like it should be darker than it is, but behind us the golden domes on the roof are faintly lit, making the darkness less opaque.

"You have a death wish," I murmur to him, wrapping the coat tighter around me as we reach the top.

He quirks up an eyebrow in amusement. "It's invigorating, right?"

The steps put us on a small terrace sunk into the roof between two of the golden domes. I almost lose my footing before Hector grabs my arm. I tense at the contact, but, as if he anticipated my reaction, he lets go just as quickly, though the feeling doesn't disappear quite as fast.

"Don't walk on there—it's sheet ice," he says in a quieter-than-usual voice. "I learned that the hard way on my first trip up here."

I nod stupidly, my cheeks flushed with cold. "Where do we go, then?"

He gestures to the short wall encasing the terrace, sitting down on the edge and sliding onto it. He moves up so there is room for me too. I copy his positioning, sitting upright on the wall, terrace behind us, and rest my feet on the tiles for added balance. The wall sits at the very top, the start of the tiled slope toward the ground. One wrong move and we could fall forward, straight off the back of the building.

"Want to talk about what's keeping you up?" he asks.

"Not right now." *Not ever* would be more appropriate, but I don't want to be unfriendly toward him—not after he's done so much for me. More than he can know. "You?"

"Absolutely not."

I find a small smile from somewhere, and his mouth turns up in symmetry with mine. "What happened to horrible truths and all that?"

"Time and a place, California. Time and a place." He scrunches up his eyes in the darkness, swiping flecks of snow out of them. "We keep running into each other at odd times. It's like we're in some sort of sync. Well, unless you're stalking me. I suppose you're finding it difficult to resist my nighttime attire?"

I glance at him, taking in his sweats, his coat—hardly suited to sleep in the first place. I roll my eyes.

We pass a moment in silence. "You didn't tell anyone . . ."

He quirks an eyebrow. "Didn't tell anyone what?"

"About what I told you on School Birthday," I say in a quiet voice.

"Not my place to say anything. Did you expect me to?"

"I don't know," I say quietly. "I think . . . I . . . well, I think I misjudged you when I first arrived."

"In what way?"

"I thought you were like a hundred boys I've met before."

"Let me guess, you thought I was"—he puts on his terrible American accent again—*"a dumb jock."*

A small smile escapes my lips.

"You did, didn't you?" He laughs lightly. "Didn't anyone ever teach you that you shouldn't judge a book by its cover, California? Even if the cover is this appealing."

I scrunch my face up. "Jesus, Hector, you're very close to ruining it."

"Well, we can't have that," he says seriously, but his smile betrays him.

I tear my eyes away and stare out at the ash-gray mountains all around us. "How did you find this place?"

"I've been here for four years, California—I told you that. And, well, I'm just one of those people who doesn't need a lot of sleep."

"Do you come here a lot?"

"Every now and then. There's talk of a new alarm system being installed that could prove problematic in the future, so I'm making the most of this spot while I can."

"Why here?" I look around, at the surrounding mountains, at the low glimmer of lights from the town across the crevasse. The silence is all around us, making me feel that there is nothing here. Nothing but us.

He doesn't meet my eye. "Would you rather be somewhere else?"

There are lots of places I should rather be, but I can't seem to summon any of them in my mind.

I lean forward slightly, and my right foot slips on the tiles, sleek with unsettled snow. I inhale sharply and swear under my breath, shaken by my momentary carelessness. "It's a pretty dangerous place to come all by yourself—it would be so easy to fall."

"And yet, Cara," he says, "you and I are being careful to stay put."

"Are we?" My voice lacks color. "Because, to me, this is just us sitting on the edge of a roof in the middle of nowhere. I'm not being careful about anything. . . ."

He holds my gaze, and I falter under its intensity. "You're being careful about everything now."

"You're wrong," I say. I want to tell him that sitting here, isolated from everything I have ever known, just reminds me that I have nothing left to lose.

He studies me again, with those probing green eyes; I contemplate what would happen if I let him see me—really see me. I am tempted, I can't deny it, but I know that temptation wouldn't lead anywhere good.

He rests his hand on my leg, and again I jump at the contact. This time, he doesn't remove it. He drops his voice to its lowest, quietest decibel, and I feel the reverberations in the air all around me. "You won't feel like this forever, you know."

I so want to be able to believe him—God, how I want that. But I can't because how I feel about G's death is never changing. Standing very still. Not moving forward. Progress is impossible. Nothing will ever change; nothing will ever get better.

"It gets better," Hector says firmly, and I wonder how he can possibly know.

19

I can't cast away the dream. It stays with me for the rest of the following day. Dream-G's reproach—*you did this*—doesn't fade, and as I try to hold myself together on the outside, I feel myself unraveling within.

I take my French phrase book into the courtyard at morning break and pretend to learn vocabulary so I can avoid talking to anyone.

Ren brings two steaming cups of tea over to the bench and sits down next to me. "Have I done something to upset you?"

"No," I mutter. Out of the corner of my eye, I watch her set the tea down next to me in a swift, careless motion.

"You've barely talked to me this morning," she says, her face set with determination. "If there's a problem, I'd rather know what it is."

I gesture to the book in my hand. "I've just got a lot to do."

She makes an impatient noise. "Where were you last night? I woke up and you weren't in the dorm."

"Couldn't sleep," I say shortly.

"You should have woken me up."

I look up from the book, irritated. "Ren, please leave it. I'm fine, okay?"

"Fine," she snaps. "If that's what you want, I'll drop it."

She stands up stiffly and disappears back into the school without a second glance. I should feel guilty; I suppose a part of me does. But guilt has become so ingrained that these days it's hard to tell.

To complicate matters, when I get to lunch, Fred is back in the vacant seat next to Hector. He turns up for dinner, too, and even joins our table in the conservatory for prep. While his hostility toward me has thawed a little since that PE class, I occasionally catch him shooting wary glances my way that I don't have the energy to return. The message is clear: we'll coexist, but I am not to be trusted yet.

Sometime in the afternoon, the school is put on lockdown. The teachers bar the outer doors and remind us in every lesson that no one is allowed in or out. On the way to the conservatory, I almost walk straight into a huge blackboard citing poor weather conditions as the reason for our containment, but when I take my seat in prep and stare out of the window, "poor" doesn't seem a strong enough description for the blizzard raging outside. It looks like someone has covered up the wall of windows with a white sheet: there is zero visibility.

Hector finds me on the window seat in the common room

after classes, watching the snow fall furiously outside. "What's going on with you?"

"Why does everyone keep asking me that? I'm fine."

He raises his eyebrows and pulls himself up next to me. "You and Ren had a fight."

"Why would you say that?"

He raises his eyebrows. "Oh, come on, Cara. She's in a filthy mood; you've barely uttered a word all day. It's hardly rocket science."

"I'm just tired," I say, not looking him in the eye. "I barely slept last night."

"Yes," he says in a bored voice. "I'm aware of that."

We pass a minute in loaded silence. Events of the past forty-eight hours swirl around inside me, poisoning my thoughts: my father's email, the half-term list, the dream, the rooftop, Fred's return.

I can't hold it in anymore. "Well, I see Fred's back to being everyone's best friend today. . . ."

A look of comprehension dawns on Hector's face. "That's what this is about?"

"It just seems a bit convenient, that's all. No one has spoken to Fred for weeks—"

"I share a dorm with Fred, California," he cuts in, pressing his fingers together thoughtfully. "We have shared the occasional word these past few weeks, you know?"

"Yes, well, he and Ren haven't. And now, suddenly, it's like the past few weeks are forgotten just in time for her to invite him home for half-term."

"If this keeps up, California, none of us are going anywhere this weekend."

"Good," I snap.

The corners of his mouth twitch.

"What is even vaguely amusing about any of this?"

"You're jealous."

"I am not jealous," I say, and I feel a sharp pain in my chest at the accusation. Am I jealous? Have I really not changed at all since I've been here?

He smiles apologetically at me. "Horrible truths, Cara. That's what you and I promised each other."

"You're pretty damn selective with the truths you choose to share with me."

He stares defiantly at me. "And you're not?"

My hands clench into fists. I use them to push myself off the window seat. I am filled with the urge to get far away from him before I reveal anything else. I should never have dropped my guard with him; I should never have let him discover part of why I'm so messed up. The only thing that frightens me more than being analyzed is being analyzed by someone with actual insight.

"Hector told me everything," Ren says when she enters the dorm later that evening.

"Everything?" I lie very still, forgetting to breathe. Not everything. Surely not *everything*.

"You're upset about Fred coming home with me."

My whole body relaxes as I let air back into my lungs. "I just think you should be careful," I eventually say, forcing myself to keep my expression blank. "A minute ago you were upset that he was being so distant, now you're inviting him to stay for the week. You're leaving yourself open for more crap from him. I mean, I know he stuck up for me the other day, but that hardly excuses him for cutting you out for the past few weeks. I don't want you to get hurt, Ren. That's all."

She sighs impatiently. "Cara, I couldn't ask you."

"It's not about me, Ren. I'm not jealous." I wonder if I'm repeating this to convince myself.

"Cara, listen—"

I cut her off. "I'm just looking out for you, Ren—that's all I'm saying. He can't have changed over the weekend. It's too quick a turnaround—"

"CARA!" she shouts, shocking me into silence. "Listen to me. I would have asked you—I wanted to ask you—but it's not that simple. My parents . . . they think Fred is my boyfriend."

This stops me short. "What? They don't know that you're gay?"

"No, they don't. And they can't know. Not after how they reacted last time."

"What happened?"

"There were rumors at my last school and they reached the parents. I was at an all girls' school. Nothing had happened then, but I knew. I tried to tell my parents how I felt—that I didn't like boys. I love my parents, but they're very traditional. We live in a small town. Everyone knows everyone—everyone is supposed to be the same as everyone. They told me I was too young to know how I felt about something like that; I needed to be around boys, and then I'd feel differently. They pulled me out of school and sent me here."

"You can't help how you feel, Ren."

"It doesn't matter how I feel, Cara. Do you know what it's like for your parents to look at you as though you're broken somehow? You can't imagine the shame. All I wanted was to be normal in their eyes."

Actually, I can, I want to say. *I know exactly how that feels.*

"Then, during my first term here, I met Fred," she continues. "His parents live in China; they're diplomats. They work at the Swedish embassy there, so he had nowhere to go that first half-term. I invited him home, and my parents made assumptions about us. We've kept it up for years."

"So after everything he's done this term, how he's behaved, you're just going to forgive him for the sake of convenience?"

"Yes," she says, unable to meet my eyes. "I have to, Cara. This is what we've always done."

I stare at her. "That doesn't mean you have to keep doing it."

She still won't look at me. "I'm sorry I can't invite you, Cara, I really am. At least now you know why."

She grabs her toothbrush and backs out of the room before anything more can be said on the subject.

20

The dream wakes me before dawn.

I tiptoe to the common room as stealthily as possible. In fact, my entrance to the common room is so covert that Hector doesn't hear me come in. His silhouette is unmoving—rigid and upright—and there is an urgency to his tone that I've never heard before. I stand magnetized to the one side of the rapid exchange in Spanish available to me, picking up nothing at all from it. Right at the end, he switches to English. "Valeria, listen to me. I'll be home soon—you just need to hang in there until then, okay?" The caller says something on the other side that I don't catch. "Look after yourself," he says just before putting the phone down.

When the line is cut, Hector, oblivious to my presence, proceeds to slam the receiver against the base repeatedly. The noise echoes around the space, building up in a furious crescendo. His expression remains tortured, and I have no doubt that if he continues, he'll break the phone. I step forward to stop him, and he swivels around, alerted by my sudden movement.

"How long have you been here, Cara?" he demands.

I step back, away from him. "I . . ."

His face doesn't relax. "Were you eavesdropping?"

"I don't speak Spanish," I say quickly.

His expression converts to relief. "Right," he says, more to himself than me.

"What's going on? Are you okay?"

He looks at me, but it's like he's not really seeing me. "I'm . . . Am I . . . ? No," he finally says. "No. I'm not okay."

He whips past me out of the room before I can ask anything else.

Hector is missing from school for the rest of the day. Ren, Fred, and I spend it watching classroom doors, waiting for him to enter, and for the first time in ages I forget about the dream; I forget myself completely.

By prep, it's clear that something is seriously wrong.

"Why is the headmaster here?" Ren asks.

Mr. King walks swiftly through the room, stopping to have a conversation with one of the teachers on duty. A blurry figure approaches our table, obstructing my vision of him, then Mrs. King comes into focus.

"Have you seen Hector?" she asks curtly.

"Not at all today," Fred says. "He wasn't in the dorm when I woke up either. Is everything okay?"

Her eyes flash for a millisecond before settling back to normal. "Oh, yes," she says. "I just need to discuss his travel plans for this weekend with him. If you see him, please could you send him my way?"

"Of course," Ren says.

Mrs. King turns back to her husband; in a corner of my vision I see her briefly shake her head at him.

Ren turns back to us. "What's going on? Where has he gone? He's never disappeared before—well, not since . . ."

Fred flashes her a warning look. "We need to find him," he says, abruptly standing up. His chair scrapes against the wooden floor. "I'll do the boys' dorms on all the floors."

"You should check the roof too," I add.

He nods once. "Good point. Ren, you do the girls' dorms, and, Cara, you can do this floor. Let's meet back in the entrance hall in thirty minutes."

I check all the classrooms, I take the hidden-door route he showed me, I even look for others I don't know about, but beneath it all I know that Hector won't be found if he doesn't want to be. Unlike my less-than-perfect plan to hide for an afternoon in a classroom (evidently known all along by the way Hector so effortlessly found me), he is doing a stellar job. Then again, he has been here long enough to know where the blind spots are.

The front door is open again, the snowfall lessened enough overnight to permit trips outside, but there are still meter-high mounds of snow at the edges of plowed paths. I lean in the doorway, half of my body exposed in the freezing air, and wait for Ren and Fred to return. If I were in his position, where would I go? I zoom in on the facts in my head. What do I know? That he had an upsetting phone call from home this morning. That he didn't show up for classes, breakfast, lunch, or dinner. That he wasn't in the dorm when Fred woke up. I was the last person to see him at around 6:00 a.m. Hours ago. But then, the headmaster and Mrs. King were only looking for him at dinner. That has to mean they've seen him more recently, doesn't it? Still, he has a head start. It's just difficult to know how much of one.

In the near distance, the cable car is lit up against the dimness of the evening. A group of students advances toward it. I realize it's Tuesday: the day we're allowed into the village for the evening. I look down at my watch. It's 8:15 p.m. and since the lift has obviously been reopened after the blizzard, everyone must be eager to finally break free of the claustrophobia of the past few days.

Something clicks into place.

"No luck?" Ren asks as she and Fred pull up next to me.

"No, but I have an idea," I say, certain now. "If I wanted to go home without the school knowing, how would I do it?"

"Well, you'd have to get to the airport first," Fred says, his eyebrows knitted together. "Taxis from here are out—they're all approved by the school, and you'd have to have a permission slip or sign it off with a teacher."

I clench my teeth in irritation. Maybe I'm wrong. "There must be a way from the town, though, right?"

"Yes, of course," Ren says. "There's a bus that goes right to the airport, but the cable car—"

I finish her sentence, "Is open again."

She takes a ragged breath in. "God, he'll be expelled if he decided to try to leave. It's the one rule the school doesn't bend on—you can't leave without permission. Even he won't be able to get away with this. We need to go now."

21

We have to wait five minutes for the next cable car. The minutes slow to an unbearable rate, every second impossibly extended. My anxiety has nothing to do with the cable-car journey and absolutely everything to do with Hector not being here. It's a different sort of anxiety than I'm used to. My hands don't shake, my palms aren't sweaty, I don't feel an empty form of dread—this time it's overpowering, like I might burst from the weight of it. Only now that he's gone do I realize how much my life here depends on him.

There's a concert on in the town center that I vaguely remember being advertised on the noticeboard in the common room. Despite the recent snowfall, the streets are heaving with people, and our progress is slow. If I imagined running to the bus stop, the opposite is true. We have to weave through the crowd, our route constantly thrown off course by people with no sense of the importance of our journey.

A stage has been set up in the center of the town square, under an old-fashioned clock tower and next to a preemptive Christmas tree, decked top to bottom in glittering white lights. We dodge around it, Fred stopping at the edge of the crowd on the other side of the square to usher me through. Our eyes meet for a second, and I see an identical desperation in his—perhaps finally we've found something, or someone, to agree on. Clear of the crowd, we press forward into a run, my feet sliding underneath me. I'm still wearing my school uniform, my black leather pumps useless against the sleek ice.

A bus comes to a standstill in the distance. My pace quickens. Then I see him, a hunched silhouette at the back of the queue, and the sight of him fills me with relief. It's premature, though; he's in that queue for a reason—a reason that could cost him his place here with us. I can't let that happen.

"Hector!" I shout, and watch him spin around. There is a moment as he sees us hurtling toward him when I think he's going to ignore us, but he steps out of the queue at the last minute as we come to a stop in front of him.

"What are you doing here?" he asks, stony-faced.

Fred clears his throat. "You left without telling anyone, without signing out."

"Yes," he says blankly. "That was my intention."

"Hector, that's pretty bold even for you. The teachers are looking for you. You'll be expelled if you leave."

His expression flickers with interest. "Hmm . . . that didn't occur to me when I left, but it's not actually a bad idea, Fred."

"Why did you come here, Hec?" Ren asks, as if hoping that a change of interviewer might provide better results. "What's going on?"

"I need to go home," he says. Ripples are visible on his mask of indifference—perhaps if we pierce the surface hard enough, his tough exterior may just crack.

"But, Hector, you're going home in three days," Ren says.

"Yes, well, I want to go now." He looks up into the distance, and his expression changes to one of disgust. I trace his line of sight. From our position, a clear view of the school is possible. The candy-box blue looks almost mythical against the black backdrop. "I hate this place."

"You don't mean that," Ren says reassuringly. "Hector, this place is our home."

"No, it's not," he says sharply. "It's a place for forgetting, and forgetting makes us selfish." He turns to get on the bus, but I position myself in front of him, blocking his way. "Move, Cara."

"No," I say fiercely. He pushes me aside; I block his way again. "You're not getting on this bus."

"Let me guess," he says nastily. "Because *it's not safe?*"

His eyes flicker dangerously; I know he's trying to wound me to get me to let him go. His impression of me is like a kick in the stomach, but I make a huge effort to look unaffected. I grit my teeth and say as fiercely as I can, "You. Do. Not. Get. To. Leave."

Behind us the bus doors close and it starts to pull away from the stop before Hector can get to it. He spins around, realizing he's missed his chance to leave. "That was the last one," he growls.

"It's fine, Hector," Ren says, nervous now. "Let's just go back to school and talk about it. Surely you can wait this out until you go home on Friday."

He hisses nastily, "I don't want to spend another minute in this place."

"You love it, really," she says in an attempt at brightness.

"No, Ren, *you* love it. You love it because while you're here you don't have to tell your parents that you're gay." He points a finger at Fred. "And while *you're* here, you don't have to get over *her*. And you"—his eyes rest on me—"you like it because you can forget Georgina died."

He stalks away, leaving us all speechless.

We stand for a moment, suspended in shocked silence. Ren is the one who breaks it. "What did he mean, Fred?"

"Nothing," Fred says quietly.

"I've never seen him like that before. It's not nothing. What did he mean, you don't have to get over—"

"Drop it, Ren," he says severely.

I try to follow Hector, thinking the last place I want to be is here when this all comes to a head. The adrenaline from the desperate need to find him seeps out of me. In its place, I become intensely aware of myself, of my frozen, soaked feet, of the revelation in his words.

"Cara, you're not going anywhere," Ren says, blocking my way. "Not until you both tell me what he meant."

Her eyes blaze and I know she's not talking about me. Whether she knows more about the crash than she's let on or she just didn't hear anything after Hector called her and Fred out, there is only one person on her mind right now. He's standing opposite her, all color drained from his face.

From the way I look between them both, from Fred's panicked expression to Ren's devastated one, I know I don't need to tell her anything. She knows how he feels about her. Perhaps she's known for a while, and perhaps Fred knew she knew as well. All Hector has done is made them recognize something that they were, up to this point, willing to ignore. It's a minor declaration, really. Still, it changes everything.

A single tear, sliding seamlessly down her cheek, betrays how fearful Ren is of that change. I place my hands on her shoulders and squeeze once.

She stands aside and lets me walk away.

Hector gets in the cable car ahead of me; I run to catch up, jamming my hand in the sensor to stop it from leaving without me. He is sitting on one of the benches when I get there, hunched over, backpack at his feet. He stands up when I enter, a mixture of regret and surprise on his face. "Cara . . . I . . ."

I slam my hands against his chest. He gives in to the shove and falls back against the side of the cable car, which sways with the impact. "I never forget she died," I say, pushing him again for emphasis. The whole carriage lurches and shudders, but I'm too angry to care. "NEVER."

As we start to move across the dip in the mountains, his voice, like his body, gives in to me. "I know you don't."

His vulnerability makes me pull back. "Why did you say it, then?"

"Because this is who I am." He gestures to himself, as though I should recognize something different about him. "I'm trouble, Cara. I warned you about this when you first arrived, remember?"

"No, you're not. But you're pushing away the people you care about. I need to know—why?"

He smiles bitterly. "Finally, you give me the psych bullshit."

"You've been asking for it for long enough. What happened earlier? Your phone call this morning . . . Where have you been all day?"

"I couldn't come to lessons. . . . The Kings let me have the day off. I was supposed to stay in the conservatory, but I couldn't be around everyone. I couldn't face—" His voice breaks off.

I search his face for answers. "Hector, what's going on?"

"My mother is in the hospital."

The cable car stops midflight, and the lights start to flicker. I take a step toward Hector and grab hold of his arm.

"It'll start moving again in a second," he murmurs. Without the noise of the pulley system, a dead sort of silence engulfs us. I don't look around; I don't look down. I just stare at him.

My legs should be buckling, my eyesight should be blurring, my heartbeat should be a loud, feral thing. All I see are his green eyes, the fear behind them. A fear that has nothing to do with the rocking, lifeless cage we're in. We're at a standstill for a moment before the carriage growls back to life and resumes its journey.

I take a ragged breath in. "Your mother? What happened?"

The muscles in his forearm tense, and I realize I'm still clutching his arm. "I don't know. My little sister Valeria says an ambulance came in the middle of the night. She doesn't know anything else."

I let my arm fall back to my side. "Friday is only two days away. You'll be able to find out what actually happened then, at least."

At least. The two stupidest words in the English language.

He shakes his head. "That's the thing. My father has banned me from going home. Mrs. King called me into her office this morning. Apparently he told her that they had a lot going on and it wasn't a good time for me to return." He looks wistfully at me. "He won't tell me anything. He says she's fine, but . . ."

"You don't believe him."

"I have to see her for myself," he says, and there's intent in the words. "I *need* to go there, Cara."

The carriage comes to a stop, and the doors open. I don't move, thinking about what I am about to ask myself to do. "You can come with me."

He shakes his head. "I know you mean well, but I'm not sure how going to the U.S. will help—"

"I'm not talking about the U.S.," I say, already beginning to regret the words. Once I say them to him, I won't be able to take them back. "I'm talking about going to my dad's. In London."

"London? Cara, I . . . Well, are you sure?"

I step out of the cable car and let my feet find solid ground. "You've still got your plane tickets?" I ask, sounding much stronger than I feel. He nods. "Well, as long as you can get permission, I'm sure."

I head toward the front doors, the adrenaline wearing off with every step I take. I go to the nearest empty classroom I can find and prop myself up on a desk. When I close my eyes, I feel the cable car rock, I see the dark mountains swirling all around us, I see Hector's haunted, beautiful, desperate face. My father's face flickers there, too, or what I remember of it.

Bile rises in my throat, and I make it to the girls' bathroom just in time.

22

I make the call before I can change my mind. I tell my mother that I want to stay with Dad. It's easier than I imagined—she takes no convincing. In fact, she sounds almost amazed. I want to tell her not to get her hopes up. A few weeks here haven't healed me; I am doing this for someone I . . . I what? I care about. That will have to be enough.

My father calls me half an hour later. I wait by the phone box, expecting it.

"I'm calling for Cara Cooper," he says hesitantly when I pick up the phone.

"It's me, Dad," I say, equally nervous. It has been a very long time since I've heard his voice.

"It's nice to hear you," he says. There is a long, awkward pause. "I've just spoken to your mum—we've arranged your flight to London."

"Thank you," I say with forced politeness.

"I'll meet you at the airport."

"Dad, there's really no need. I'm seventeen."

"I know. It's just a long time since you've been in the city," he says. Whether he means it this way or not, it feels like a dig. He quickly continues. "And I moved into a new flat six months ago, so I wouldn't want you to get lost."

Next it's my turn to talk without thinking. "I know; I got your email." I close my eyes in regret. What I am actually saying is *I got all of your emails and didn't reply.*

"I'd be more comfortable if I met you this once," he says, pretending not to notice.

"Well, if you have to . . ."

"I'll see you then," he says self-consciously, getting ready to hang up.

"Wait, Dad," I interrupt quickly. "There's just one thing. I said to a friend of mine that he could stay with us. I hope that's okay?"

"He . . ."

"His name is Hector. He's visiting family in London and needs a place to stay."

"And he's not staying with them?"

"He can't. It's complicated," I say shortly. "It's not a problem, though, is it? I already told him you'd be cool about it."

I don't know why I bother asking the question. We both know there is only one answer. He has wanted me to visit for five years and I am taking advantage of that. When I mentioned Hector's name, he must have known this was the reason that I was coming to stay. But either because my mother told him to agree to any of my demands, or he just knows it's the only way I'll visit him, he doesn't object.

"Of course not. It'll be a bit of a squeeze; my new place is even smaller than our last one. But I'll work it out somehow. Looking forward to seeing you."

"Okay, Dad, see you then."

On the way to ending the call, my hand freezes, the receiver dangling in midair. I close my eyes and my face scrunches from the weight of our conversation. I know he's still there, holding on to the open line between us—a line that hasn't been open for a very long time. There is a moment when I consider drawing the phone back to my ear, saying something else.

There is another moment when I hang up the phone.

23

You can come with me. It was such a simple offer, yet I made it blindly. There is a reason I haven't been back to London for five years, and there is a reason I didn't want to go anywhere this half-term in the first place.

I spend the following day secretly hoping Hector's father won't give permission for him to come with me. Or that my father will email the school to tell them he's not comfortable having Hector stay. So many factors have to align before my words actually come into being.

All of us spend the day tiptoeing around each other. Ren and Fred are overly polite to one another, both barely speaking to Hector, who, after a brief apology at breakfast, has proceeded to treat the day as though nothing has happened. And both of them seem to be avoiding me after Hector dropped the G bomb last night—I haven't yet established what both of them know, and I don't want to. I have a feeling that all of us want to take an eraser to last night and scrub it out.

Hector confirms the worst at dinner. "All's been approved— I'm coming with you, California."

"That's good," I say, silencing the part of me that wants to cry out *I take it back. You can't come, because I can't go. Just the trip in itself is insurmountable, let alone actually having to confront my father in the flesh after all this time.*

I'm sure Hector assumes we've kept in contact all these years. For a year or so after my mother and I arrived in the U.S., she made me speak to my father every few weeks. I think, even though she would never pick up the phone to him, there was a part of her that felt guilty for taking me halfway across the world. Then, as I got older, I had a realization: if she refused to speak to him, I could too. I stopped picking up the phone, stopped replying to all the messages. He keeps trying, always via email, but his messages are less frequent now. They're pretty basic and inconsequential, but I don't blame him. How long can you keep communicating with a brick wall?

After the crash, he tried to come to the U.S., but I made my mother stop him. What made him think that I'd want to see *him* then? What right did he have to come and try to make amends when I was at my lowest, when he hadn't tried to come out to the U.S. when I was at my highest? The crash didn't give us another chance—it just solidified the distance between us. A distance that spans more than an ocean.

"When was the last time you were there?" Hector asks. The question is tentative, as though he already knows he might not like the answer.

I swallow nervously. "I haven't been back since we moved."

Two tables away from us, a boy a few years below us knocks a glass over. Cheers erupt as it smashes into tiny pieces and the boy flushes scarlet. I welcome the ensuing commotion, a distraction from the deadly silence now hanging over our table.

I know that Hector must be fully considering the extent of what I'm doing for him. I briefly wonder whether he'll tell me that it's too much of a sacrifice, that he doesn't expect me to do this for him, that we don't have to go after all.

His eyes narrow, almost wincing, before he reaches out an arm across the table and lets it rest limply between us. "I appreciate it, Cara."

He was willing to be expelled to see his mother, so I doubt there's much he's not willing to do. This time I'll be the collateral damage.

I keep my hands folded on my lap, my gaze settling back onto the broken glassy fragments spread across the floor. It is, after all, impossible to shatter when you're already in a million pieces. How much messier can it get?

24

Half-term arrives; we wait in the conservatory for our taxis. Madame James trudges through the groups of people handing back phones with named luggage tags taped over the screens. Perched on the edge of the table next to me, Ren and Fred sit awkwardly, their bags piled at their feet. Ren's mother has arranged for them to be collected and driven the whole way to Lyon. The journey is over four hours—and I'm not envious of them in the slightest. I can't help thinking that Hector's outburst—brutal as it was— might be just the thing they needed. If the icy tension between them continues the way it has these past few days, Ren's parents are going to see straight through the show they've been putting on.

Hector and I are called forward at around two for the taxi his father had already arranged for his original trip. I did try to engineer the journey by train, but he quickly shut me down, telling me it was a convoluted one that would take us more than five hours. So when he stands up and hooks both of our bags over his shoulder, I direct my focus onto him, keeping myself in the present and not on the crippling tightness in my chest. It takes everything I'm made of to distract myself from the tingling sensation in my legs, the building crescendo of panic in my chest, and my shallow, incompetent breathing.

I feel the stares all around me, circling, waiting for me to lose it—because that scene is inevitable, isn't it? I tell myself I have to do this. I made Hector a promise; this isn't about me.

"Cara, wait," Fred says, following me out into the corridor and pulling me aside. He glances around—Hector is already way ahead—then continues when he's satisfied we won't be overheard. "I know it's not really my place to say anything, but I need to talk to you before you go."

I raise my eyebrows. I'm tired, I'm anxious, and I'm doing something massive as it is. I don't have space in my head for him to get involved. "Fred, Hector's coming with me so he can see his mother, that's all. There's no need to be scared I'll turn him against you. It's just a week."

"It's not me I'm worried about," Fred says cautiously.

"Hector's a big boy; I think he can look after himself."

He closes his eyes, his irritation visible, then forces them open to address me again. "Listen . . . he hasn't told you everything."

My patience starts to wane. "I get it, Fred. You and Ren were here first; you've known him the longest. You don't have to—"

"Cara, that's not what I mean. He's opened up to you more

than he ever has with us," he cuts in. There is just the tiniest hint of bitterness there—he's holding back for me. "You must have noticed how he is around you. It's like, you walk in and he lights up. . . ."

I feel my face flush. "Only because I'm new. He sees me as a challenge."

"Not in the way you think. There are times when he's with you that I almost see his guard drop."

"Even if that's true," I say, "why does that worry you?"

"Cara, Hector runs rings around everyone all day long. He spends his life holding everyone at arm's reach."

For a moment I see a glimmer of how hurt Fred is. "He doesn't do that with you, Fred."

He doesn't draw breath. "He's always done that with me, Cara."

"Why are you telling me this?"

"To warn you, I suppose," he says. "You've got your own stuff going on. And, well, the places he'll take you might not be places you're ready to go."

"I don't underst—" I start, willing him to stop.

"You're not the only one who's suffering, Cara," Fred says, ignoring me. "I can't tell you any more. Just be careful."

"Careful of what?" I ask, irritated now. "That I don't hurt him? Or that he doesn't hurt me?"

He shrugs. If I didn't know he has a hostile streak in him, I'd say he was embarrassed. "Feelings make things complicated, and the both of you have got more than enough of complicated already."

Hector reappears at the other end of the corridor and calls down to me, "California, we don't have all day. We've got a plane to catch, remember?"

"Coming," I call back, shooting one last glance at Fred. His expression is apologetic; mine is furious.

25

Fury is good. Fury gets me into the car. I let Madame James tick me off her list, then I slip straight into the taxi next to Hector without a second's hesitation. I strap myself in and turn to check Hector has done the same.

"A present for you," he says, holding out something made of beige flannel. "It's an eye mask. Put it on."

"I'll be fine," I say with forced confidence, because as the car begins to move, I realize two things:

1. On my journey here, it was almost dark. With the shocking clarity of daylight, I'll see our descent in high definition, my fear focused and distinct.
2. The car will be tilting downward as it takes the hairpin bends, which will be much, much worse.

"I stole this from Fred specifically for you, California. Courtesy of a Swiss airlines flight to Beijing, you will now have a carefree journey. So stop resisting and put the damn thing on."

I do as he says and am immediately grateful for it. Now that I'm in the car, I'll have to stick this one out. The driver can hardly let me out on the side of the mountain if I lose it. *Oh, God, I'm going to have to stay here—of course I am going to lose it.* My hands begin to shake, then I feel a cold, steadying pressure in my right hand as Hector takes hold of it, my sweaty fingers entwined with his. At his touch, I feel anchored, as I did the night I told him about the crash. At his touch, I feel a little less alone.

Fred's words do the rounds again. *Feelings make things complicated, and the both of you have got more than enough of complicated already. . . .*

A kinetic charge fills the space between us; I wonder if he feels it, too, or whether I am making it up. We have over two hours crammed next to each other ahead of us, and I am confronted by a different sensation. One I most certainly shouldn't be feeling—one that has *complicated* written all over it.

Despite cheating with an eye mask, when we arrive at the airport I feel triumphant. I start to wonder whether doing the things that fill me with horror—and coming out the other side undamaged— might be what helps me the most. As we trail through the airport, I'm submerged in a cloud of calm.

Our tickets weren't booked together, so we can't sit next to each other on the flight. This, judging from the tension in the taxi, is for the best. But when we stand in the long queue at the gate, Hector seems agitated.

"I'll ask the person sitting next to you if we can swap. I'm sure if we explain you don't like flying, they'll understand," he says. His concern makes me smile. "What? Why aren't you panicking?"

"I'd have thought you'd consider that a good thing?"

"I do. I just don't understand how you're so calm. You've just spent two hours wearing an eye mask."

"I'm not afraid of flying, Hector."

He frowns. "That doesn't make any sense."

I start to rummage through my backpack to find my boarding pass. "What part?"

"All of it. You won't step in a lift—don't think I haven't noticed you climbing all those stairs every day—you almost had a panic attack when you first went in the cable car, you're fine as long as you wear an eye mask in the car, yet you had a freak-out when we all were supposed to get on a bus."

I feel a flush of embarrassment flood through my skin, but I make myself hold his stare. "Thank you for reminding me."

"No, but come on, Cara. Claustrophobia has to be the worst on airplanes."

"I never said I was claustrophobic."

I can almost see his brain working tirelessly to figure this one out. "So it's about control?"

"Yes, I suppose," I say, not really sure how to explain it to him. Whether verbalizing it will make me seem even sillier.

"But surely on airplanes you have the least amount of control."

"And that's the exact reason I don't mind them. They're not my responsibility."

"But you're not responsible for cable cars, lifts, chauffeured buses, or cars either," he says. He looks so stumped by this that I realize I'm going to have to explain it to him. Which means he's going to think I'm crazy.

We hand our passes over and are ushered through to start another queue. We walk side by side down the Jetway toward the plane door.

"Okay, think of it this way. If the method of transport is already scheduled, think train or airplane, then it's not my fault if it crashes because, whether I was on it or not, that plane or train was always going to leave when it did. But if I get in something, an elevator or a cable car, and it moves because I've pressed a button or whatever, then I am responsible if something goes wrong. I was the person who told it to move—it wouldn't have moved otherwise."

"There are holes in that explanation," he says.

"Which are?"

"The buses on School Birthday. The taxi today. They were both scheduled."

"Yes," I say, trying again not to remember what happened that day, "that's true. But cars and buses are different. The reason why should be clear to you by now."

"Well, as far as I see it, you're already breaking your rule quite effectively. Car trip today. Cable-car jaunts. You're proving yourself wrong. Everything's looking up."

"I wouldn't get ahead of yourself," I say quietly. "Those trips weren't made with the intention of proving myself wrong."

"No? Why did you make them, then?"

"I did those trips because I had no choice."

His forehead creases sternly. "You had a choice, Cara. You always had a choice and you made those trips anyway."

We reach the plane. Hector's seat is rows ahead of mine, so I plunge forward down the narrow aisle.

"Wait, Cara," he says. "Are you sure you're going to be all right?"

"Absolutely fine," I reply brusquely. "If we crash, please know that I take great comfort from the fact that it's highly unlikely we'll survive."

A few seated heads turn my way in horror at this; Hector scrunches up his nose in disgust.

"You asked for no filter," I remind him. "That's what this looks like from my side."

26

My father is waiting in the arrivals area at London's Gatwick Air-
port. I spy him first, feeling everything that's happened—or hasn't
happened—between us pulse out like a homing beacon. His blond
hair is now almost completely gray, his frame fuller than I remember. Even though I'd recognize him anywhere, he is unfamiliar to me. His eyes light up when he sees me—I feel him
taking me in, trying to establish how I look now, who I am now.
He steps forward out of the waiting crowd and I have to fight the
urge to step back.

"Hi, Cara," he says, leaving a two-meter gap between us. He
knows better than to come any closer. We stare at each other for a
painful moment and I feel my world implode. What was I thinking? I'm not ready for this—I never properly prepared myself
for it.

Hector stretches out his hand into the space in front of us. My father looks away from me to take him in. "You must be Hector," my father says. There is an element of wariness to his tone. If he'd behaved like a father should, if he'd stuck around, I'd maybe tolerate this reaction. But he hasn't, so I allow it to become the first strike against his name on this trip.

"Thank you so much for letting me stay with you, Mr. Cooper," Hector replies in his most charming voice.

"Call me Thomas," my father says, awkwardly shaking his hand. "Here, let me take Cara's bag."

Hector, who has hooked one of our bags over each shoulder, hoists them farther up his back. "Ah, don't worry, sir. I've got them," he says.

My father looks taken aback by Hector's formality. "Shall we get going, then?"

We follow him through the crowd, Hector brushing me lightly on the elbow as we walk side by side to the train station.

"*Sir?*" I hiss at him.

He lowers his voice so only I can hear him. "I have a lot to achieve this week, and there may be a time when I need your father on my side. This is what I call groundwork."

"That's calculating of you," I say. It was stupid of me to expect any less, I suppose. He spends his life at Hope successfully doing the exact same thing with all of the teachers.

"It's the way of the world, California," he replies. "You have to build your defense when you can. Preferably before the crime has even happened."

His words allow me to see the trip through his eyes. He's not here to make this easier for me; he's here with a purpose. He must have calculated a plan to see his mother. I need to remember that.

"I don't expect you'll be able to wrap my father around your little finger like you have the teachers at Hope," I say warily. "I doubt your"—I gesture up and down his body—"will have the same effect."

He laughs aloud, letting his arms flow down his body in imitation of me. The action is so girly I almost laugh. "My what?"

"Oh, you know," I say, my cheeks hot with embarrassment.

"Don't you worry about me, California," he says, still smiling. "I've got this one figured out."

"How?"

His expression changes as we board an escalator. "If you think your father will be a tough nut to crack, let's hope you never have to meet mine."

At my request we travel by public transport to his apartment. It takes a train journey, a bus trip, and a ten-minute walk before we're standing outside a redbrick terraced house with a lurid yellow door. Even though we've missed rush hour, it's a Friday night, so thankfully all the methods of public transport we took were busy enough that we were pressed up against a selection of strangers and didn't have to talk to each other.

Now, however, my father seems nervous as he turns the key in the lock. "I'm in the upstairs flat," he says, "and, just to warn you, it's pretty tiny."

We head up a narrow flight of stairs to find there is just one bedroom, a small kitchen, a bathroom, and a slightly larger sitting room, where a pile of bedding has been stacked on one of two sofas. We linger in the doorway, our minds asking the same question.

"One of those is a sofa bed," my father says. "I thought, Cara, you could have my room, Hector the sofa bed, and I'll sleep on the other sofa."

"Dad," I start, suddenly very conscious that I can't allow this to happen. Hector and my father *cannot* share a room for a week. "You don't need to move out of your room for me. We'll be fine in here."

"Absolutely," Hector says. He sits down on the smaller sofa and pats it firmly. "Honestly, I'm more than happy here. It's unbelievably kind of you to have me in the first place. I wouldn't want to put you out."

My father shifts his weight from one leg to the other, clearly uncomfortable but unsure whether to say anything.

"That's settled, then," I say.

"Um," my father mumbles, "Cara, could I have a quick word?"

I roll my eyes and follow him through to the kitchen, brushing away the feeling of awkwardness building up in the small space. "What's up?"

"I don't really feel comfortable with you sharing a room with your boyfriend. You are still underage and, well, I don't really think it's appropriate. I know your mother would agree with me."

"I'm seventeen. Hardly a child. And Hector is not my boyfriend."

His eyes cloud over with relief. "He's not?"

"Just a friend," I say, then to freak him out add, "Anyway, even if he were my boyfriend, what are we going to do with you in the next room?"

He clears his throat. "I suppose it's okay, then." I nod impatiently. "Right, well, you must both be hungry after your trip—I thought we could order pizza?"

"Sounds good, Dad," I say, feeling a little guilty with how sharp I've been with him. We have invaded with absolutely no notice, after all. Then I catch myself. This is nothing compared to what he's done in the past. I don't owe him a thing.

I drop myself down on the sofa next to Hector. "Everything okay?" he asks, not looking up from his phone, which he's been practically glued to ever since we were given them back in the conservatory.

"He thinks we're dating," I say, pulling an uncomfortable pillow out from behind my back.

He looks up with a smirk. "Well, it makes sense," he says, and for a second I hold my breath, waiting for what he's going to say next; then he just says, "After all, I am very good-looking."

I stare at him in amazement. "Hector, you can't say that about yourself!"

The sides of his mouth twitch; he's trying not to smile. "You think I'm handsome, though, right?"

I feel my face heating up. "That's not the . . . I . . . I honestly don't know what to— Are you . . . Are you being serious?"

He starts to laugh. It's one of those deep, genuine, infectious ones that acts like a magnet, pulling everything toward it until I can't help but laugh too. His eyes flicker with satisfaction.

I shake my head. "God, you can be arrogant, Hector."

"Confident," he says with a wide, mischievous smile.

"Arrogant," I repeat.

He rearranges the pillows behind his back and looks down at his phone again. "Well, California, as long as you're around to keep me in check, I can live with that."

I pick up the remote and switch the TV on, in need of a distraction while I re-cage the little bird inside me that's trying to unfurl its wings. Reruns of a talent competition fill the screen. I let the indoor fireworks and lurid colors paint the screen, my eyes blurring into the distance. Every now and then, they fix on familiar objects in the room. An ornament of an owl, the spines of some battered paperbacks with familiar titles and author names, a navy zigzagged rug. It's not the same flat that I grew up in, but the possessions are the same. I remember asking my mother why we didn't have any of our things when we arrived in the U.S., and she'd said that we didn't need things, just each other. Now I'm older, I can see she said this to placate a younger me. We left with a suitcase full of clothes and nothing to remind us of what we'd left behind.

I pull my eyes away from my surroundings and swivel to face Hector. "What are you looking at?"

He lowers his voice out of earshot of my father, who we can both now hear clattering around in the kitchen. "I'm trying to find out what hospital my mother is in. If she went in an ambulance, it has to be one of the ones nearby—my bet is either Chelsea and Westminster or St. Thomas'. It's not like she's famous or anything, but my father has had quite a lot of press coverage recently, so I suppose they might report on it in the tabloids."

"Can't you just ask your sister?"

"She doesn't have a mobile," he says. "And if I call the house, there's a chance my father will pick up."

"Would that be catastrophic?" I ask. "He must be expecting you to call, you being in the same city and all."

He shoots me a look. "He doesn't know I'm here."

"What?" I almost shout. He shushes me, checking that my father hasn't overheard. I lower my voice to a whisper. "He had to give permission for you to come with me, so he must know."

He winces. "Well, he did give permission; he just doesn't know that he did. My father isn't very good at email, and I know his password, so I fixed it all from the school computers."

"Hector!" I hiss. "What were you thinking? If anyone finds out, you'll be in so much trouble."

He adjusts his expression from guilty to unrepentant. "I need to see my mother, Cara. I'm prepared for the consequences of that, whatever they are."

I think of him at the bus stop. He was willing to be expelled without a second thought; he was willing to impersonate his father to wangle a trip to London because his father intended to keep him away from his mother no matter the circumstances. For the first time I wonder whether Fred was right. What hasn't he told me?

The doorbell rings in the background.

"Hector, if your sister doesn't have a cell phone—"

"Mobile," he interrupts.

"Whatever. If she doesn't have one, how did you and her have all your early-morning conversations without your father knowing?"

"My father goes for a run most mornings at five. When he leaves, she calls me from the landline—she has the number of the phone box in the common room. After—" He stops himself and starts again. "Well, two summers ago we made a pact. Switzerland is an hour ahead, so every morning I'd wait for her to call at around six-thirty our time. Sometimes she doesn't, but sometimes she does. It's the only way we're able to speak about the things that we don't want our father to overhear."

Before I can ask him what those things are, my father walks in with two pizza boxes. I could be imagining it, but Hector looks relieved at the interruption.

27

I wake to the sound of hail hitting glass, and with an idea.

A gray light has begun to sneak through the gaps in the curtains, sending a thin beam across the bottom of my foldout bed and onto Hector, who is midsleep. Soon after we had dinner last night, both of us crashed, exhausted after a day of traveling. Just before Hector fell asleep, he muttered the plan for today: to call all the hospitals and see whether they'll tell us if she's there. My idea is much better than that.

I decide to give Hector longer in bed—longer to be unaware. Today is a day that could hold a number of outcomes—most of which I'd like to avoid.

For someone who told me they didn't need a lot of it, the sleep he's in now is silent and absolute. He doesn't stir as I extract myself from the sheets and riffle through my duffel for my toiletry bag. Even with his mouth slightly open and his cheeks creased with pillow marks, he looks as attractive as ever.

I take my clothes to the bathroom to get dressed and catch my reflection in the mirror above the sink. For the first time since the crash, I mind how I look—actually mind enough to do something about it. I search around in my bag and find a crusty concealer stick. I wipe away the majority of the muck on the top and start dabbing it under my eyes. I don't have much else in the way of makeup—nothing compared to the whole bag of it G and I used to share in the U.S.—but I do finally find a pot of peach lip balm.

As I go to the kitchen to make tea, a memory swims to the surface of my mind. I'm in the bathroom at school before class, waiting dutifully as I did every morning for G to put on some makeup.

"Peachy Dreams?" she says, staring at the little pot with an incredulous look on her face. "Honestly, they make up the stupidest names for these things."

I pull out a different, dark shade of red. "Would you prefer Ravishing Raspberry?"

"That's not an actual one?"

"Or Curious Clementine?" I say, pulling out another.

She starts to giggle. "God, next it will be Brilliant Banana. . . ."

My father, outfitted in garish sportswear, walks into the kitchen, shaking me into the present. His ensemble, royal blue leggings and a crisp, lightweight jacket that rustles when he moves, looks like he walked into a store and let the assistant have the time of their life.

"You're up early," he says through a yawn.

I divert my gaze away from the Lycra and focus on stirring the tea bags around two mugs. "What time is it?"

"Almost eight," he says.

"Hardly early."

"Well, you are a teenager."

I roll my eyes. It feels so predictable. I can just imagine him poring over a *Teenagers for Dummies* guide before we arrived.

"I'm going for a run," he says. "While I'm gone, why don't you have a think about what you'd like to do today?"

"Hector and I are just going to do our own thing," I say, watching the disappointment taint his face. *No,* I think, *you don't get to be disappointed with me.*

"Okay, well, as long as you're back before seven. I'm making dinner for us all." He starts to head down the stairs, turning back on the bottom step. "Oh, and there's a spare set of keys on my bedside table."

"Thanks," I say, picking up the two mugs and heading back to the sitting room, where Hector is still fast asleep. I perch on the arm of the sofa bed, trying to work out the best way to wake him.

After a moment, he reaches an arm out and paws my knee. "Don't be a creep, C."

My whole body flinches at the nickname, tea surging out of the two mugs I'm holding, the scalding liquid spattering my jeans. For a blink of a moment, I'm back in that school changing room again, in complete awe of the girl in her mismatching sweats. Afterward we would walk home through our local park, putting the world to rights—something we'd do every day after school for the next three years. Then we're in the mall, picking out cheap metal jewelry. She passes a necklace to me. It's silver—or pretending to be—a simple monograph at the end of a plain chain. "Look," she says. "G for me, C for you. G and C—they even sound the same." We buy them for the grand old price of two dollars each. We put them on straightaway, me wearing hers and her mine. Even when she's not around, I find myself periodically checking that it's still there. Flash forward three years. The G necklace is bloodied and broken in a clear bag full of my personal effects. The C—and the person wearing it—never to be seen again.

"Never call me that," I snap.

He pulls himself up to a sitting position, rubbing the sleep from his eyes. "I didn't realize it was such a big deal."

"Yeah, well, it is."

"Won't happen again," he says, taking one of the mugs of tea from me. He blinks repeatedly, trying to wake himself up. "What time is it?"

"Past eight." My voice has a residual sharpness to it.

He sits up taller. "Is it? Christ, I never sleep this late. You should have woken me."

"I've had an idea: what if, instead of calling all the hospitals, we just asked someone from your dad's office where your mum is? Doesn't he have an assistant or something?"

He sighs, takes a sip of tea, and sets it down. "She'd recognize my voice."

"But she wouldn't know mine," I say hopefully. "You tell me who I need to pretend to be, someone she'd give that information to. It's worth a try at least."

He stands up, finally alert, and grabs my face, planting a strong kiss on my forehead as he passes me to unplug his phone from the wall. "You, California, are a bloody genius."

My forehead burns, unused to the contact, or the feeling that contact leaves. I check myself; there are a lot of things I am supposed to be feeling now—this is not one of them.

He gestures to the charger in the wall. "Do you want this? In fact, where *is* your phone? Your dad gave me the Wi-Fi code last night if you want it."

A sick feeling swirls in the pit of my stomach, because if I know one thing it's that I don't want the code. "That's okay," I say in a thin, unconvincing voice. "I'll get it from you later."

He looks at me with curiosity. "You really are one of the strangest people I've ever met. Don't you ever go online?"

I move over to the window, picking out a random person on the street to focus on. I watch as he cowers, pulling his jacket over his head to shield himself from the downpour. "Not anymore," I eventually say.

How can I tell him that there are things on there that I don't want to see? That if I go online, I get an overpowering—and frankly masochistic—urge to Google G. That I did it once after the crash and it was enough to make me swear off the Internet for life. It wasn't just the pictures of the wreckage I couldn't look at—it was everything else. It was her Facebook page, her Twitter feed, her Instagram photos. All the parts of her life that she put on display—things that, when I looked again, didn't seem to represent who she was at all. And then there were the messages posted from people who knew her, or knew of her. The outpouring of gushy messages from people who were cruel to her in real life, or who hadn't ever bothered to get to know her. I couldn't bear it that they were clinging to her death as though it was something social. As though it was something to talk about. I remember one particular tweet that ended my Internet use altogether. It was from a girl in my grade, Bella, who had always been poisonous to G.

> I can't stop crying. The world will be less bright
> without you Georgina #WithTheAngels

The message said it all. If she'd actually been remotely close to G, she'd have known that G hated her name. Only parents were allowed to call her Georgina. Bella was piggybacking on the grief felt by the people who had actually known her. The tweet was an insult to G and everyone who knew her.

I hadn't wanted to look online in the first place. It was my mother's idea. She thought I might find some comfort from the posts. G's parents had told her how overwhelmed and amazed they had felt from all the kind things people had been saying about G, and my mother must have thought that I needed a bit of amazement in the aftermath—maybe amazement would shock me out of the half-person I'd become. I scrolled through the posts for five minutes and I couldn't find a single piece of comfort. In fact, it left me repulsed and led me to spend five days without once seeing the sky.

I pull myself out of the memory and pick up the landline; my fingers hover over the keypad. "What number am I calling?"

My plan works like a dream. After much deliberation, Hector decides the safest bet is to go with his father's sister Alice, since all of his mother's relations are Spanish and my accent ability is pretty basic. We get a name and we get a department: intensive care unit at St. Thomas' Hospital.

I push my luck at the end. "How's she doing?"

"No change, I'm afraid," the secretary replies. Hector waits for me to relay the information, his face dropping when I do.

"It's a start," I tell him. "We'll go there this morning, and we'll know more. It'll be better then."

"She's in *intensive care*?" He looks at me and there's something vacant about his expression. "I mean, I knew she was in the hospital, but . . . my father . . . he said . . . he said she was fine."

I try to remove all pity from my expression. If I've learned anything this past year, it's that pity is impractical; it doesn't change a thing.

I leave Hector to shower, wondering how we're going to pull this off. It's a Saturday, and Hector's father isn't supposed to be working, so chances are he's at the hospital. Hector is adamant that his father can't know he's in London; on this, I agree. All of this will have been for nothing if we're found out too soon.

I step into my father's room to retrieve the apartment keys and feel myself stepping into an exhibit. It is both a place I know and a place rooted firmly in the past. Children's drawings; a poorly sewn attempt at a toy chicken; my parents' wedding photograph gleaming from a perfectly polished silver frame. More photo frames. Too many photo frames.

A movement catches my eye—a series of baby photographs fill the screen of my father's desktop, rotating in and out of focus on an image reel. I am his screensaver. I rush over and shake the mouse, getting rid of the images. A newspaper article remains on the screen. I draw in a quick breath as a family of five stare out at me. I recognize Hector immediately in the center, flanked by both of his parents. A young girl with identical dark coloring to Hector beams out on the far left, and on the right a boy that could be Hector's twin if he wasn't a few years older. A shadow of coarse stubble frames his face, and he's taller, if that's even possible. There is a red ring around him, the newspaper's way of pulling him out from the rest of his family. I look down at the caption and find his name: Santiago Sanderson.

"Ready to go, California?" I hear Hector shout from a room away.

"Just a minute," I call back, quickly scrolling up to minimize the window.

At the top of the article my hand freezes, the headline screaming out. For a second before I shut the page down, I forget how to breathe.

MINISTER'S SECRET HEARTBREAK: THE SON HE COULDN'T SAVE

28

Rain falls at a diagonal, creeping underneath our umbrellas, the downpour finding places to dampen us just where we thought we were safe.

We don't speak for the entire journey, a journey where the poisonous cocktail of feelings I have collide with each other. Why didn't he tell me that he'd lost his brother? How could he have kept such a huge event from me after everything I've told him? Presumably this is what Fred wanted to warn me about before we left. . . . Why couldn't they have all just told me this from the start? Didn't they trust me?

On our way to the hospital, I watch him out of the corner of my eye. Finding that article has shaken me awake, and I start to see the fractures in him. Maybe they were always there, but I couldn't see past myself before. There's also the possibility that, deep down, I always knew; I just didn't want him to be falling apart when I was so broken. Did I choose not to see him that way, even though he chose to see me exactly as I was—as I am?

The hospital towers up against the riverside, an ugly gray-brick slab of darkness housing a multitude of physical injuries and plenty more mental ones. I wonder what the thoughts going on inside the building would look like if they were written on the walls. Whether it would be a place that anyone would ever go again, or whether there would be enough hope inside to counteract the pain.

"Okay, so we'll need to find her without running into my father, and without anyone remembering us—or that we came here at all. We can't risk anyone mentioning to my father that they saw me," Hector says. His behavior is, understandably, more uptight than normal, but it's clear that he has no notion of what I discovered this morning.

As we head along a concrete walkway to the automatic glass doors of the main entrance, I continue to store the questions that are burning within me. Now is not the time, clearly, but mixed in with shock is a small feeling of inevitability. I suppose I've known he has kept secrets from me; I ignored the warnings, too wrapped up in myself to delve any deeper than felt easy.

To our right, on the other side of the Thames, Big Ben and the Houses of Parliament loom up, their elegance a kind of morbid juxtaposition to where we are now. For a moment, I am distracted by them, until the roar of traffic brings me back to the present and I notice, beneath us, a series of ambulances parked at diagonals waiting to be needed.

I have a realization. "Won't your father be there all the time by your mother's bedside?"

Hector half smiles. "That's not something we need to concern ourselves with."

"What do you mean?"

"He'll visit her, sure, but he's not the doting-husband-by-the-bedside type."

"Oh," I mumble, wishing I could say something to change what he just told me. I plow on instead. Adopting a determined, practical approach might be the only way I'm able to cross those doors. "The key is to look as though you belong wherever you are. Remember, you have every right to visit your mother. As soon as you look a bit lost, someone will call you out on it."

"And you know this because?"

"You forget I've spent a good chunk of time in a hospital."

He stops abruptly. "Are you going to be okay going in?"

"Fine," I say, feeling anything but. After all, the hospital is where I discovered that my whole world had fallen apart. "But, you know, there's a chance that when we get there, I won't be allowed to come with you." I don't vocalize my next thought, or the subsequent shame I feel straight afterward: I secretly hope I won't be allowed.

"No, I want you with me," he says with such finality that I grab his arm. I push forward, dragging him with me, because, for all of his faults, and for all of my anxiety, I'm reminded that right now this is hell for him. And he's terrified.

We bypass reception for a large wall map, like the ones you find in shopping malls. The intensive care unit is in the east wing;

we follow signs, finally stopping at a nurses' station. The area has a highly charged energy about it, signs about hygiene cover the walls, and a distinct smell of alcohol gel permeates the air. I'm reminded again of my own time in intensive care back in the U.S. I remember waking up in a place almost identical to this—and I remember waking up with the crashing, earth-shattering realization that G would no longer be in my reality. Not ever. For a second, I feel the same incomprehension, the same anxiety, all over again.

"Who are you here to see?" the nurse asks me, pulling me back into the present.

"Maria Sanderson," I say quickly. I note Hector keeps his eyes rooted to the floor.

"She's down the corridor on the right," she says, gesturing. "But you should know, access to her is restricted. Her husband has provided a list. Let me check whether you're on it."

Hector takes a step closer to the desk. "I'm her son."

She surveys him with uncertainty, then picks up a piece of paper. "And your name is?"

"Hector. But I doubt you'll find my name on there. This visit is . . . unexpected. I've come from abroad." He pulls out his most persuasive voice—a voice that always gets results. I doubt this will be any different. "Surely you'll be able to make an exception for that."

"If your name isn't on here . . . ," she starts, her voice noticeably less confident.

"You're going to stop him seeing his own—" I begin, but Hector places a hand on my arm to silence me.

He holds her gaze, staring her down until she relents. "Go on, then. Just don't get in the way of the doctors or nurses."

We don't hang around long enough for her to change her mind.

I see Hector's mother first, through a glass panel in the door, in a small room filled with machines. She lies unconscious, hooked up to a labyrinth of tubes, connected to bags of fluids and blood. She even has a tube coming out of her mouth, breathing for her. The whole situation is more serious than I'd imagined; she can't even breathe for herself. And I'm struck by the fact that she doesn't look alive. Her skin is pale, almost yellowed, her arms much thinner than the picture I set my eyes on this morning. Hector places a palm on the glass, reaching out to her—wherever she is now—and all color drains from his face, mirroring hers.

"I'm going inside," he says. I stay put, knowing that even if I did want to accompany him, there is no place for me here.

Another nurse leaves the room as Hector goes in. I stop him in the corridor. "What happened to her?" The door is still open a crack, but I know that Hector won't hear us.

"Head injury," the nurse replies. Through the glass, another nurse gives Hector a plastic apron to put on and makes him coat his hands with antibacterial gel again. "I'm afraid I can't tell you any more at this stage while her condition is still so uncertain."

"Is it uncertain?"

His expression tells me everything I need to know.

"Please could you tell him I'll wait for him outside?"

I direct one last glance at Hector, hunched over his mother's bed, and I hear him whisper, "Please wake up." He talks so quietly, yet his words are like nails on a blackboard to me. I know those words. I know the feeling behind them. I said the exact same thing to G's lifeless body as we hung upside down in that car. And I meant them as fiercely as he does now.

I hope to God his have a better outcome.

29

Hours later, when the streets are lit by the glimmer of headlights from passing cars, Hector finds me. I am sitting on a plastic bag on a wall outside, the rain finally exhausted.

"My father came in at two," he says, sitting down next to me. I offer him the bag; he shakes his head. "Did he see you?"

"No, I made sure I waited until he'd left before going back in."

"The nurses will tell him."

"Hopefully not," he says, rubbing his hands together next to me. "They said they wouldn't. They might give me a day's grace. That's what I'd do."

I nod, hoping he's right. "How is she?"

"No change, but I know a little more. A doctor came in after you left. He said they're keeping her sedated for now to assess the damage her fall caused. She tripped on the way up to my parents' roof terrace, fell down the stairs, and hit her head. Apparently she had a high dose of sleeping pills in her system—enough to make her really drowsy. They think that's why she fell."

"Does she usually . . . ?" I try to think of a way to word the question. "Well, is it usual for her to take pills to sleep?"

"Not unusual," he says in a bleak voice. "She's been struggling since . . ." His eyes lose focus. "Well, she's been struggling."

We walk the whole way back to my father's apartment and somehow manage to get through dinner. I dodge all his questions about how we spent our day and put all my efforts into deflecting attention from Hector's deflated form.

When it's time to go to bed, the atmosphere in the room feels different. Hector perches on the end of the sofa bed, hunched over his phone. I drop down next to him and watch him set an alarm for 7:00 a.m.

"Is that okay?" he says, tilting the screen toward me.

I nod once in the semidarkness, then whisper, "Are *you* okay?"

Hector blows air out through his nose, his mouth curling into a pained, taut sort of smile. Without thinking, I reach out and rest my hand on his wrist. The light from his phone screen goes out, and I pull my hand back, sharply aware of our proximity.

As my eyes adjust to the darkness, he lies backward next to me on the bed. Eventually I lie back, too, making sure to keep space between us. He's still close, closer than he's ever been; my eyes are in line with his chest, which rises and falls with his breath.

I twist my head to stare at his face; his eyes are closed and he seems much younger, much less sure of himself in the dim light. "When were you going to tell me about your brother?"

His eyes snap open, finding a point on the ceiling to fix on.

"I don't know whether I ever was," he eventually says, not bothering to ask me how or for how long I've known. "I liked that you didn't know that part of me. You knew me how I wanted you to know me. I wasn't brother-less with you—just who I am now."

"Me knowing doesn't change anything, Hector."

He pulls himself onto his side until our faces are a few inches apart. His eyes appear much darker than their usual green, and I feel them searching my face, looking for a reason to remain silent. After a long moment, he breathes out. "My brother was named Santiago. He killed himself two years ago, right after he left Hope."

"I'm so sorry," I say. My hand reaches out again, brushing against his bare arm, looking for a way to comfort him. Knowing it's not that easy.

He bristles at my touch. "Don't be," he says. "You didn't kill him; he took care of that himself."

I make myself hold his gaze; I make myself keep my arm where it is. He looks almost deranged with grief. I've seen it before—on the faces of G's parents when they first came to see me in the hospital. Impenetrable and implacable.

"I can't decide which way is better."

I pretend I don't hear the cracks in his voice. "What do you mean?"

"Is it better to have your life taken from you, or to take it yourself? I mean, at least when Santi died it was something he'd chosen—that makes it better, surely."

My hand contracts around his arm. "Hector, at our age, there is no *better* way to die. None at all."

He turns over again onto his back, closes his eyes, and presses his palm firmly against his forehead. "So, now you know why this is a thing . . ." He gestures between us. "I know what it feels like to lose a best friend too."

I see it now, why he's managed to get to me where the others haven't. Why I've been able to tell him so much. We're in the same obscure place, him and me.

"Which is why you now hold Fred at arm's length," I say, my thoughts drifting. I can finally understand how they're so close but at the same time on completely different levels. Hector can't bear to replace Santiago, so he pulls back from Fred, never allowing him everything.

"The very same reason you haven't been completely open with Ren," he says. He's right, which is silly because in everything— looks, personality, values—Ren is G's opposite. Yet I can't let her in, in the same way. I can't let her replace G—it would be an injury to my relationship with G. It would be like saying G's replaceable.

She's not.

My next words come out as a whisper. "Do you ever wonder . . . Do you . . . I . . . Well, I don't understand why I'm the one who survived, why I'm the one who's okay."

"All the time, Cara." He breathes out very slowly before continuing. "I wonder about it all the time."

"You said to me once . . . You said it gets better?"

"It does. You learn to live with it; you *have to* learn to live with it. But I can't tell you if how you feel will ever go away; I don't know myself whether that's possible. I'm still devastated."

And even though his voice is flat and emotionless, I understand him. Because sometimes grief isn't tears or public outcry. Sometimes it's quiet rage and empty space that words and sound can't articulate.

I tilt my head in his direction, and he tilts his to face me. We stare at each other as the minutes pass, and I think about how silence can say more than a thousand words. I don't know how the next moments happen, whether it's me moving or him, but the inches of space between us seem to shorten.

Alarm bells should be going off. We shouldn't be this close. It's reckless. More than that—dangerous. For the longest moment nothing happens. His eyes search my face, reading for a reaction, perhaps. Wondering if I'm going to freak out, like he's seen me do so many times before. Eventually he just asks, "What's going on in that head of yours?" I open my mouth to say something, but he gets there first. "And don't make something up."

"I wasn't going t—" I start to say, and he raises an eyebrow. "My head is a mess, Hector. You don't want to know what's in there."

His hand finds a place on my arm, and my skin feels like it's scorching my T-shirt.

I breathe out, the breath catching in my throat, and whisper, "There are moments when you make me feel like I'm not crazy."

He loops his arm around me and pulls me against him. For a

moment, I tense up, my chest tight, my shoulders high, then he just says, "Ditto," and I give in to it.

Our faces hover millimeters from each other, his nose resting against mine, our eyes locked in the darkness. All sound is extinguished, and it's just me and him—there aren't any best friends, or brothers, or parents, or anyone apart from us. Then he kisses me, and every ounce of anticipation disappears.

I'm surprised to find that here, I may have finally found a place where I imagine myself surviving.

30

I wake up with Hector's arm draped across me, trapping me under the duvet. I don't know what time it is, only that it's early: the sun hasn't risen and the room is swamped in gray shadow. His tattoo is exposed before my eyes, and I let myself stare at the large figure eight etched into his skin. Part of the line is thicker than the rest—the thicker line makes up a large *S*. He pulls his arm back, making me jump, and when I look up into his face, his eyes are open.

"It's an infinity symbol," he says quietly. His phone starts vibrating on the table next to us, but he doesn't move to get it.

"What does it—" I whisper.

His eyes are fully open now; he uses them to give me a withering look. "You know what it means. Aren't we past that?"

I pull myself out from under his arm, suddenly distant. I want to tell him that I don't know where we are.

I don't know where I want us to be.

In one night, everything seems to have shifted. I'm not ready for the shift. *What happened?* I wasn't myself; he wasn't himself. I should never have let myself get that close to him when we were both in such an emotional state. All I know is that something that felt so wonderful and inevitable last night feels so totally different in the ashy light of day.

Feelings make things complicated—God, if I haven't learned that, what have I learned? And Fred was right; we're both made up of too much complicated as it is.

Hector fumbles for his phone and puts it to his ear. I climb out of bed, grab some clothes, and head to the bathroom to change while he's talking. I stumble in, locking the door behind me. The uneasiness builds inside of me until it almost reaches sickness.

What was I thinking last night? Why did I let him kiss me? *Why did I kiss him back?*

I grip my arm, feeling the bulge of the scar through my top. I shut my eyes to block out the flashback swimming into my vision. I dress quickly and, with a deep breath, force myself to go back into the room. I need to repave the distance between us now, before it's too late. I let my barrier fall too far last night, and I have to rebuild it.

He stands with his back to me, staring down at the road through the now-opened curtains, phone pressed to his ear. Seeing him in person crumbles some of my resolve, and I end up staring at him for a minute too long. His voice is a decibel louder than a murmur of Spanish, and even though I can't understand a word, it's clear something is wrong. He hangs up soon after I enter, and the look he gives me makes all the things I was going to tell him irrelevant.

"Was that your sister?"

He nods once, sitting down on the bed, but tilts his body away from me.

"What's happened?"

He drops his head into his hands and groans. "This trip . . . It's not going as planned."

"Hector?"

"He knows," Hector says. "My father knows I'm here."

When we arrive at the hospital, it quickly becomes clear that today won't be anything like yesterday.

Before we can go to Hector's mother's room, a nurse directs us into a side room, where two men are waiting for us. I recognize Hector's father immediately from the newspaper article. There is no hello. No it's been six weeks, I've missed you, son. No how are you. No I'm so sorry about your mother. Just, "What the hell were you thinking? Coming here was unbelievably arrogant, Hector. Even for you. I don't need you here at a time like this— I've just had to dodge a pack of reporters."

"Have you really?" Hector asks. I see now he's not going to bother himself trying to charm his father.

"Oh, for God's sake, Hector, this is not a joke. I sent your sister out of the city and said you weren't allowed to come home for good reason. I need to manage this situation without any of you around."

"*Manage* this situation?" Hector repeats, anger blazing from his eyes.

"You know how much work I've been doing with mental-health charities. If the papers misrepresent what happened, it could ruin everything I've worked so hard for."

"Good," Hector replies fiercely. "Maybe now your supporters in this country will realize it's stupid to put their faith in someone like you."

His father stands up taller and, without meaning to, I recoil. "Someone like me? What's that supposed to mean?"

"Someone who puts his career above his family's well-being. Someone who spends so much time pretending to support everyone else that he doesn't even realize that the people who actually need the support are in his own home."

His father's face doesn't flinch. "That's what you think, is it?"

I feel Hector's fury rise up next to me like a wave. I feel it climbing and climbing, preparing to crash down on top of all of us. "How many more people have to hurt themselves before you realize it, Dad? First Santi, now Mum."

"Your mother fell down the stairs and hit her head."

"But Santi didn't fall, did he, Dad? He jumped." Hector draws in a ragged breath. "And Mum, she wasn't taking all those pills because she was feeling a bit tired, was she? She wasn't on the rooftop to look at the view, was she? When are you going to get what you're doing to them into your head?"

"This is not my fault," his father says. The man next to him tries to pull him aside. He looks like an advisor of sorts, someone trying to deflate the scene exploding around us. Right here must

203

be what Hector's father was afraid of. A perfect news story in the making. "You shouldn't be here, Hector. You are supposed to be at school."

"You are blinded by ambition," Hector growls, ignoring him. "You've put everyone in your life under the microscope, Dad. You've put the people closest to you in a place where they feel they have to hide how they're feeling, or risk costing you your career."

"Once again you're letting emotion cloud your judgment. None of this has anything to do with my job."

"It has everything to do with your job. You think anything less than perfect is a weakness. You haven't given anyone's less-than-perfect feelings the time of day. Why did Santi jump, Dad? Who made him feel that he couldn't stay?"

His father clears his throat. "Your brother was ill, Hector. An illness I have been trying to raise awareness for ever since."

"An illness you only accepted after he'd died. An illness that you don't accept in Mum. An illness that somehow you've managed to garner sympathy for. I've been following the news coverage of you. It's disgusting." Hector's fury has spread out into the corridor, opening wide like the jaw of a crocodile, pulling in passersby and threatening to crush them, suffocate them. "What would all these mental-health organizations say if they knew what you said to your son when he was alive, Dad? *Come on, Santi, buck up and act like a man. Get a grip, Santi. You're being self-indulgent.*"

"Enough," his father finally snaps.

Hector continues, unabashed. "How were you planning to play Mum's accident to the press?"

"With the truth," he says firmly. "I'm going to tell them that your mother fell over and hit her head."

"And the pills? What are you going to say about them?"

"That's private, Hector. Nobody needs to know about them."

"Well, *I'm* not going to lie for you," Hector says. "I'm going to tell everyone how desperate and marginalized you make the people around you feel. Career collateral—I can see the headline. Finally breathe some truth into all those stories."

His father's face pales. "Your mother wouldn't want you to do that."

"Well, thanks to you," Hector says through gritted teeth, "she can't tell me what she wants herself."

"She can," his father interrupts.

Hector freezes. "She's awake?"

His father nods curtly; Hector pushes past him out of the room without another word. I feel a sudden rush of relief at this news, that now she's awake everything we've done to get here has vindicated him. From his father's furious glare, I know that's probably not the case. But it's okay. The worst thing that could have happened has, miraculously, been avoided.

After a long minute, one where I watch Hector's father pull his features back in place like a pro, he finally focuses on me.

"My son seems to have forgotten his manners," he says smoothly. "I'll have to introduce myself. Rupert Sanderson, Hector's father."

"I know who you are," I say. I've just witnessed the explosion, so there is absolutely no point in wasting time with pleasantries at this stage. "I've been here the whole time."

He raises his eyebrows and his features contort in an unfamiliar, angled way. I doubt, bar an unpredictable temper, there is much Hector has inherited from this man. "I see," he says, guarded. "Hector is staying in London with you?"

"Yes," I say, hoping he misses the possessiveness to my tone.

He smiles. "And you are?"

"Cara Cooper."

"Well, Cara Cooper, you won't have him bothering you any longer. I'll send someone to pick up his things from your house later today, if you could kindly give Henry your address." He gestures to the man at his side, loitering next to him.

"He's not bothering me. I was the one who offered to have him," I say quickly. Defensively. It's stupid to be this defensive, but somehow, in the two days we've had together here, and despite the awkwardness of this morning, I feel like we've achieved far more than we came for.

"I'm sure you did," he says. "Which is typical of Hector, really. My son has always had a way of getting what he wants, no matter what it costs. I'm sorry you had to be that cost. Him coming here has caused a great deal of trouble. It was very selfish of him to use you to get here."

"It's not like that," I say, feeling my voice waver.

"Hmm . . . ," he says. "Well, I'll let you go, Cara. Thank you for having my son to stay. Very kind."

I watch him stalk off toward his wife's hospital room.

—

I wait for Hector to reappear in the intensive care relatives' room. It is a miserable place full of waiting people, all of their worlds hanging in the balance. Their fear, their amplified emotions, project outward and fill the space. It's catching: the longer I stay here, the more overcome I feel. For most of them, this is, or will be, one of the worst days of their lives. I wonder if this is how my mother felt waiting for me to wake up from surgery after the crash, whether her desire to leave was as overwhelming as mine is now. I don't blame her for insisting I be discharged at the earliest possible opportunity—finally I understand that insistence.

I am hit by the sudden urge to hear her voice, to apologize for something. Well, for everything, really. To tell her all the things I haven't been able to say to her, or to say nothing at all. Just to listen to her trying to soothe my screaming brothers in the background, or for her constant conversation, sentences jammed so closely together to avoid any kind of silence. But mostly to check she hasn't given up on me yet.

Please don't give up on me yet.

I take my phone from my pocket but don't dial her number. My finger hovers; I take a deep breath and click onto the photo button. The photos are still there—of course, they are. I mentally shake myself. What did I think was going to happen to them? Did I really think they'd disappear with her?

I gulp down the surrounding air to steady myself and then pull up a picture. It's the day before the New Year's Eve party.

G and I went to the mall to get dresses. The first photo I click is her wearing a short-sleeved navy-blue dress.

"We need to really wow everyone," I remember her saying. "This isn't the one."

"It's just a party," I'd replied, but she'd just shaken her head with that impatient look she had.

"Oh, come on, C. You know it's not *just* a party. It's *the* party. Tomorrow night, things are going to change."

The next photo is of me. I'm wearing green sequins, and all I can think is *Yes, G, everything is going to change.*

I look up just as Hector walks briskly past the room. I jump up, switching off my phone again, and head after him.

"Hector!" I call out.

He spins around. "You're still here?" All his fight from earlier is gone, replaced by someone who looks and sounds drained.

My forehead creases in confusion. "Are you . . . ? Is your mother . . . ?"

"She's awake and talking, so that's something."

"That's wonderful, Hector."

He nods silently at me.

"Your dad wants to send someone over to the apartment to collect your things." He continues to nod vacantly. "I want you to know that you're welcome to stay with me. I mean, I know it's tiny and mostly uncomfortable with my dad there . . ."

He clears his throat. "I have to go home."

His response should make sense—this is what someone from a normal family would do. Then again, normal families probably don't have relationships that hinge on so much resentment. Normal families probably don't explode at one another in hospital corridors. Someone from a normal family doesn't have to make an illicit trek across Europe to see a mother whose life is hanging in the balance. His response should make sense; his response is what I want, isn't it? Distance.

Why does it feel like a slap in the face?

"Of course," I say, trying to hide the irrational bud of hurt.

His forehead creases momentarily. "My sister is coming back home later, and I need to go and pick her up."

"Yes, of course," I mutter again quickly, cursing myself for being so selfish. Today is not about me.

His eyes scan my face. "Just so you know, I'd . . ." He clears his throat. "Well . . . I'd much rather be going back with you."

My eyes snap up to his, and I try to read his face, trying to decipher where we stand with each other.

"You'll let me know how everything goes?"

He pulls his phone out of his pocket. "Put your number in there." I feel him watching me as I input the number. His next question is tentative. "Are you going to be okay with your dad?"

"Of course. It's only a week. I'm sure I'll manage." I force a smile, but I can tell it's flat and unconvincing. "I didn't give anyone his address for your things."

"I'll tell them," he says, his words stiff. "And thank you for, you know . . . getting me here."

He looks at me like he wants to say something else. The silence pools around us, full of unsaid things.

"I should go."

I nod, taking my own cue to leave. I start to walk away, turning back at the last minute. I open my mouth to say something else, but no words come out. We stare at each other for a moment; then he disappears down the corridor in the opposite direction.

31

Along with the PG Dictionary, Poppy, Lennon, G, and I started Secret Squirrel. If you said "Secret Squirrel" before you told the others something, that thing automatically added itself to the blacklist of things that were never, ever to leave the room. If you told anyone about a Secret Squirrel, we threatened to release all of the things you'd ever added to the list to the whole class.

Lennon used to say things like "Secret Squirrel, I don't have a nail on my third toe."

Poppy's were almost exclusively boy-related, like "Secret Squirrel, I played golf with Tom Saper on Saturday night."

G's were things like "Secret Squirrel, I bought a top to wear on Saturday night, kept the tag on and then took it back."

Had they come out at school, I doubt any of these would have been of particular interest. Except for maybe mine: "Secret

Squirrel, I have never actually been on a date. Not once." This would have destroyed my reputation.

Poppy and Lennon used to tease me about it; they'd say I wasn't the dating type, then spiral into giggles. They had practiced explanations, of course:

"Oh, Cara, don't be annoyed. It's a compliment!" Lennon would say. *Of course it is.*

"Yeah," Poppy would add. "Dates are so overrated. Do you remember when I went on that date with Jake—it was awful!" Which is categorically not what she'd said at the time. It's funny how, when the guy doesn't ask you out a second time, memories transform.

G never joined in with the teasing. Later, when it was just the two of us, she'd tell me I was too good for the boys at school. But that wasn't it, and we both knew it. I wasn't short of admirers per se: I had things with guys all the time. It was just that no one ever really wanted to spend time with me one-on-one.

Until Hector.

G's face fills my mind. I can't help thinking about all the hours we spent discussing boys. I wonder what G would have thought about Hector, whether she'd have thought him date-worthy. I think of her seeing me with Hector when she hasn't even been gone a year. Would she expect it of me?

Anger boils up inside and I feel sick. *What the hell is wrong with me?*

My father appears and sits across from me on the sofa. I don't react when he enters, keeping my gaze fixed out the window and my ear tuned in to the traffic outside.

"Hector's family is on the news," he says.

"I've heard," I say blackly.

"Did they know he was in London?"

"They gave permission for him to come and stay, didn't they?"

He makes a huffing noise. "Is he coming back here tonight?"

"No?" I despise how I phrase my answer as a question, like if I leave the chance for him to return, he might just do so.

The doorbell rings and I jump up, keen to get away. I push myself down the stairs and open the door. A woman I've never seen before stands there. "I've come to collect Hector's belongings," she says.

My father, who's followed me to the door, replies for me. "I'll go and round everything up."

When he's gone, I lock eyes with the woman. I should ask her if everything is still okay with Hector's mother. If she is still getting better. If Hector is okay. If he's made up with his father. I realize as I stare at her that a part of me was hoping Hector would come himself. In the ensuing silence, I can only think of G's face, which makes me unable to say anything at all.

My father descends the stairs a few minutes later with Hector's things, and in an instant the woman is gone.

On my way back upstairs, I can't shake my own stupidity. Of course it wouldn't be Hector ringing the doorbell. I've done what he needed me to do, haven't I? Like his father said, all he needed was me to help him get here. Nothing more.

He doesn't owe me anything, and I don't deserve anything from him.

"You're disappointed it wasn't him," my father says, resuming his place on the sofa and breaking the silence that has come to settle in the room now that it's just the two of us. I sink down into the opposite one, acutely aware that this is the first time we've been alone in the same place for five years. "He needs to be where he is now, Cara. Family sticks together in tough times."

"We didn't," I reply nastily. All of my anger is suddenly directed at my father. Years of resentment soar up. Now that Hector has left, there is no one to distract me from it.

He winces at my words. "That was different."

"How was that different?" I ask irritably, the seams of my carefully constructed composure starting to split. Hector. Kissing him. G. G's face. I feel myself unraveling at an unprecedented speed. "You abandoned us."

"Oh, Cara . . ."

I look at him, struggling for words, and the anger inside me roars, urging me on. "You've had *five years,* Dad. *Five years* to prepare your bullshit explanation and you can't say anything at all. It's pathetic."

He hunches over, drops his head into his hands, and for a second I think he's going to admit defeat. Then he draws himself up, sweeping his hands through what's left of his hair, jaw set, eyes determined. Ready to engage.

I don't let him speak. "If you hadn't left, we'd never have gone to the U.S. I'd never have met G. I wouldn't have been driving for over a year. I'd never have gotten in that car. G would still be alive, safe and far away from me."

I know I am linking things that shouldn't be linked, that I am projecting how I feel onto him, but it feels so good to let everything out—like how it must have felt for Hector this morning.

My father clears his throat. "I understand you need someone to blame, and I am happy to be that person. More than happy. In fact, I deserve it. But, Cara, you can't live in hypotheses. It's nonsense to torture yourself with hindsight. It doesn't lead anywhere. I know you've been struggling, but it won't last forever. When your mum told me about how you were back in the U.S. . . . Well, look at you now. You're coping brilliantly after everything you've been through this year."

"Brilliantly?" I leap up from the sofa, prepared to storm out, then remember that I am already in my "bedroom" and there's nowhere to storm to. I keep my back to him instead and stare out the window. "I should never have come here. It was a stupid idea—"

"I'm so glad you did." He shifts in his seat, tilting toward me. "Cara . . . I know I owe you an explanation, which is so completely overdue. The thing is . . . well, I don't really know how to start."

I drop back down onto the sofa and scrunch a cushion against my chest. "Hmm, I don't know . . . How about 'I ran off with your mother's best friend, Cara'?" I say in my most scathing voice. "I mean, that's the truth, isn't it?"

The color leaches from his face.

"What, Dad? It *is* true. You shouldn't do things you can't talk about." The last words catch in my throat.

He remains silent, as if trying to locate the necessary language. It's strange, because there's a part of me that would rather he stayed that way, a part that doesn't want him to try to justify what he did, but there's another part that does, a part that wants there to be a good enough reason to forgive him. Wonders if such a reason could ever exist.

"I made a mistake," he says, and he actually puts his hands up in surrender as if to ram the point home.

I raise my eyebrows. *"You don't say.* Well, where is she, then? Are you still together?"

"No. She went back to her husband."

I study his face, trying to gauge his reaction. "Did you love her?"

He shakes his head. It's a finite movement. "No."

I feel myself frown; he's telling the truth. "Why did you do it, then?"

He presses the heel of his hand against his forehead and squeezes his eyes closed for a long moment. "Sometimes, Cara, people just make terrible choices. I could tell you that there were things that led me to it, but what's the point? The result is the same—I did it in a moment, and as soon as I did I couldn't take it back. I don't know what to tell you, except that I am sorry, so sorry—and there isn't a day that goes by when I don't regret that choice. If I'd known you'd go to the U.S. . . . ."

I stare blankly at him. "What? You wouldn't have done it? But if you thought Mum would have taken you back, you'd have done it anyway?"

"That's not what I meant—"

"That's what it sound—"

"Cara, please, let me finish." He rubs his palms over and over on his jeans. "There are no excuses. I knew better than to do what

I did; I was stupid and selfish, and arrogant, and a thousand other things. Please know that I have been paying for that choice every day since."

I stare at him in silence for a very long time. He waits while the words circle around my head. I pull them apart and put them back together again; I make sense of them and I don't. They're all he has; I'm not sure they're enough.

"Saying 'people make terrible choices' doesn't absolve you of what you did," I say eventually.

"I'm not saying it does; I'm just trying to be honest with you. I think you deserve that, at least. And then, when you're a bit older, when you're presented with a choice, you'll think about me and have a benchmark. You'll choose right."

A shudder passes through me. "Will I? I've made some *awful* choices lately."

My father winces. "A car accident isn't a choice, Cara. Things happen all the time we don't have control over."

"Don't you dare start telling me these things are down to fate—"

"Well, Cara, you have to consid—"

"Fate is bullshit, Dad. Fate is for people too weak to consider causality. I opened the car door, I put the key in the ignition, I drove within the speed limit. If I'd gone faster or slower, maybe things would be different—we wouldn't have been in that exact spot at that time. But I didn't." My voice is level, lifeless. "I made the choices; I was the cause. She is dead because of me."

I start to rub my arm, the patch over my scar, conscious that this conversation has taken a turn and not able to remember how we got here. For a long moment, he doesn't say anything. I wait for him to say the things I've heard a million times over:

It's not your fault. You didn't kill her. It was an accident. It's going to be okay. . . .

"We all carry scars, Cara" is all he says, watching me closely, and I have the sense that he is seeing far more than my mother, stepfather, and all the therapists in the state of California combined. He stretches his hand across the space between us. I don't know why but I let him rest it on mine. "Keep doing what you're doing. You know more than most that life is a fleeting, fragile thing—hold on to it where you can. You have to trust that things will change."

There are a million things I want to say to him. Yet, now, I can only voice six words. "I can't forgive you for leaving."

"I know," he says with a pained expression.

I want to tell him that a part of me wants to. Just like I want to tell my mother that I don't blame her for sending me away when neither of us could cope.

Just like I want to tell G that I'm sorry. *I'm so sorry, G. It should have been me. I can't understand why it wasn't me.*

32

That night, G visits me in my sleep again. When I wake, the full force of everything that's happened hits me anew, leaving me breathless and in a state of panic. I try to remember when I last had the dream—not since Hector went missing before half-term. It's the sympathy of others that brings it back, I'm sure of it. My father wouldn't tell me things will change if he knew what I've kept from him. From all of them.

The rest of the week passes in a blur. I pretend I have more homework than I was given and spend whole days cooped up in the sitting room, drawing on my exhaustion to ensure early nights. Even though I am unbelievably tired, I try not to sleep to avoid seeing her each night. It's all wrong: the dream her isn't anything like how she was in real life.

When I think of G, I think of gentleness, and kindness—

of someone who'd allow herself to be laughed at for wearing the wrong tracksuit if it was to stop someone else from being targeted.

She was *always* the glass half full to my empty. She was the kind one; I was the bitch.

I knew all this at the time; I abused all this at the time.

Time slows to an unbearable pace, and I will the days into passing, making dangerous promises to myself. If I can just get back to school, I'll be honest. . . . If I can just sleep without interruption, I will tell them everything. . . .

Hector doesn't call, so instead I'm stuck with my dad filling me in on all the news reports: Hector's father gave a public statement that his wife had been in an accident and was healing well. There was no mention of any pills.

I keep my phone on, permanently by my side for the rest of the week. Just in case.

I expect Hector to be on my flight, but he's not. When the plane leaves the airport, I automatically pull on the sleep mask, determined to get back to school without incident.

I step out of the taxi, hit by my first wave of freezing air. This time, I'm glad of the temperature. The relief on returning here is both bizarre and comforting. This arrival is almost identical to my first one, yet I notice things I didn't notice before. Like how the surrounding mountains have perfect, meringue-like peaks. The colors are brighter, less muted than before. I make myself promise: this time around, I will fight like hell. This time around, despite what will inevitably come after, I will be honest. It's the only hope I have.

I send my bag up in the elevator and climb the steps to the sixth floor. I have to stop to catch my breath at the top, and I briefly glance over to the door on my left, which leads to the boys' wing. Despite everything, I find myself wondering if Hector's here yet—if he's coming back at all.

All thoughts of him are swiftly put aside when I enter our dorm. Ren is already there, sitting at my desk. She spins around on the chair. "Thank God you're back," she says. "I've had the most awkward week with Fred, and I've just been sitting here waiting for you and reliving it."

I smile, dumping my bag down on the floor.

There's a different feel to the room and I try frantically to place it. Ren's eyes dart behind her, and I follow their track until I see the change. On the corkboard above my desk, three big photographs have been pinned up. One is of the back of Hector and me on the swings. The second is of Ren and Fred playing minigolf, taken by Fred, his long arm visible in the shot. But it is the third picture that is the most surprising. A black-and-white photograph of my mother and the twins that looks like it was taken recently.

"How did you—" I start, looking over to Ren, who is watching my reaction closely.

"Madame James gave me your mum's email address—I hope you don't mind?"

I feel a surge of something—something I'm not able to verbalize. I move forward to hug her. She makes an odd noise, a combination of surprise and something else, then she hugs me back.

"Thank you," I whisper. And I realize I have to do this now before I can change my mind. I was wrong before; Hector was wrong. It *is* wrong to hold back from the people we care about. Ren isn't G, but there's space in my life for her too. She can be my friend. I can let her in—more than that, I *want* to let her in.

"Ren, there's something I haven't told you. . . ."

She swallows nervously. "I know about the accident, Cara. So does Fred."

As much as I want to tell her, I feel it again. The guilt, the dishonesty—everything I've kept from them. "Did Hector tell you?"

She doesn't quite meet my eye. "Fred and I Googled you last week."

Then, like the coward that I am, I feel relieved. She only knows the facts. "That's one way to find out, I suppose. But there's more to it than just that."

I have to tell her everything; I force myself to.

She turns her desk chair around so that it's facing the middle of the room and sits down, gesturing for me to do the same. "I'm listening."

I stare into her deep brown eyes, so innocent and unknowing, and brace myself to tell her the rest. I do plan on telling her everything—I really do—but somehow I end up telling her the story I told Hector.

"Thank you for being honest with me," Ren says as Madame James enters the dorm to check attendance and take away our

222

phones. A little part of me dies at her sincerity. I should back-track. I should tell her the truth. But then she starts telling me about her week with Fred and I convince myself the moment for truth is gone.

I've told myself that a lot.

33

I'm a coward. I've made a million excuses for why I can't tell any-
one what I did, but this is the only one that's true.

When I climb up to my bunk, there is a note on my pillow
that just says *Rooftop. Midnight.* I don't try to sleep, instead lying
motionless for a few hours until it's safe to get out of bed and go
to the common room. The fire-escape door is open an inch again,
propped ajar.

I grip the handrail as I climb the stairs. The frozen metal
peeps through sections where the paint has chipped away, and
the cold scorches my ungloved hands.

For some reason, as I make my way toward the ledge, I can't
get the image of my father alone in his apartment in London out
of my head. He deposited me at the departures lounge, watched
as I disappeared through the arch to security. I looked back at

him and I saw the sadness on his face. It was all wrong: he should have been happy that finally, after five years, we'd spent a week together, but instead I knew he'd recognized that there wasn't an easy fix to everything he'd broken.

I remember how, when we got to the U.S., I didn't understand why we had to leave. For a while I thought my mother was weak for turning her back on our whole lives in England. I shouted terrible things at her; I told her that she couldn't be bothered to try, that she'd given up. She stayed calm throughout, and it infuriated me then. I wanted a reaction; I wanted her to take us home.

"There are two types of lies," she said. "White and black. White lies are justifiable, because you tell them to protect other people, but there's no justifying black ones—those are just told to protect yourself."

It was a few months later, only after I overheard her and Mike talking about Dad's affair, that I understood. And in all the dilemmas that came after, I never questioned why she always came back to this. "Black and white," she'd say. "Respect yourself enough to know the difference."

Hector is sitting on the wall of the terrace. "California," he says in greeting. "I was hoping you'd come."

Seeing him again lifts something in me. He waits for me to climb the rest of the stairs as if nothing has happened. There's no flicker of anything on his face; it's like I wasn't in the hospital with him, like he didn't tell me about his brother, like I haven't already revealed so much of myself to him. He behaves normally, like he's normal and I'm normal, and it's totally normal to be meeting each other here, on the rooftop of a six-story building at midnight. It's exhilarating and terrifying in equal measure. And the thing that terrifies me the most is that when I'm around him, I almost believe it.

I climb to the top of the stairs and pull myself up onto the wall, turning to face him. There's a moment when we just stare at each other, where all the bravado drops away.

"Are you okay?" I ask, searching his face for a clue.

"Almost," he answers, zipping up his coat right to the top.

I have the strangest urge to unzip it slightly, but I hold myself back.

"And your mother?"

"Better." He winces. "She checked herself into some holistic rehab center outside of London. You know, to stop relying on the sleeping pills so much." He turns away from me; there's a rare streak of vulnerability about his expression. "I did try to call you."

"I must have missed—"

"You gave me the wrong number," he cuts in. There is something cautious about the way he says it.

I frown; it takes a single moment to realize what I've done. My hands ball into fists by my side, scrunching snow up into them. "Oh, God . . . Did you . . . did you call her?"

He nods once and my stomach knots itself together.

"I was looking at photos in the hospital. . . . I must have accidentally . . . You must think I'm crazy."

He raises his hand; it hovers in the air before he rests it for a tentative moment on my leg. At his touch, I feel that thing again. That warming, hopeful swooping sensation in the pit of my stomach. I pull my leg out from under his hand, but before I can read his reaction, he's up on his feet.

"Come on," he says. "I'm going to give you a tour of the domes."

Confused, I pull myself back onto the terrace. He holds out a hand to help me over the low wall, right into the center of the roof.

"Remember that's the area to avoid," he says, pointing out a spot on the tiles. "Stay close to the walls."

We skirt the central golden dome, dimly lit by outdoor spot-lights. "Hector, what are we—"

"That's the town, but you know that," he talks over me. "And if we go over to the left dome, you'll be able to see the chapel, right over there in the far corner. Do you see it?"

I nod at him, wishing he'd stop behaving as if nothing happened. *"Hector . . ."*

"And that, California," he continues, pointing to a gap in the trees on a nearby mountainside, "is where the old railway station used to be. There used to be another cable car that came across to us here. It used to be a hotel, I think, but they got rid of the cable car when the station closed. A train derailed during the war or something—I don't think the line has been used since."

I frown, irritation gripping me from inside. Why won't he let me speak? "Hector, *please.*"

He spins around to face me, his figure backlit by the light bouncing off the domes. "I'm trying to distract you, California. I can almost see your mind whirring in there—you're about to tell me something unnecessary."

"I'm about to tell you something truthful," I say through gritted teeth.

"Don't," he replies. "You're going to dissect London. Let's just . . . not. Not tonight."

"What part of London are you talking about?"

"All of it," he says back. "Just stop overthinking everything. You're having the most magical nighttime tour. You're in Switzerland now, on a bloody rooftop."

"What is it with your family and rooftops?" I immediately cover my mouth with my hand as pain flickers on his face. "I'm sorry, I don't know why I said that. I don't know . . ."

"Cara, what the—" he starts, and his voice is gruffer than before. "Why would you say that?"

"I'm a bitch, Hector," I say, my voice rising.

He stares at me with narrowed eyes, and it's almost more than I can bear. I rush toward the stairs, right over the tiles he warned me about. Just as I feel my balance go, he's behind me, his arm grabbing me around the waist, keeping me upright and forcing all the breath out of my lungs.

I feel his height behind me, him so close to me. He doesn't remove his arm from around my waist, and for the tiniest second, I lean back into him. It is probably the last time he'll opt to be this close to me.

"Cara, what's going on?"

"Please don't be nice to me," I beg. "Not now."

He tilts his head over my shoulder. "What's happened?"

I consider just coming straight out with the truth: you can't be near me because I've done a terrible thing—an unforgivable thing—and when you know, you'll understand. I feel my stomach contract like it's warning me: *You don't have to do this.* But I do. I have to tell him.

"I've kept something from you."

He releases me from his grip, then directs me back onto safe ground until we reach the low wall of the terrace. He pulls me down to sit back in our usual spot, tilting my legs so I'm partially facing him. I oblige only because I can no longer feel my limbs.

"Go on," he says, staring down at me with confused, clouded eyes.

"I keep having this dream. I'm back in the car."

"A repeat of the accident?"

I suddenly feel very cold, a cold that has nothing to do with the temperature up here on the roof. "Not exactly."

He starts to blow on his fingers. The movement is distant— or maybe that's just me. My body feels separate from the words coming out of my mouth. All I feel is the adrenaline, the blood rushing up to my throat making it close to impossible to speak.

"You know dreams aren't real, right?"

I'm filled with a sense of urgency. "I know it's not real, Hector. In the dream, she's me and I'm her. Or at least, she's the one who survives and I . . . well, I . . ."

"You die?"

I nod once. "Just before I do, she tells me something. . . ."

"What does she say?" he prompts. "Come on, California— you can tell me."

It's the name California that incites me. He's not taking me seriously; he thinks this is a joke. "She says, 'You did this.'"

He clenches his jaw, his frustration visible. "We've been through this before, Cara. The accident wasn't your fault. You've got to stop coming back to this point—"

I flinch away from him and my voice starts to shake. "She's not talking about that."

Something flickers behind his eyes—perhaps he can already see it on my face. So finally, with the tone the question deserves, he asks, "What did you do?"

There are two types of lies; I know this now, and I knew it then. Yet, somewhere along the line, I chose to lose sight of the difference.

34

New Year's Eve, San Francisco

The doorbell rings in the distance. I check my reflection one last time in the mirror—I'm wearing the dress bought especially for tonight: the green sequins chosen for a purpose.

In the car, G starts talking about the party. "James says he wants to talk to me about something important. . . . I think to-night's the night."

"He's going to make it official?"

"Let's not jinx it, okay?"

"Okay," I say, and force myself to smile.

She moves on to talking about Scott, so I dig a quarter out of my bag to distract her. She tosses it into the air and the events of the night are set in motion.

We separate when we arrive and I end up lingering in the

room closest to the door, arranging Doritos in bowls with Lennon. She makes a loaded comment about my outfit; I make one about hers. All is well with the world.

She announces the arrival of the boys just as Poppy appears with some gossip about James and G.

"Don't say anything," Poppy says, "but I think she's got it wrong. James told me last week that he didn't want to be tied down. . . ."

There's something gleeful about the way she says it, which reminds me that to Poppy, information is information—as long as she's the source, she's happy. James arrives just in time to put an end to our conversation. I watch as G practically throws herself at him. When they separate, we lock eyes across the room.

Scott draws up next to me, and I weigh how my night is going to play out. I decide in an instant: tilting my body toward him, playing with my hair, fluttering my eyelashes.

I do my absolute best, and I make sure James sees it.

I play my part well—I've practiced it enough these past few months. I integrate myself at the party. I pretend to enjoy myself. I pretend I'm relaxed, easy . . . not charged up with heightened senses, not full of anticipation.

An hour or so later, G clumsily throws herself down next to Scott and me on the sofa.

"James and I are official," she announces, her words slurred.

I'm quick to hug her, holding on to her for longer than normal, mostly to hide the confusion on my face. I glare at James over her shoulder, a tight feeling in my throat.

He starts to mouth, "I don't know how . . ." But G pulls herself free of me, rushing over to tell Lennon and Poppy, and I get up and walk away too.

James pulls me around by the arm at the bottom of the stairs. "Wait, Cara. You haven't let me explain."

I glower at him. "It's a bit late for that, isn't it?"

"Please . . . just hear me out. Let's find somewhere private." He drags me up the stairs to the nearest empty bedroom he can find.

I stare at the far wall, my back to him. "You said you were going to break it off with her."

He gives me a desperate sort of look. "I tried, Cara."

"Not very hard!" I spin to face him, disbelief rippling under my skin.

"I was telling her how I needed to talk to her, that I really liked her *but* . . . It was like she wasn't listening to me properly, and then she just sort of started talking over me and said she'd been excited about tonight forever, and she was really excited we were going to start the year together as a couple."

"And you didn't think to correct her?"

He takes a step toward me. "How could I? She was so happy and smiley and I just, well . . ." He raises his hand to my cheek; I bat it away. "Cara, please—"

"*Please?* What do you want me to say, James?"

He takes another step toward me, this time placing both

his hands on my cheeks, tilting my chin up to him. "You're the one I like, Cara. You know that, right? I'll fix this somehow, I promise."

I feel that swooping sensation in my stomach, and when he leans in to kiss me, I kiss him back, drawing closer to him until my arms are wrapped around his neck. Everything around us seems to melt away.

The bedroom door crashes open, and James's grip on my waist becomes slack.

"Is this a joke?" G says, and her voice has a cold, terrifying quality to it. I turn to see the outline of her glowering at us from the doorway. She looks between us both, and her face flashes with a rainbow of emotion: shock, confusion, fury, devastation . . . betrayal.

She addresses James. "You just asked me out. What are you doing with *her*?" She says the word *her* like it's a filthy, revolting thing.

I take a step toward her, my arm outstretched. "G, I can explain—"

She bats me away, her eyes brimming with tears. She teeters slightly, and I remember how much she's had to drink. "*You.* Of all people."

"*G . . . ,*" I plead. My heartbeat is in my head, pounding violently in time with my accelerated breathing. Time, I know, is all I have—the words that will count are the ones I say right now. And I can't think of a single one.

"God, you really are a slut, Cara," G says with more venom than ever.

234

The word hangs in the air, searing my skin like a branding iron, and I realize that if I don't get out of here now, the house will probably collapse on top of me. I barge past both of them, charging down the stairs. I pull G's handbag off the kitchen counter and start rummaging inside it for her keys.

A chill spreads through my entire body. What did I expect to happen with James? He'd end it with G and we'd come out as a couple? My rib cage feels like it's contracting, pushing all the air out of my lungs. I am filled with the urge to flee, to get away from all of this. I remember his face inches from mine, his arms around my waist, his lips . . . All the things that moments ago felt so good now feel very, very wrong.

Lennon pulls on my arm. "Come and dance with us."

I violently shrug her off and finally locate the keys; then, what feels like seconds later, I'm outside, reversing the car.

Palms slam down on the hood. "Where do you think you're going in my car?"

G moves toward the door and, in one swift movement, is inside. I expect her anger to follow her in, but for a long moment, the slow rumble of the engine is the only noise in the stationary car.

Eventually she turns to me and says, "Tell me it was just that one kiss."

I try to look at her, but I can't.

She inhales sharply. "I've stood up for you, you know that?"

Her voice is quieter now, more loaded. A part of me wishes she'd scream and shout at me—that, surely, would be better than this.

"This past year," she continues, "people have said some really bitchy things about you, about how many guys you've gotten with. I've *always* had your back."

"Oh, G, I had yours too."

She laughs nastily. "You didn't have my back. You saw your opportunity and stuck a knife in it."

She turns to face the window. After a moment, I lean across to get her seat belt. She pulls the strap across her chest herself, but our hands brush in midair and she flinches away from me, dropping the latch. I click it into place for her as silent tears fall down her cheeks.

I utter my next words when we're on the highway, streams of rain lashing against the windshield. "I'm sorry, G. I don't know why we did it."

She twists her head around, her cheeks now streaked black with mascara. "You did this, Cara. *You.* My *best friend.*"

There is the glaring screech of a horn, the stark blaze of headlights, and then the world explodes.

35

"It wasn't your friend Poppy who kissed him," Hector says, his tone somewhere between confused and horrified—exactly where it should be. "It was *you*."

I can't look at him. "It was me," I repeat in a very flat voice.

"And the whole you-liking-Scott thing was just something you made up for my benefit? You never liked him at all?"

"I . . . well, I used him, I suppose. It was G who wanted me to date him. I think she wanted us to have boyfriends who knew each other, but I wasn't interested."

His voice is very low, almost inaudible. "Because you were interested in her boyfriend."

I nod, wishing I could shake my head. Wishing none of this were true.

He exhales loudly and then starts to laugh. It's not a laugh of amusement, though; it's one of those bitter, disbelieving ones.

"Oh, Cara, you don't make it easy for yourself," he says in a voice loaded with exasperation. *"Why?"*

I consider backtracking and telling him that I was drunk after all. That I wasn't myself. That it only happened once. In other words, I consider telling him more lies.

Silence fills the air all around us—I'm the one who has to break it. But how can I answer him? How can I tell him that, above all, it just felt good to be liked, desired? I relished the attention, because when G started seeing him, I felt left out. I was tired of being, as Poppy put it, "not the dating type." I felt lonely, so when James came on to me, I welcomed it. That's all it ever really was: I liked feeling a little bit less alone.

"I . . ." I struggle for words.

In the moonlight, I watch his exasperation turn to something else. And just for a moment I see it: judgment. The nighttime air solidifies, closing in. Even though it's hopeless, even though it was me who chose to sabotage my relationship with Hector by telling him this, the survival instinct in me rises up.

Even though it's crazy, I want him to understand. I have to make him see that I'm not a monster.

"It made sense at the time. I could rationalize it in my head. There were a hundred reasons why it was worth it."

"And now?" he asks, and the question is ridiculous. Of all people, he knows there are no reasons. None at all.

"I know it was wrong," I say quickly, hoping this may somehow placate him. Stupid, really, since it doesn't even placate me. "I don't expect you to . . . Well, I know . . . I know it was unforgivable."

He doesn't move, doesn't react. Doesn't offer any sympathy for how I feel now or try to empathize in some way to make me feel better.

"Not unforgivable," he says finally, "but somewhere close."

I give up fighting; I give up trying to redeem myself. There's nothing to be done. It's too late for redemption—too late for everything with him. Or, more importantly, with her. I take a series of shallow breaths before speaking. "If she were here now, she still wouldn't have forgiven me. I'm sure of that."

He stays deathly still. "No?"

I shake my head, knowing he can't see me. My mouth feels obscenely dry, and I am filled with the urge to get far away from here. I place my hands on the tiles on either side of me and start to push myself up.

He doesn't try to stop me. His stillness has a powerful effect. By not moving, not reacting, he manages to wound me more profoundly.

A voice in my head asks, *Can you blame him? What did you expect? That he'd tell you it was fine to betray your best friend because you were jealous of her? That it was understandable to do that to her because you felt insecure? That he liked you more for being honest about what you did? That now that she's dead the impact isn't the same? But you know it's worse now, and you only have yourself to blame.*

I can't concentrate on anything other than the voice, so at first I don't notice her there, her long red hair flickering in the wind. Then I see her: she must have followed me here. The look of shock on Ren's face makes me feel physically sick. I move toward her and for the second time tonight forget to be careful on the icy tiles.

It happens in slow motion, then all at once. My feet slide underneath me. My pelvis collides with the roof. My arms fly up, my fingers snatching uselessly at the ungraspable air. My whole body starts to slide toward the edge.

Hector grabs hold of my right arm, yanking my downward progression to a halt. My feet are inches from the gutter and six stories of free fall.

I close my eyes, a starfish on the roof, and try to remember how to breathe.

"Okay?" Hector asks, his voice spiked, gruff . . . transformed by adrenaline.

I shake my head repeatedly, not opening my eyes, and try to curb the rush of adrenaline that has invigorated me too. I try to temper the profound feeling of gratitude that I'm still alive. After all, there are so many reasons why it would be easier to fall.

My wrist starts to ache. I tilt my head back to find it still encased in Hector's grip. He hasn't loosened it even though I'm no longer in danger. My sleeve has fallen back, my scar a vivid zigzag in the dim starlight.

He grabs my other arm and hoists me back up next to him on the wall in one swift movement. When I am back in safe territory, I look for Ren, catching a final swish of her hair as she disappears down the stairs.

"I'm so sorry," I say in a breathy, desperate voice. "I tried to warn you. I'm a terrible person."

After a long pause, Hector says, "I can't make this better for you, Cara."

"I know," I say, and stare at him, eyes pleading, willing him to understand. "I had to tell you. I know the timing is horrible—I know you've got things going on and, compared to what you're dealing with . . ." I don't know how to finish. "You had to know," I add desperately. "I'm sorry."

He nods. "Horrible truths."

I swallow nervously. "This is the worst."

"I hope it is, Cara. I really do." He gestures down the stairs. "You should find Ren. That window won't be open for long." Then he turns back to face the darkness.

36

I wasn't at G's funeral. I'd just gotten back from the hospital and wasn't well enough.

This is another lie.

I was bruised, bandaged, traumatized, but I could stand. I could have been there.

I remember Mum and Mike coming home, Mum's face blotched from tears, her hand gripping Mike's a little too hard. I had been peeling the same orange for over an hour, chipping away at its tough skin with what I had left of bitten-down fingernails. I remember thinking it should hurt but not being able to feel a single thing.

I remember thinking I was out of my body, because this couldn't actually be real.

Mum sat down next to me on the sofa and said all the requisite things I imagine people say after a funeral. "It was a beautiful service. An amazing turnout. Georgina was very loved, wasn't she? Her father gave the eulogy—he was such a credit to the family."

Yes, she was loved, I wanted to scream. *Of course she was loved. She's still gone. An amazing, well-populated service doesn't change that.*

"Georgina's boyfriend seemed like a nice guy," Mike said. "He was sitting at the front with the family. They seem to have really taken him under their wing."

"James sat with Mr. and Mrs. Canter?" I asked, and they both stared at me. Probably because it was the first time I'd spoken all day.

"Yes, darling," Mum said. "We met him after. He asked about you."

"How was he?"

"What do you mean?"

"Exactly what I just said. Did he look okay? Was he upset? How did he behave?"

She gave me a strange look. "He was devastated, Cara. Obviously."

My teeth gritted themselves together; a surge of anger scorched through me. I was shocked by the feeling—by feeling anything at all.

I remember getting up, telling my parents I was going for a walk, seeing their surprise at me electing to leave the house. I somehow navigated the two blocks to James's house, lame and bandaged as I was, and banged on the door again and again until he answered.

Behind him, I could see that friends from school were there. Lots of them. And I remember feeling like I wanted to throw up. What was this? A wake after a wake? It made me sick to see them all there together—without me. Without G.

"Cara," James said, stepping out onto the doorstep and pulling the door behind him. "You look—"

I cut him off. "Are you having a party?"

"It's not a party," he said, and I was glad to see he looked horrified by the assumption. He stared at me for a moment, as though he didn't know what else to say to me. It hit me then more than ever what an idiot I'd been. "What are you doing here?"

I tried to conjure a reason in my head for what we did. I tried, I really did, to find a redeeming feature about him. Even one might have made it easier.

Dear G, I cheated with your boyfriend, but it was worth it because . . . because . . . because nothing.

"You need to stay away from the Canters. I swear to God, James, if you even . . ."

His face transformed into anger. "If I what, Cara?"

"They've just . . . they've just lost—" I tried to get the words out, but they tangled themselves around each other, so I just said, "They do not need you spouting your bullshit in their lives. If they knew what you'd done to G before . . ."

"Shh, Cara—keep your voice down." He looked anxiously back at the door.

"You haven't told anyone, then?"

I felt confused. If everyone didn't know, why hadn't anyone come to visit me at the hospital?

"Of course not," he said, and he looked at me like I was mad. "You and I are the only ones who knew."

"And G," I said, and her name snagged in my throat. "And here you are acting like the doting boyfriend. It's disgusting."

The muscles in his jaw clenched over and over. "I genuinely cared about G, you know," he said very quietly.

The front door sprang open, and I heard Poppy's voice say, "James, who are you talking to?"

Her eyebrows rose when she saw me, and she took in my bruises and bandages but didn't look me in the eye. Lennon appeared behind her moments later. "Cara, what are you doing here?"

All warmth from years of friendship turned to ash.

I recalled my mother's words from the day before: "When something terrible happens, you discover who your friends are. This, Cara, is a sink-or-swim situation. You need to call the girls—they'll help you keep afloat. That's what friends are for."

Poppy and Lennon didn't know the full extent of what I'd done and still they stood back and watched me drown.

37

After all those years of friendship, I was hurt that Lennon and Poppy didn't try to see me in the hospital. I was also relieved. I didn't want them to know what else I'd done.

It's strange that after just a few months of knowing Ren, I feel so different about her—even if she doesn't feel different about me. She pretends to be asleep when I get back to the dorm and leaves in the morning without a word. I don't blame her. I could have been honest with her from the beginning. I had a chance last night to tell her the whole story and, once again, I didn't.

After everything I've kept from her, Ren has every right to let me go, but I have to do whatever I can to stop her. I get myself dressed but descend the stairs slowly, daunted by the task ahead.

Hector is waiting at the bottom, his back pressed against the wall, his legs lazily propping him up as he drinks out of one of two cardboard coffee cups he's holding. He passes one to me without a word.

I take it from him, but I keep my distance; there's no way to know where I stand with him anymore. "Where did you—"

"They're for the staff," he says in a bored voice. "I think you should give breakfast a miss. Ren's there and she's fuming." I direct a slightly desperate look at him, but he just shakes his head. "Come on—let's go for a walk before class starts."

He chucks a school coat at me from a nearby rack and walks out the front door before I can stop him. He takes long strides up one of the paths that weave between the buildings. The sky is a cloudless aquamarine, but there is a sharp, minus-temperature bite to the air. As it's early, the snow around us is mostly untouched; it glistens provocatively under the glare of the sun.

I have to jog to catch up with him; a splash of coffee erupts from the mouth of the cup onto the frozen ground. "You're still talking to me?" My words are tentative, coated with anxiety and disgustingly hopeful.

"I have questions," he says, and there's a thoughtful quality to his voice. He stops, pivots toward me and back again, then starts walking at a slower pace. "Quite a few, actually."

I walk in time with him now, keeping a yard between us. "Ask me anything."

"What happened after you got back from the hospital? Have you seen any of them since?"

"Briefly," I say, and tell him what happened after the funeral. I tell him about James, how we could barely find words for each other. I tell him about the girls, how they looked at me like I was a stranger. I tell him that it truly hit me on that doorstep that G had been my life jacket—without her, I didn't know how I would survive.

We reach the chapel on the far edge of the mountainside. Hector gestures to the jagged stone steps that lead up to the entrance. We sit at different levels, me above him, at a tilt to face each other. I can feel the freezing stone through my thick skirt and tuck the tail of my coat underneath me.

He takes a long sip of coffee, his brows creasing together. "Do you still have feelings for him?"

"For James? Why would you ask me that?"

He assesses my face then, as though he's unsatisfied with my response, and says, "It's a simple yes/no answer."

"No. Obviously." I stare down at the ground. "What do you want me to say? That when G died, every feeling I thought I had for him died too? Because that's true. I just didn't think you needed it spelled out. I haven't been secretly pining for him these past few months, Hector, if that's what you're asking."

"I don't know what I'm asking, Cara," he says in a quieter voice than before. "I don't know what I want you to say. I'm trying to digest what you told me last night; I'm trying to get a clearer picture of everything."

"The picture's bad," I say in a low voice. "If I can't justify any of it, you won't be able to."

A black bird with a bright red beak lands on a nearby tree stump; we watch in total silence as it sits there, stretching and nibbling at its wings. Silence with Hector has never felt empty before now. I'm horribly aware that this is the moment he'll make up his mind about me. It hits me that if I keep talking, I might be able to delay his decision.

"In London, after you left," I start, and he tears his eyes away from the bird, "my dad and I had this sort of weird heart-to-heart. . . ."

He quirks an eyebrow, interested.

"He told me to use him as a benchmark. He said, when it comes to it, I'll think about what he did, how he screwed up, and I'll make sure I never do something like that."

"It's not bad advice."

I wince. "Just a bit too late. I've already made the same choice as him."

"Cara, they're not related. I mean, it's not like you got a cheating gene from him."

"I know, I know. It's just, well, I've judged him—hated him—for years for what he did. And yet I did pretty much the exact same thing."

"What are you saying?"

"You're allowed to hate me. I'd understand if you did."

I can't quite work out his expression, what it means. "I don't hate you, Cara," he finally says.

"I don't want to make the same choices as him. I've seen what happens. . . ." My next words are little more than a whisper. "I'm afraid that it's already too late. That I'm like him. I . . . I can't be like him."

"Don't look at me like that," he says, grimacing at my expression. "I'm afraid of it even more than you are."

"That I'm like my dad?"

He shakes his head. "That I'm like mine."

We stare at each other for a long time. "You're nothing like your father."

He smiles. "You met him for, like, five seconds."

I stare at him with steely determination. "Yeah, well, I just know these things."

He stands up abruptly, brushing the snow from his legs, and reaches out to pull me up too. He doesn't let go of my hand and at the last minute pulls me into a hug that has an air of resignation about it.

"Wh—" His coat muffles my words.

"Let's stop talking about this. There's nothing to be done," he says. "And to be honest, I think you've punished yourself enough for everything, don't you?"

And there it is. What I haven't dared dream of. Forgiveness. Acceptance. From Hector. A rush of something hot and prickly rises at the back of my throat. The world around me feels surreal, so I cling to him, balling some of his jacket up in my fist, wishing I could find the words to tell him what this means to me.

But he pulls back, extracting himself, and I realize, forgiveness or no forgiveness, everything isn't how it was before. I still haven't got a read on him—I still don't know where we are with each other.

"We should go. Classes start soon." He ushers me onto the path that leads toward the school. As the conservatory windows come into focus, his pace slows ever so slightly. "One last thing."

"Yes?"

"Why did you lie? It would have been so much more straight-forward if you'd just come out with everything at the start."

"I could barely admit what I had done to myself. And then you were being so understanding. You were so . . . How could I tell you?"

He puts a rough hand on my shoulder. "That's weak, Cara."

"It's also true."

The school is abuzz as the rest of the students catch up after a week apart, and I spend the day searching for a moment to talk to Ren.

In biology, we are asked to get into pairs for a new project. It becomes painfully clear, when Ren doesn't volunteer like she usually would, that without her I don't really know anyone else at Hope, besides Hector and Fred. Thankfully, I am partnered with a tall girl named Teresa. She has an open, kind face and a neat Afro. Most importantly, she doesn't seem too bothered to be paired with me, smiling and moving into the seat next to me without objection. As we work, I keep sneaking glances at Ren, huddled in conversation with Hector; she doesn't return the look once.

After prep, I watch Ren walk straight out into the courtyard in the direction of the swings. I follow her there, a sick anticipation building inside me. I know I have to face her, but an invisible force slows my legs.

I stop yards from her, dropping onto the swing farthest away. She doesn't seem surprised by my approach—I wonder whether she came here knowing I'd come too. It seems like the sort of thing she'd do. Kind.

I suddenly realize how important she is to me. I suppose I've known all this time—I just haven't let myself believe it. I make up my mind in an instant: If I need to beg, I will. Whatever I do, I need to make it right with her. "Ren . . . I'm so sorr—"

She doesn't wait for me to finish. "Would we have been friends then?"

I hesitate for a second, then resolve to be truthful. It's now or never. "No. I wouldn't have given you the time of day."

She nods repeatedly, as if reassuring herself of something. "Because I'm gay?"

"Not everything is because you're gay."

She raises her eyebrows. "Not everything is about your accident—you can't keep blaming everything on it."

"I'm . . . I'm not."

"I've been thinking about last night, about why you lied. Hector says it's because you care about us—"

"I do care about you," I say, seizing my chance.

"But you could have told us ages ago," she says impatiently. "Instead you've weaved this whole web for yourself. You've linked everything that has happened so it's now a big entangled mess."

"Everything *is* linked."

She shakes her head harshly. "No, it's not. You're confusing two things that aren't related. You didn't crash that car because you were seeing her boyfriend behind her back. You crashing that car wasn't some sort of karmic judgment for how you behaved.

"You made crap choices, but they were your choices, so own up to them. You could have said no to her boyfriend, but you chose not to. You could have told me the truth last night, but you chose not to. I'm not upset with you for what you did—that was in the past; you can't change what happened. But you can choose what happens now. You can stop deliberately lying to your friends, Cara. And we are your friends, aren't we?"

"I tried to tell you," I say in a very small voice. "I did want to, but I was scared, I think. I thought you'd stop talking to me, that you'd hate me for it, which of course you have every right to do. You've done so much for me already; I was afraid if I told you, you wouldn't want anything more to do with me."

She gives me a look as if to say, *Well, that's happened anyway, hasn't it?* "You lied to me; you told Hector the truth. On the same night."

And I realize what it looks like to Ren. Like I've put a boy before my friend. Again. But it's not the same. I wish I could tell her it's not the same. That wasn't why I told Hector—I wasn't trying to get him on my side. It was, in fact, more like the opposite: he was getting too close. I needed him to see me for who I am.

"Ren . . . I see how that might look, but—"

"Listen, Cara." She cuts me off again. "I don't know what happened between you and him over half-term. I know you told him weeks ago about the accident—I'm not upset with you for that. He's pushy as hell when he wants to be. When I asked him about it, he told me to wait for you to tell me yourself, and I was fine with that. I understand why you would be more cautious with me, but surely you have seen by now I'm not trying to replace

G. When we became friends, I didn't even know about her. All I have tried to do is be a good friend to you—"

"You have been amaz—"

"Let me finish," she interrupts.

I fall back into silence, gripping the wooden bench until splinters embed themselves under my fingernails.

"It's going to take some time before I properly trust you again."

I nod over and over again, stunned by her tolerance. I resolve to do everything I can to make this up to her, to somehow make this better.

"I'm so sorry, Ren. I wish I could take it back; I wish I could have told you everything from the start. I wish I could have done everything differently. Please know how sorry I am."

I put every ounce of sincerity that I can muster into my words. They're all I have; I have to make sure they're enough.

"Okay, Cara," she says brusquely before disappearing back into the depths of the trees. "But *please*. No more lies."

38

The following morning, even though I've been awake for hours, I can't get out of bed. I should be jubilant that Ren has found it within her to give me a second chance. I should be more likable than ever, more charming, more repentant, more everything . . . but all I can think about is the fact that I'll never be able to tell *G* how sorry I am.

Ren leaves for breakfast without me, which should be all the incentive I need to get up and out of bed. I'm not fully forgiven yet. But I can't bring myself to move, my body heavy and numb, and for the first time in ages, I keep my eyes fixed on my scar. My usual urge to hide it is replaced with an unadulterated fury that roots me to the spot. I want to scream and rage at it. I want to rip it off my body, cleanse myself of all this trauma. How can this be it? How can this be all I got from a night that took so much?

I am more rested than I've been for a while, and this angers me too. I close my eyes, willing myself to sleep, since the dream wasn't part of my sleep last night and that feels wrong. Haven't I been trying to avoid this dream for weeks? Haven't I woken up horrified from seeing her face? Why now do I so desperately need to see it? Why am I suddenly so terrified of not having the dream?

Someone opens the door without knocking.

"You need to get up," Hector says. "You're going to miss a thrilling history lesson if you don't get out of bed."

I don't have the energy to be surprised that it's him—that he's here in the girls' corridor once again. Or maybe I am just finally not surprised. I tilt my head down to face him. The effort even this small movement requires is momentous. "How—"

"I had an inkling." He raises his eyebrows theatrically. "You weren't at breakfast. Ren says you've called a truce, so I assumed there must be a problem. Come on, California, get up. You're not out of the woods with her yet, and, anyway, we have a test next lesson—pop quiz. Isn't that what they call it where you're from? You love a good pop quiz."

"Pop quizzes are supposed to be secret, Hector. That's the whole idea—they're popped on you when you least expect it."

"Yes, well, I know to expect it because I've seen the papers dated for today," he says.

I stare at the ceiling. "From Monsieur Thauvin's desk?"

"Filing cabinets," he says conversationally. "It was quite a task too. They are actually very difficult to break into. I think he's rather suspicious of me." He clears his throat. "Anyway, I haven't come for idle chitchat. I'm here to get you up."

After yesterday, I should be making an extra effort with him too. I should try . . . but I just shake my head.

He gestures up to my bunk. "Do you want me to actually come up there and get you? Is that it?"

"You wouldn't dare," I say. The alarm in my voice cuts through the numbness.

"Come on, California—you know me better than that." He crosses the room and takes hold of the ladder up to my bunk. We spend a moment in a silent standoff and then he starts to climb toward me. "I'm coming up. . . ."

"Please, Hector, I just need today. I can't . . . I'm feeling . . . I just want to be quiet."

"You're fine, Cara," he says, businesslike. "You're doing fine."

Looking at him, so eager, so determined to show me I am not struggling, fills me with shame.

"Come on," he says, tugging at the corner of the duvet. "You can always get a sick note or something if the day really is terrible."

I raise a hand in resignation. "Leave me to get dressed."

His face erupts into a brilliant, devastating smile. "I'll wait for you outside," he says. And I know him well enough now to realize that he would wait outside my dorm all day just to prove a point.

It takes me twice as long as usual to get dressed, but I do it for the boy standing outside my door.

"Take your time, why don't you?" he says, placing his hands

on my shoulders and marching me down the corridor. He calls the elevator, which opens immediately. "Get in."

I don't know why I do. Maybe it's because, after he's forced me out of bed, I want him to think that I'm somewhere close to normal. Maybe it's because, when he's around, I believe I can do impossible, ridiculous things. Whatever the reason, I propel myself forward into the cage. His impatience mobilizes me—that much I've already seen.

The elevator rattles to a halt between floors.

"What's going on?" My anxiety spreads out, filling all four corners of the elevator. I look at Hector for his usual reassurance. "Why did it stop?"

"I don't know," he says, indifferent. "Why are you asking me?"

"You seem to have an answer for everything else," I snap.

"Perhaps it's broken."

"Perhaps it's broken?" I repeat, feeling the terror build. "Well, fix it!"

"No can do. We'll have to wait."

I sink to the floor, my back scratching against the side of the elevator. "For how long? Everyone is in class until lunch. We could be here for *hours*."

"I am not a telepath," he says, sitting down against the opposite side of the elevator and stretching out his legs. They touch the wall behind me, emphasizing how small the space that we're trapped in is. "And before you ask, no, there isn't an alarm button."

"I can't be in here," I say, and hear my own desperation. My heart beats fiercely in my chest. The walls of the elevator begin to blur, tilting inward.

"Of course you can," he says, shifting forward onto his knees until our faces are inches apart. I expect him to say something to wind me up but instead get plain sincerity. "You can because you have to."

My breath shortens even more. "You don't understand. . . ."

"Understand this," he says, and then he places his hands on either side of my face. I am so surprised by the movement, I forget to breathe, all my concentration contained in this moment. The focus I'm putting on his face distracts me and, in the background of the moment, the walls stop closing in on us. "Nothing is going to happen to you here."

I look at him with wide, desperate eyes. "Why are you doing all this for me?"

"I'd have thought that was obvious," he says, pulling me to my feet. We stare at each other; intent crackles in the air all around us. The seconds tick on, and a part of me wonders what he's waiting for. But instead of stepping closer, he takes a step back, just as the elevator whirrs to life. Instead of the relief I expect, I feel only disappointment.

"You see?" he says as the elevator rattles to the bottom. "That wasn't so bad, was it?"

I am breathless, which has nothing to do with the erratic workings of the elevator, but my hands are still. I search for enough courage to tell him some of the thoughts that are racing around my brain, but before I find it, a panel of buttons comes into view and I notice a red button with STOP printed on it in bold. I glance between him and the button and a look takes over his face. It's brief, guilty, and tells me everything I need to know.

I've been played.

My composure explodes. Without thinking, I lift my hand and slap him hard across the face. "Fuck you, Hector."

I run out of the elevator and straight through the double doors outside. I stop running only when I'm gripping the cast-iron fence. I let my body double over. Hector follows, stopping just behind me. Now even the open space doesn't feel big enough; I want to be as far away from him as possible.

What have I done? I've allowed my life to stretch out of proportion. A minute ago I was feeling disappointed I wasn't trapped in an elevator with him.

G is dead.

Gone.

And that's what I was thinking about. Hector.

"What do you want from me?" I scream at him, emboldened by rage. "What the fuck do you want?"

"Cara, listen—"

"No, *you* listen!" I shout. "First you tell me your secrets, then you kiss me, then I tell you all mine, and then you *forgive* me, of all things. You forgive me!" I force a harsh, disbelieving laugh. "Then this. You trapped me in the elevator when you knew . . . you knew . . . You are purposely messing with my head. Is this a game to you? Am I a game?"

"Don't be angry with me," he says quietly. "I just wanted to show you that you can do it."

"*You wanted to show me* . . . Do you want to know what happened the last time I was trapped in a small space like that? I was hanging upside down in a car next to my dead friend. For *hours*. And do you have any idea what that feels like, Hector? Hours trapped next to your best friend while her body turns cold. Do you? Of course you don't. No one has ever cut you out of a car before."

And all of a sudden, I'm back there. Deep green threads hang from my body, crudely stripped from the dress. There are sequins on the dashboard, roof, everywhere, mixed in with the blood spattered across thousands of shards of glass. She's there too: pale, broken, lifeless. And I reach out for her, but my right arm won't move. I look down at it, at the ragged, bone-baring cut. My vision blurs, but no, I must stay present. I must wake her up. I try to reach her with my left arm, but the seat belt is rigid, keeping me in place. So I shout at her, willing her to regain consciousness. *Wake up, G. Please wake up.* I repeat the words over and over, thrashing against the seat belt, trying to get free, trying to wake her up. *Wake up, G. Please wake up.*

Hector puts a hand on my shoulder. "Cara, I—"

I shrug him off, furious. "Stay away from me, Hector. Stop thinking you can make me better by forcing me to do things. What did you think? That you would be the one who could magically heal me? You couldn't help your brother, you can't help your mother, but if you help me it will make up for that? No more, Hector. I'm not a remedy for your ruined family."

Pain flickers across his face, but I don't care. I am so completely furious I can't feel much else. He takes a deep breath and steps toward me, his arm outstretched. I knock it far away from me. He takes another step closer anyway. "You're already better, Cara."

"No, I am not," I say, almost spitting with nastiness. "Just because I'm finally being honest with you doesn't mean that I'm cured. Doesn't mean that I'm moving forward. LOOK AT ME! I'm a total mess. How is this me getting better?"

He lowers his voice. "It's okay that it scares you, Cara. That's how you know it's real, that it's progress."

I laugh; it sounds cruel, unhinged. "You think it scares me that I'm getting better?"

He doesn't hesitate. "Yes. I know it does."

And there it is: the truth. I've admitted what I did—and I'm still alive. Hector's and Ren's forgiveness has shown me that I can move past this. Now I've voiced my guilt, there's nothing left to part with. If I'm honest, if I fight like hell, I could pull myself out of these gray, ashen days, I could make new friends, I could allow myself to date, to feel again. I could start to rebuild my life. The dreams will stop, and I'll start to sleep again.

This truth is the most devastating of all.

If I don't dream about her, won't I forget about her? If I move forward, doesn't that mean she gets left behind?

And I know, deep down inside in a place I haven't allowed myself to venture before, there is a part of me that doesn't want to move forward. That doesn't want to be a person who doesn't have G in the periphery of my vision. Because if I consent to living without her, it will mean I am letting her go, and if *I* let her go, won't everyone else feel they can too? Then G's death will become nothing. She'll become a faint spot in our memories, a spot that we hide from to avoid falling back into our grief. She was too special—too important—to become just a memory. If I'm not grieving for her, if I'm not feeling guilty for what I did to her, I'm getting over her death. And I can't accept that. I just can't.

I feel myself crumbling, shattering into tiny, irreparable fragments. Hector wraps his arms around me and I lash out, struggling against him, unable to bear his touch. I am fury; I am agony. And it hurts like it has never hurt before—blinding, incomparable, unstoppable pain.

I give up fighting him just at the moment I break down. The world caves in darkly around me as the devastation takes hold.

There is no relief to the sadness. None at all.

39

I can't see an end to the tears.

I cry for the months I haven't been able to.
I cry because there's so much left unsaid.
I cry for the void G has left in my heart.
I cry until I lose all sense of time.
I cry until I can no longer see through the tears.
Until I feel as though I am going to be sick.
Until I can't breathe.
Until I collapse.

40

I wake up to the sound of voices. It takes a moment for my eyes to adjust to the room. It's not my dorm—instead I find myself in a normal-level single bed, one in a long line of beds separated by green and white striped screens, like the awnings on the front of the main building. I vaguely remember coming here, someone helping me into pajamas before everything lost focus again.

I feel a weight on my arm, the scarred one, and look down to where someone is lying on it, her face masked by a mass of red hair.

"Where am I?" The words come out as a croak, my throat sleepy and scratchy from crying for so long. After so long.

Ren sits up, her face flushing with relief. "You're in the San," she says.

I clear my throat and blink furiously. "The what?"

"Um, it's the special room run by the sister—the school nurse,

I mean," she explains. "This is where you go when you're ill. Not that you're ill," she corrects herself. "It's just that, well, you passed out, Cara."

I look at my hands on top of the covers. They're colorless, unmarked. "How long have I been out?"

Another voice answers. "Almost twenty-four hours," Fred says, his voice stiff. I let my gaze drift up to where he's standing against the far wall. He's not alone: Hector is next to him.

"I've been asleep for a whole day?" I press my cheeks. They feel inflamed, my eyes raw despite resting for so long. I vaguely remember waking up several times in the night, tossing, turning, and abandoning all attempts to properly wake myself up. Shame kicks in and I do my best to turn away from it. "On a scale of one to ten, how puffy do I look right now?"

I expect a rude answer from Hector—I expect him to play the game like usual—but am instead confronted with stern sincerity. "You look absolutely fine, Cara."

He's wrong. I should be worrying about the fact that I had a cataclysmic breakdown in front of him. I speak directly to him. "I'm so sorry . . . I had no idea that was going to happen. I—"

He cuts me off, not looking at me. "You don't have anything to apologize for."

There is something I can't place in his voice—something close to anger. I wonder briefly how we're both here, both irrevocably bruised by grief, yet in completely different states. How has he lost his brother and managed to stay upright? How has he managed to live without his brother's death defining him? Then again, maybe I only see what I want to see. It's tough to know how much he's changed, because I didn't know him when his brother was alive. Equally, he's only known me as who I am after G's death. And while I live and breathe that night, I only established Hector's loss five weeks into knowing him. What does that say about me? That I'm so self-involved I can't be anywhere without my trauma draped around me, and he's found a way to manage his? Or his loss surges through him every other second like mine does, but he's better at hiding it than me?

The door opens and Mrs. King enters. "Oh, good. You're awake, Cara." She takes in my audience. "You three are still here? Well, it's almost time for breakfast. Time for you lot to start your day. You can catch up with Cara later." None of them move. She claps sharply, the sound echoing in the space. "Off you go."

As though jolted awake, all three of them snap to attention. At the door, Hector glances back at me and our eyes meet. His are strange and unfocused, as though they don't see me.

After they leave, Mrs. King moves over to the bed next to me and sits down. I prop myself up with my pillows. The effort it takes is momentous; I feel, even though I have been asleep for hours, like I haven't slept in weeks.

"They wanted to stay the night here, you know," she says.

"Even Fred?"

She smiles knowingly. "*Even* Fred. Sister Helen was having none of it. Instead they ended up staying awake all night in the common room, or so Madame James tells me. She gave up trying to get them into bed at around five this morning. They just kept going back. They wanted to be here when you woke up. I think, more than anything, they wanted you to know that you have nothing to be ashamed about."

"I'm so sorr—" I start to say.

She mimes zipping up her mouth. "Grief can't be ignored, Cara. You've bottled it up for too long. Yesterday . . . well, it was bound to happen."

A silent tear slides down my cheek; I wonder if this is how it's going to be from now on. Whether by letting myself cry, I've just opened the floodgates.

"How are you feeling?"

I search for the right words but I can't summon any at all.

"Hector told me what he did," she says, placing her hand on my arm. "That trick with the lift. If it helps, he has assured me that he feels terrible, but even so, I want you to know that he'll be suitably punished. I'm going to have him on school service for the rest of the academic year."

"School service?"

"Oh, you know, all the duties no one ever wants to do. He'll be putting the younger years to bed, among other things."

"Ren does that."

"Yes," she says, "but Ren volunteered. Before you arrived, she always struck me as someone who was quite lonely. I think, more than anything, she volunteered because she wanted something to do in the evenings. Hector, however, has never been one for extra-curriculars."

"It's not his fault that I . . . well, you know, lost it," I say quietly.

"I don't blame him for holding the elevator, really. I suppose I should have expected it from him."

She groans and says under her breath, *"That boy."*

"No, but what I mean is, I think I'd probably been building up to this for a while. He has, in his misguided way, been trying to help me."

"I think you're right," she says, taking off her glasses and starting to clean them on her sweater. She looks thoughtfully at me. "You two have become quite close. He's going to miss you."

My heart skips a beat. "Miss me? Why? I'm not going anywhere, am I?"

"I spoke to your mother this morning. She wants to fly over here and get you."

I sit up taller on the bed. "She wants me to leave Hope?"

"Yes, I think that's her intention."

Everything that has happened in the last few days slams together in quick succession. The roof. The elevator. The tears, unstoppable and devastating. But then there are the other things. Hector forcing me out of bed when I didn't think I could move. The three of them around me when I woke up. I've never had friends by my hospital bed before. I consider what it would feel like to lose them too. What my life would be like if I wasn't here. A pain sears through my chest.

"You can't let her do that," I say urgently.

"You'd like to stay?"

"Staying is the only chance I have," I say, because however hard it will be to stay, it will be far worse to leave. At her expression, another thought consumes me. "Unless you want me to leave? I know that I've caused quite a few problems since I've been here."

Mrs. King frowns. "Of course I'd *like* you to stay, but it's not really a case of what I'd like."

Relief floods through me. "I'll call her. I'll tell her I want to stay. She'll have to let me."

"I promised her I'd get you to call her when you woke up." She pulls a phone out of her pocket but pauses before she passes it to me. "But before you do, I want you to know that you can leave here, Cara. If you think you would be happier back home, I don't want you to feel pressured to stay. Mr. King and I try our best to make this a place where our students are happy, but I know that it's not always possible. We've helped a lot of people here, but we have failed a few too. . . ." Her voice trails off and I wonder whether she's thinking about Hector's brother.

She stands up. "I'll come back in a bit. Call your mother— she'll be desperate to speak to you."

"You cried," my mother says, as though she can't quite believe it.

My voice breaks. "Mum—"

"It's okay, Cara. I'll come and get you. It was a stupid idea to send you there. I just thought . . . I was desperate."

I take a large gulp of air to steady myself. "I don't want you to come and get me."

"I can understand why you're upset with me. I can understand why you wouldn't want to see me after I sent you there, but we'll get you home and—"

"I want to stay, Mum," I say, and there is conviction behind my words. "I have to."

"You don't have to, darling. You can come home. I should be there with you," she says. I hear her uneven breathing and wonder whether she, too, has finally succumbed to tears.

I shake my head, then remember she can't see me. "I have to do this alone."

"I'll fly over."

"No, Mum, it's okay. Really, I'm okay." It's not exactly true, but I'm closer than I have been for a while.

"Your teachers, your dad, well, they all said they thought you were managing," she says through ragged, honest breaths. "I've just let you be there . . . I've barely heard from you . . . and I just thought it was better to give you time."

"It was better. Sending me here was the best thing you could have done, Mum."

"It sounds like you've done more there than you would ever have done here." Her voice becomes more hesitant. "And it was good for you to go back to London after so long."

"I guess it was."

"Honey, are you really sure about staying?"

"I really am, Mum."

"When you come home for Christmas, we'll talk more about everything, okay? You do want to come here, don't you?"

"Of course," I say, confusion clouding my voice. Then it hits me: she's jealous, afraid I'll ask to stay with my father again. I feel a sudden rush of love for my ridiculous mother.

"I'm going to fly over and get you then," she adds brusquely. "No arguments."

"Okay, Mum." And then I add in a tight, apologetic voice, "I'll call you more, keep you updated. I promise."

She starts to laugh. I hear the sadness there, the regret . . . the relief and the love. And even though there are tears streaming down my face, I start to laugh too.

Mrs. King reenters the room half an hour later. "So, what's the verdict? Are you staying or leaving?"

I hand her back her phone and brush away the residual tears. "Staying."

She beams. "Wonderful. That really is wonderful, Cara."

"Should I go to class?" I ask, thinking about how this is School Birthday all over again. Will everyone have heard what happened already?

She shakes her head. "I think maybe you should give yourself a day. Take a break, give yourself a bit of time to process. I also think, and I've discussed this with your mother, you should have some sessions with our school counselor going forward."

"And my mother agreed with you?" I say, my eyebrows raised.

"Talking about it helps," she says. "You've already seen that, haven't you?"

And I suppose in a way I have.

41

That evening, the common room is abuzz with excited chatter, which I quickly realize stems from a large poster that has been pinned to the noticeboard. THE WINTER BALL is written in ornate gold calligraphy, with the date, the last night of term, printed underneath.

Voices grow quieter when I enter, a hush spreading through the space. I consider backing out just as Ren calls my name. She beckons me over to where she and Fred are perched on the window seat. She scoots closer to him to make space for me next to her. "We were worried . . . well, we thought maybe you left."

Behind them, through the bay window, the sky is split into bands. Wedges of color—blood orange, lilac, and a deep navy blue—meet together as the sun sets.

I drop down next to Ren, feeling myself at the center of their attention. "It was a possibility," I say in a low voice, relieved when the conversations around us start up again. "My mother threat-ened to come and get me."

"But you're staying?"

"I'm staying," I say, watching for her response.

"That's good news," Ren says. I can tell that she means it.

"Where's Hector?" I ask, suddenly conscious of his absence.

"His school service started today," Ren says, standing up, "so I imagine he's manhandling the younger years into bed. Which reminds me, I'm on the rotation for the girls tonight too. I'll see you in the dorm, Cara." She rests a hand on my shoulder. "I really am glad you're staying, you know."

Fred and I sit across from each other in silence when she leaves.

"You were right about me after all," I offer, resigned to finally addressing the hostility between us. He did wait by my hospital bed; I owe him this, at least.

"You *were* hiding something," he replies, slightly sheepish.

"Yes." What more can I say?

"I wasn't trying to be nasty for the sake of it—you know that, don't you?"

I don't know how to answer because I realize I haven't really tried to know him at all.

The remaining light outside begins to dim; flurries of snow swirl through the air, finally settling against the windowpanes. I try to think of something to say to him. The only two times Fred and I have been left by ourselves we've argued, and when we catch each other's eye in the awkward calm left to us, I know we're both thinking the same thing.

"I'm going to call it an early night," he says, standing up.

"Me too," I say.

When we split on the landing to go our separate ways, I suppress a small smile of relief. Maybe there's a chance for him and me.

I get through lessons the following day without incident and stay late in the conservatory after prep to catch up on the work I missed while I was in the San. It's almost deserted now, with just a few stragglers left. In a far corner, the librarian hands Hector a towering pile of books. I wait for him to look over at me, but he never does, positioning the books on a nearby table and starting to sort them into piles.

I pack up my stuff and approach him timidly, intensely aware that we haven't spoken properly since I fell to pieces in front of him outside the school.

"I've barely seen you all day," I say in a low voice.

"Yeah, it's been a bit of a busy one," he says, not looking up from the books.

For a moment I think he's going to ask me something; then he takes one of the piles, turns his back, and starts to climb a set of stairs to the balcony level. I watch him through the dark wooden railings as he slides books into slots in no apparent order.

"Look, Hector, about what happened—"

He freezes, gripping one of the shelves. "I took it too far."

"It's not your fault."

He looks at me properly for the first time. "Cara, I can't do this anymore."

I climb the stairs to the balcony so I'm level with him. "Do what? You haven't done anything."

He smiles, but it's a sour sort of smile. "Look, Cara, when you said the other night that I was hoping to heal you . . ."

"I was angry when I said that, Hector. I'm sorry, I didn't mean—"

He holds a hand up to stop me. "You were right. I've been trying to help you, Cara."

"And you have been helping."

He laughs, but it's an empty, echoing sound that speaks of endings. "No, I haven't."

"Well, I never asked you to."

"Yeah, well, I could hardly ignore you. You should have seen yourself when you first arrived here."

"I know, I know—I was in a bad place."

"Cara, 'bad' doesn't even get close. You had this look like you were either going to check out permanently or you were going to check back in again, but you hadn't quite decided. I recognized it immediately—"

"Because of your brother," I interrupt.

"I overlooked my brother," he says bitterly. "I wasn't likely to make the same mistake with you. And you were doing so well. You've been so much happier, Cara; I wanted you to realize how far you'd come. I thought accomplishing the lift 'breakdown' would solidify that somehow in your mind . . . but, well, everything with you has become very tangled. You've let me become too involved in your life, and I've let you become too involved in mine. The truth is, it was never meant to go this far."

There is a heaviness in my stomach that is becoming worse by the second. "What do you mean?"

He won't look me in the eye. "Cara, I . . . I can't prop you up anymore."

"Prop me up?" I stare at him for a moment, at his serious expression, at the ferocity behind his eyes. Is that really all it is between us? I'm a project for him, a way for him to assuage some of his own guilt? I inhale sharply. "What are you saying?"

"I'm saying that right now I think it's just better—"

"Better if what?" I ask, and I hear the desperation in my tone.

"If I leave you alone," he says, and the words have weight.

I stare at him, willing him to take them back, but his expression is blank, unreadable.

"Fine," I force myself to say. Then I push myself down the stairs before he can see how his words have wounded me.

I rush down the corridor to the front hall, the dark paneled walls blurring as I blink back tears. I'm so determined to get to my dorm, away from everyone before I finally succumb to them, that I collide with someone at the base of the stairs. I take a step back, and my new biology partner, Teresa, comes into focus.

"Whoa," she says, gripping the banister to right herself. On seeing my expression, she adds, "Are you all right?"

"Fine," I snap.

She gives me a questioning look but doesn't probe. "I've been looking for you. You know there's a letter for you on the table in the mailroom?"

"A what?"

She smiles kindly. "A letter."

"For *me*?"

She nods. "It's been sitting there all day. Sorry—I should have picked it up, but I wasn't sure whether you'd left it there on purpose. It's just through there." She points to a door to our right.

I mutter a hesitant "thanks" and push open the door to reveal a heavy mahogany table. There is one letter left in the center. At the sight of the handwriting, I momentarily forget to breathe. The untidy scrawl is as familiar to me as my own mother's. In G's house, her mother, Karen, wrote notes for everything. G would raise her eyebrows when we found them in the strangest of places: on the remote, telling us we weren't allowed to put the TV on until we'd finished our homework; on the fridge, telling us what special snacks she'd made for us. We even practiced imitating it to fake sick notes for PE. Her letter has come at an opportune time to remind me that my progress is in complete opposition to the wreckage I've left behind.

I slip the letter up my sleeve and head straight to the dorms, where I pull it out and smooth it against my knees. The postmark is unfamiliar: this letter hasn't been sent from the U.S. I draw a deep, measured breath and carefully unstick the envelope. Inside there is a postcard. The caption reads: VENEZIA PONTE DI RIALTO. The image sends a jolt through me. G was longing to go to Venice; her parents had promised to take her after she graduated from high school. A few summers ago that was all she talked about.

"Imagine, C, a whole city floating on water," she'd said.

The postcard begins to tremble in my vision, but I force myself to turn it over.

To Cara,

We finally decided to make the trip to Europe—seeing as we can no longer do it with Georgina, we thought we'd do it in memory of her.

It's been a long time, I know, but we'll be in your area next weekend and thought we could pop by your new school. We've spoken to the head and it's all arranged, so we'll see you Saturday next.

Karen and Ted

I feel myself sinking. This is why they've written. I haven't seen either of them since the hospital. They only visited twice; we all knew why they couldn't face it. Every time they saw me, they asked the question I ask myself daily: Why did I survive and not their daughter?

I show the note to Ren when she returns to the dorm an hour later. She sits patiently dissecting it with me again and again. There are no "best wishes" at the end of the card, but then I have never had any mail from Karen, so I don't know whether that is something she does. And then there's the "To Cara" part. It feels formal, detached—she used to call everyone darling. Wouldn't she have addressed it "Darling Cara" if she really wanted to see me?

A note appears on my bed the following day. It's from

Mrs. King, telling me someone will come find me when the Canters arrive.

I forget Hector; I forget everything else I'm struggling with. Instead I am preoccupied with questions.

Why, after all these months, do G's parents want to see me when I'm halfway across the world?

How is there anything more left to say?

42

There is a winter market going on in the town, and the whole school is allowed to go. Ren ushers me out after prep, telling me that it will be a good distraction from the Canters' impending visit. I don't object, eager for an excuse to get out.

Hundreds of little wooden stalls fill the main square, their roofs bowing low under a thick layer of untouched snow. Lines of multicolored bulbs zigzag around the town, strung between the buildings. The tree in the center of the square has been re-decorated, masses of tiny ornaments dangling from its branches.

We move between the stalls: one is decked head to toe in glittery Christmas trinkets; another has a table set out with every color of woolen scarf imaginable. Then there is the row of food stalls, where mulled wine perfumes the air. We huddle in front of one that has small models of buildings made entirely of chocolate and try samples of cheese at another, and spoonfuls of chutney piled on warm baguette. Eventually tired of wandering, we stop to buy tankards of hot chocolate at the edge of the market. Fur rugs cover benches made entirely from ice.

"What was she like?" Ren asks tentatively. I don't have to ask her who she's talking about.

"Umm . . ."

"You don't have to say if you don't want to," she adds. "Sorry, I don't know what I was thinking. I shouldn't have asked."

"No, it's okay," I say, then take a long sip of hot chocolate to stall for time. It's thick, sickly sweet, but strangely calming. "I just don't really know how to answer. She was a lot of things."

I try to think of how best to describe her. If I'd been asked the same question a year ago, I'd have said she was pretty, popular, fun. None of those words seems to mean much anymore.

"She was like you?" Ren prompts.

I swallow. "She was better than me. More trusting." The words stick in my throat.

I search for an acceptable way to sum G up, desperate that I can't find the words. I try to picture her, but the only image of her I can summon is in the car. I am filled with a sense of urgency to paint her right before . . . before what? Before she fades from my memory?

"She didn't let people get away with things," I say quickly. "She was loyal like that. She stood up for her friends."

"Do you think she'd have liked it here?" Ren asks, her glance flitting back to the bright lights of the square.

"She'd have hated the cold but loved the dating potential," I say, the corners of my mouth twitching. "She was always saying she wanted to go out with a European boy."

Ren smiles. "Well, we don't exactly have the best selection here."

I laugh, then take this as an excuse to change tack. "You and Fred seem okay, though?"

She makes a huffing noise. "It's still a bit weird between us," she admits. "I don't think he'll come home with me again, I'll put it that way."

"Maybe that's for the best?" I offer.

"Maybe?" she says, and it sounds like she's asking herself a question.

"You could tell your parents the truth, you know."

She looks at me with a mixture of admiration and skepticism. "And you could stop being so proud and tell Hector how you feel about him."

I choke on a sip of hot chocolate. "I don't . . . I . . . There's nothing to . . . Stop trying to change the subject."

She laughs at my expression, loud and unguarded. "See, it's not so simple, is it?"

"It *is* simple," I say without a glimmer of humor in my voice. "Hector told me he doesn't want to spend time with me anymore. He said . . . he said he was tired of propping me up."

She stares at me with an impatient look. "He didn't mean that, Cara."

"Oh, I'm sure he did. He said we were too involved with each other. That he'd leave me alone from now on." I drop all bravado, feeling myself wince, and say more quietly, "You should have heard the way he said it."

"People say terrible things when they're in pain."

"But it makes sense," I say. "At first I didn't understand why he was paying me so much attention. Then, when I found out about his brother, it became a bit clearer. I thought he and I, well, I thought we understood each other."

"You do." She shakes her head, sloshing a bit of her drink onto the fur rug and rubbing it hastily to remove the stain. "Listen, Cara, he's still shaken up from London, I think. Sometimes he takes a week or so to settle in again when he comes back to Hope. I think home is really hard for him—this time especially so. And I think what happened the other morning gave him a bit of a shock." She smiles apologetically.

"I think you're being overly generous," I say. "He admitted that I've been a kind of project for him."

She sets her mug down and looks up at me fully. "If that's all it ever was, he'd never have spoken to you about Santiago. Cara, after what happened with his brother that summer, he spoke to me and Fred about it just once. He told us he never wanted to talk about it. He didn't want our pity, sympathy, or anything. He just wanted to forget. I doubt he's talked about it with anyone since it happened. Until you."

I shake my head. "And his sister."

"Well, maybe they talk about it during the school holidays. I don't know much about that."

"Or when they speak on the phone?"

She shakes her head. "Hector rarely calls anyone while he's here. I mean, he speaks to his mother occasionally. But that's it."

"That's not true," I say, confused. "He waits for Valeria to call every morning."

She raises her eyebrows at me, looking genuinely surprised. "That's news to me. Although it makes sense—Fred does say he wakes up ridiculously early. So there you have it. Why would he have told you any of that—things neither Fred nor I know—if he thought of you as just a project, if he didn't care about you?"

"You're not supposed to hurt the people you care about."

"People always hurt the people they care about." Her mouth forms a pitying smile. "That's why it hurts so much."

It does hurt—it hurts far too much—and Hector's words still sting like fresh cuts.

"I can't talk about this, Ren," I say, and I make sure my tone leaves no room for argument. "Please. I can't talk about him anymore."

43

Over the next week, I don't venture to the rooftop again. In fact, I don't run into Hector outside school hours at all. If I do wake up in the middle of the night, which happens less and less frequently, I force myself to stay in bed. And because I am dreading the arrival of G's parents, time seems to speed up.

After lunch on Saturday, I head to the conservatory under the pretense that I have more work to do. I take a set of stairs to the balcony level, then climb again and again until I'm far away from anyone. The higher I get, the darker the room becomes, the transparent roof now misted from a thick coating of snow. I wonder how the glass doesn't break from the weight of it, how it manages to hold itself up.

I find a nook on the fourth level between two sets of book-shelves, carved out of the same dark wood. I pick a random title from one of the shelves and pull myself into the nook, resting the book on my knees and opening it somewhere in the middle. I don't attempt to read it; the words blur in front of me, my heart thumping loudly. I try with all my might to calm it down, but the more attention I pay it, the more ferocious it becomes. My body and my mind pull in opposition, leaving me somewhere in between, until I start to hear the thumping of footsteps out of sync with my heartbeat. Just at the moment all the noise threatens to become too much, all sound becomes muted.

"So this is where you've been hiding out." I look over to the stairwell, where Mr. King clutches his side dramatically. "Quite dangerous of you to make a man of my age climb so many stairs."

My mouth opens in alarm. He's hardly old—maybe in his late fifties. Up close, I see that streaks of gray cut through his brown hair and his skin sags just slightly around his jawline. He is wearing a navy-blue suit, a yellow tie with snowflakes on it, and his thick, black-rimmed glasses. After a moment, he smiles.

"Slide over," he says, sitting down next to me in the wooden alcove. It is a semicircle designed to hold one person. The sides curve up, so when he sits, we end up uncomfortably close.

"Are they here?"

"Almost," he says, picking up the book I'm pretending to read and snapping it shut. I notice the title for the first time: *Medieval Life: A Social Study*. "Light reading?"

"I wasn't really reading it."

"In need of a distraction?" he says. I nod. "You know, I suspect you and I should have spoken earlier. My fault entirely." The skin around his eyes crinkles. "But, well, we have a connection. I, too, lost my best friend when I was around your age."

"I'm sorry," I say, the words slipping out of my mouth. They are meaningless, of course. They are the lame, instinctive reaction to tragedy.

"Don't be," he says. "I wasn't with him when it happened, like you were. And he was a bit older than your friend, though not by much. He died in his early twenties. But still, I'd like to think he had a bit more time to actually live. School, well, it's not real life. It's just something you have to do, isn't it? After you leave here, you'll be able to make choices for yourself. Proper choices about the things you actually want to spend your time doing. Not mandatory lessons and set bedtimes—soon you'll be able to make your own rules. Not that my friend and I paid much attention to the rules when we were your age, mind you. I shouldn't be telling you this," he continues. "Don't want to encourage you. Mrs. King will be furious with me."

I feel myself smiling. "Mrs. King has been very kind to me."

"She's a special woman," he says. He gestures around to our environment. "I couldn't have done any of this without her. She didn't know my friend like I did, but she saw how his death affected me. She brought what she'd learned from that experience here."

"What was that?" I ask, not able to help myself.

"That living and surviving aren't the same." He turns so he's looking me straight in the eye. "She's helped a lot of students, my wife. And it's not a game or a PR stunt for the school—she does her absolute best to ensure the students get the best of their time here and considers it a personal strike if they leave worse off than when they arrived. Particularly since . . ."

I fill in the gap. "Santiago."

"Hector told you?" he asks, his eyes flickering behind his glasses.

"His death . . . it's not Mrs. King's fault," I say.

He gives me a meaningful look. "But it's very easy to holster the blame, isn't it?"

I direct my gaze away from him, out into the distance, through the glass wall and outside, where, for once, snow isn't falling. The trees don't move, as still and tense as I am.

Mr. King stands and holds a hand out to pull me up too.

"If I've learned anything in this life, Cara, it's that you can still feel dreadful, overpowering guilt even if something wasn't your fault."

I stand up and follow him down the stairs. "What was your friend's name?"

"Charles Hope." He smiles as I realize the significance. "It's been almost thirty years since he died, can you believe that? It's amazing how time passes."

My next words slip out involuntarily, and I instantly hope he hasn't heard them. "I can't stand it."

He turns halfway down the stairs, confused. "Why?"

"I'm scared about aging more than ever now."

"But you're a teenager," he says, bemused. "Doesn't every teenager just want to grow up? I know I did. All Charles and I wanted back then was to grow older and wiser, to shrug off the restrictions of youth. We didn't want to be young—we wanted to be old. We thought getting older meant our lives would get better."

I take a deep breath and think of G. Destined to be forever

seventeen, never aging, never experiencing any of the things we thought we'd do together, things I've done without her in the last year. "The older I get, the younger she stays. The distance between us just grows greater, and there's no way to turn back."

"Of course you can't turn back," he says.

I feel myself frowning. "What do you mean?"

"You've already borne the worst, and you have survived. You can't go backward, only forward. Time is only relevant to the living, Cara. This time now is yours."

I consider his words, then disregard them. "What's the point in any of this if at the end we just die? Disappear into oblivion. Nothing we do ever lives past us."

"But it does," he says. "Your friend might be gone, but everything you built with her lives on. She'll be a standard for you—for what you expect from friendships. For how you carry yourself into new experiences, things you weren't able to do with her. For how you love. She'll be with you, inside you, for the rest of everything."

"It's not enough."

"It has to be," he says. "It's a cruel lesson to learn at your age, Cara, but at some point in your life it's inevitable, as it is for all of us."

"The lesson that we all die?"

"I'd say the lesson you've learned is that you are alive."

"I know I'm alive," I say, impatient now.

"Do you?" He narrows his eyes. "Do you really?"

44

It's too late to turn back. Even though I know the Canters' trip to Europe wasn't made with the intention of visiting me, they have surely gone out of their way to travel here. You don't go anywhere through Hope; it is on the edge of a mountain, isolated and contained—exactly the features I've grown to love.

I can't help noting, as I follow Mr. King down the green-carpeted corridor, how reluctant I am to make this journey—delving back into the deepest, darkest depths of my past. A past I am trying to step away from, one that everyone is telling me I have to find a way to leave behind.

When Mr. King opens the door to the study, two sets of eyes lock on me. They are sadder than I remember; they are memory and reality meshed into one.

Mrs. Canter stands up. "Cara."

How do you greet the bereaved parents of your best friend?

You cry. Well, that's what I end up doing. You step forward. Your words become garbled. You try to articulate how sorry you are. You end up falling to pieces.

"Oh, darling," she says as she steps forward and pulls me into her arms. Over her shoulder, I watch Mr. Canter look on. He, also now standing, slips his hands anxiously into his pockets. "We didn't come here to upset you. That's the last thing we wanted."

"I don't understand why you wanted to come," I say through sobs.

"To see you, of course," she replies, squeezing me tighter against her chest and starting to rub my back in reassurance. "To see how you're doing."

It's almost worse this way. How can she find the strength to comfort *me*? How cruel of me to allow it. I pull away from her and step back, giving her the distance she must want from me.

"Cara, why don't you come in and sit down?" Mrs. King comes into view. She motions around the room, which is set up differently from my first time here. A sofa has been moved to the center, directly across from the fire, the two armchairs angled to face it. I find myself in one of the chairs. Weeks have come and gone since I was last here; so much has changed.

"Mrs. King has been telling us a bit about what you've been up to," Mrs. Canter says encouragingly. "I gather there is quite an exciting ball coming up."

"I'm so sorry."

She frowns. "Why are you sorry?"

"The ball," I start to speak, hearing the catch in my voice but unable to control it. "It's silly. . . . It's irrelevant."

"Why is it irrelevant?"

The words tumble out of me. "Because G can't go. Because I'm alive. Because I'm living her life—or the life she should have had. And I took that from her. I'm sorry. I'm so, so, so sorry." My face is wet; I can't lift my hands up to wipe the tears from my cheeks.

I can't tell whether I'm making any sense.

Mr. Canter clears his throat. "Cara, you didn't take anything from Georgina." His face scrunches into lines—far more lines than I remember being there before.

"I took everything from her," I sob.

"You drove the car, Cara," he says. "You were driving the car when the truck smashed into the side of it, but you are not responsible for what happened."

Of all people, I don't expect *him* to say that; I don't expect *him* to feel that. My body involuntarily reacts to the words. The knots of tension balled up inside me loosen themselves a little.

"She got in the car because of me. We'd had an argument," I say, looking between them, waiting for Mr. Canter to take his words back. For Mrs. Canter to step in accusingly. She doesn't flinch, just stares at me with something close to pity in her eyes.

"Cara, she didn't have to get in the car," he says. "She made that choice. It goes without saying that if either of you knew what was about to happen, neither of you would have gotten in that car. It's not your fault."

"We lied to everyone about what we were doing that night," I say, trying to give him another reason to condemn me. Trying to find something.

"You did, Cara," he says, "and it took us a while to come to terms with that. But you did exactly the same thing that all of your friends did that night. You're a teenager—you're supposed to break the rules."

"I thought . . . I thought . . ."

"You thought when we stopped visiting you that we didn't want to see you because you were to blame." I nod, and he exchanges a look with Mrs. Canter. "Guilt, Cara—it's a powerful emotion. It's consuming. It stops you from seeing the bigger picture. Karen and I, well . . ."

"We felt a lot of it ourselves," Mrs. Canter cuts in. She turns away from me, and I catch a tear falling down her cheek. "We blamed ourselves for not asking more questions about where you were all going that night. We blamed ourselves for not holding our own New Year's party that she'd have had to stay for. For not being there. For not being on the road to flag down the truck." She presses her fingertips into the corners of her eyes. "This guilt, Cara, it eats you alive—it ruins memories; it distorts everything."

"We felt we were the ones who let her down," Mr. Canter says, giving his wife space to catch her breath. "And for a while, neither of us was strong enough to be near anything or anyone that reminded us of Georgina, which of course included you. We didn't know how to support ourselves, so we weren't in a place to support you."

I shake my head, unable to process what I'm hearing. "You had—you still have—every right to be separate from me. And I know it won't help, but don't think for a second I don't hate myself for taking G away from you."

"But she wasn't just taken from us, was she? You lost her too. We didn't have the capacity to see past our own grief in the aftermath." Mrs. Canter sits up taller now, a stern look taking over her face. "But, Cara, I want you to know something: it's much easier to hate yourself than it is to forgive yourself. And you need to forgive yourself, darling."

I know that what they're saying is really no different from what everyone else has tried to make me believe over the last year. And even though I've come a long way, it never felt justifiable in my head to let go of the guilt completely. I think, above all, the Canters are the people I needed to hear this from—only their forgiveness is final. Only their forgiveness makes it true.

I stare at them with a mixture of disbelief and relief. I search their faces for signals that they're just saying this to placate me. There are none.

My next words are stilted, breathless. "If I'm not to blame, then it's just a freak accident. If G died in a freak accident, then the whole world is upside down. She was too good—too significant— to die like that."

"But it wasn't a *freak* accident, Cara. Whether he meant to or not, that trucker drove into you. He took Georgina from all of us. I can't imagine what it's like to be the only survivor in something like that, but we're not resentful of you because you were the one to survive. We're grateful that you're here—that you survived. It's the only good thing about that terrible night."

Mrs. Canter and I lock eyes. She pats the sofa between her and her husband, and as I go to sit, Mr. and Mrs. King leave the room. The Canters each take one of my hands in theirs. Mrs. Canter pulls up the sleeve of my sweatshirt to reveal my scar. She traces it with her finger, and I have to put all my effort into not flinching.

"How can life go on without her?" I whisper.

"Because it already has," Mr. Canter says, looking desperately sad. "Because none of us can stop it."

I shake my head furiously, as though denying it might make it a possibility. "We had so much left to do together."

Tears slip down his cheeks, and he squeezes my hand. Suddenly I realize how selfish I'm being for saying this. For making this about me. They, far more than I, had so much left to do with her. They'll never see their daughter graduate from high school or college; they'll never watch her fall in love, walk her down the aisle, hold any of their grandchildren. For the first time, the loss of G separates itself from my own personal grief. It is her parents'. It is her relatives'. It is everyone's who knew and loved her.

I sink against them both, and we stay like that, wedged comfortingly together on the sofa, for an undeterminable amount of time. A time during which I consider what it will really mean to have a future without G. What it will mean for all of us.

Mrs. Canter pushes herself forward to the edge of the sofa. The movement is labored, and from looking between them, I know they are trying to hold themselves together for my benefit. "Cara, we're going to cancel Georgina's cell contract when we get home. You haven't called for a while—"

I take in a sharp breath. "How did you—"

"You're not the only one who wants to hear her voice," she says, hugging me tight against her side. "But we need to draw a line now, darling. We need to try to look forward."

A single sob escapes my lips. "There will always be so much left unsaid."

"We know," she says, her voice wistful, full of the same longing that I live with.

Of all the people I've talked to after G's death, I'm secure in the knowledge that her parents do know. They know most of all.

45

The Canters' departure brings another onslaught of tears. When they go, even though I felt only dread before it happened, I'm grateful for their visit. I suppose I always knew I'd have to face them eventually, but I never imagined that I would have such a genuine second chance with them. However wonderful this feels, it is also a double-edged sword. I can't help thinking that in death there are no second chances; I'll never get to say the things I wish I'd said to G when she was alive. I won't get to apologize, justify, or validate. There is nothing except the gap she has left, time that continues at a merciless pace and my progressively unreliable memory.

When I return to the dorm, Ren is there. From the way she quickly picks up a book when I enter, I get the sense that she's been waiting for me. For a moment, the whole situation seems absurd. How is it possible that I have someone—a friend—waiting worriedly for me?

Her eyes scan me up and down, presumably trying to assess the damage. "Have they left?"

I mumble a yes.

"Are you . . . well, how are you doing?"

I swallow, buying myself time. I let myself sink into my desk chair and, a few moments later, I start to tell Ren everything.

We spend the afternoon walking in the grounds, wrapped up in multiple layers to combat the fierce cold. In the distance, the vicious sound of cannons interrupts the otherwise still air. I look at Ren with fearful eyes.

"They're setting off avalanches," she explains, as though expecting this to calm me.

"Excuse me?"

"Oh, don't worry, it's perfectly safe. They're just small, controlled ones. They do it when the snow builds up to stop them from happening naturally—those are the ones we have to worry about. The noise will become a familiar friend next term—that's when it really heats up." She grins at my expression as we start to walk back to school.

I play the words *next term* over in my mind. She says it like it's inevitable. I can't help thinking it wasn't when I arrived here, and that somehow managing the Canters' visit was the final hurdle.

I really have come too far to turn back.

46

Talk of the Winter Ball begins to dominate the corridors at Hope. By the first week of December, the conversation is all about who is going with whom.

It strikes me, as I climb up the stairs after classes, that the conversation was entirely the same in the U.S. We used to spend hours plotting who was taking whom to things like this, who would get the most random invitation—who wouldn't get asked at all. There's something about organized parties that has always filled me with dread, though. Lennon had a couple of guys on rotation who she'd rely on, Poppy would always wangle herself an acceptable date, G would always be fine, but me . . . I never ended up going alone, but I never got asked weeks in advance like they did.

I worried what people thought of me there; I don't worry

about that in the same way anymore. This time, I just try not to think about it.

As soon as I decide I'm not going to involve myself in any ball-related conversations, Teresa pulls me aside in the girls' corridor. "Cara, I was hoping I'd catch you," she says. "Have you talked to Ren since dinner?"

"No. Why? What's up?"

She shuffles uncomfortably. "Well, it's just . . . it's a bit awkward because Fred asked me to go with him to the ball next week."

I feel my insides deflate. "He did?"

She nods, hesitant. "I . . . I don't know. I just assumed he'd go with Ren, like he did last year, but, well . . . he said he wanted to go with *me*."

"That's good, Teresa," I say. When I see her reaction, I try to be more enthusiastic. "I mean, that's great. Isn't it? Do you want to go with him?"

"Yes, but I don't want to go with him if it's going to hurt Ren's feelings. I asked her if she minded and she said no, but . . . I don't know. If it was me I think I'd mind."

It strikes me as typical that Fred would have asked someone so decent—someone it's hard to dislike. "When did you tell her? Recently?"

"Just after dinner," she says.

"Did you see where she went after that?"

She gives me a worried look. "Oh, God, I knew it was a bad idea. I'll tell Fred no."

"Don't do that," I say. "Ren wouldn't want you to say no because of her. If you like him, you should go with him. Listen, can we talk a bit later?"

I don't wait for her answer, pushing my way past my classmates and back down the stairs. I find Ren in the art building, as I knew I would. She smiles weakly when I approach.

I pull a nearby stool closer to where she's working and lower my voice. "Are you okay?"

She shrugs in an attempt at nonchalance, but her face betrays her. "Did you speak to Teresa?"

I nod solemnly.

"It's ridiculous for me to feel like this."

"It's understandable," I say, putting an arm around her.

"Is it?" she asks. "Why can't Fred ask someone else to the ball? It's not like he and I are dating. He's free to ask whoever he wants; in fact, I should be glad that he's finally asking someone else. Why can't I be happy for him?"

The answer is simple. "Because he's always been yours."

She shakes her head. "But that's so unfair of me. I know Fred hasn't been very nice to you and has been so insanely complicated this term that you probably can't see it. But, you know, through the years I think I've always just relied on him for things like this. I think I took him for granted. I knew he'd ask me. I knew he'd want to spend time with me. And that made everything easy. But . . . well, after this term, I'm not sure anymore. And anyway, it's not like it's fair of me to ask that of him, yet I still expect it. I should be thrilled for him. What's wrong with me?"

"Nothing is wrong with you, Ren. It's a perfectly human reaction."

She reaches over and squeezes my hand. "Cara, what are we going to do about this ball?"

"I don't understand why it's such a big deal not to go with a date."

"Would you have gone to prom without a date?" When I don't respond, she smiles. "Exactly."

"Can't we just go together?"

At this, she starts to laugh.

"What's so funny?" I say, bemused.

"Oh, I appreciate the offer, but I thought you were trying to keep your head down."

"You could go with Hector, then, couldn't you?"

She looks at me strangely, like she can't quite believe I've suggested that. Maybe because since we went to the winter market, I haven't mentioned his name aloud. I've seen him in every class, of course, but we haven't actually said a word to each other. Somehow he always seems to be leaving the dining room when Ren and I arrive, and I don't know where he is during prep, whether he's there, hidden in one of the high alcoves, or whether he doesn't turn up at all. I try not to look, but when I do, he's nowhere to be found.

I clear my throat. "What's so horrible about that?"

"Nothing," she says quickly, "nothing. It's just . . ."

I feign nonchalance, a sick, twisty feeling in my stomach. "He already asked someone."

"I highly doubt that," she says, watching me closely. "He's been so busy with all of his various punishments, I bet he's barely thought about it. I mean, I haven't heard of him asking anyone. Do you want me to ask him about it?"

"No," I say, quick to shut her down.

She nods; I know that she understands because she doesn't push me. "I wonder if we've left it too late. Maybe there's no one left."

I look at her seriously. "Listen, there's something important I've been meaning to ask you."

"Go on. . . ."

"Will you do me the honor of being my date and accompanying me to the ball?"

At the sight of her expression, I laugh. It echoes around the room, pulling the attention of the handful of other students still dotted around the large space. Somewhere in the middle of the laugh, it sucks her in too.

The following day, when we arrive early to history, Joy and Hannah are already in their seats with fixed smiles that speak of nothing good. We move over to the desk across from them, as far away as possible.

"Ren, I've just heard the news," Joy says innocently, her eyes filled with pity. "I'm so sorry."

"The news?" Ren repeats.

"Your 'boyfriend' has asked someone else to the ball," Hannah says, putting the word *boyfriend* in quotes with her fingers.

Ren swallows. "He's not my—"

"Oh, I'm sure you'll find someone else to go with," Joy says. "Most of the boys are taken, but we all know that you'd rather—"

"Enough!" I slam my books down loudly, making her jump. "I'm sick to death of hearing your irrelevant little commentary on everything."

Joy sits up straighter in her chair and eyes me with loathing. *"What did you just say?"*

Before I can say anything, Ren sits down into her seat and says in a fierce, determined voice, "You heard exactly what she said."

Monsieur Thauvin dashes into the room. "Everyone in their seats, please."

I slide into the seat next to Ren and find Hector directly opposite me. The corners of his mouth rise in the tiniest hint of a smile, but I turn in Ren's direction.

"Thanks," she mutters under her breath.

"You were the one who shut that down," I mutter back.

She doesn't say anything else, but there's something like triumph splashed across her face. Her lips fuse, and I know right there that she's suppressing a smile.

By the time we get to dinner, the whole year seems to be talking about our run-in with Joy and Hannah. A nervous energy seems to have built up as the day went on.

"I don't understand what the fuss is about, really," I say to Ren, helping myself to paella from a large dish in the center of the table. "You've stood up to them before, haven't you?"

"Well, yes," she says, "but it wasn't as clear-cut as that."

"Surely other people have too?"

The satisfied expression remains fixed on her face, just as it has all day. "Of the girls . . . no one has ever had the last word."

"Do you think we've heard the end of it?" I ask, eyeing their table, where they're deep in discussion.

Ren takes the spoon out of my hand. "You know, this time I think we have."

A surly-looking man walks into the room. I recognize him immediately because he has no place here. Mrs. King appears close behind him and they both start to walk toward us, him marching through the tables, searching the faces that look up at him with curiosity.

"What's he doing here?" Ren whispers.

"Hector's mother's okay, isn't she?" I whisper back, and my stomach twists itself into sudden knots.

Ren nods firmly. "Yes—much better, apparently; I asked him about her this morning."

As they approach, I hear Mrs. King say, "Rupe, I'll tell him you said goodbye. It's probably best to leave it."

I look quizzically at Ren and mouth, "Rupe?"

"Tell you later," Ren whispers back.

"I'm not just going to let him storm out," Hector's father snarls. They both stop at our table, where Mr. Sanderson glowers down at me. "Have you seen my son?"

Again, I'm struck by his abruptness, his lack of greeting. "Not this evening," Ren answers for me when I don't say anything; I don't trust myself to speak at all. She looks up at Mrs. King. "He's all right, isn't he?"

Hector's father glances between us in annoyance. "He's absolutely fine. Just making a scene, as usual."

Mrs. King flashes a smile, but it's strained. "We'll leave you to your dinner, girls." Then she turns to Hector's father and adds more forcefully, "I'll let Hector know you've left and said goodbye."

His eyes remain cold, darting dangerously around as she ushers him out of the room. Her hand tugs on his arm in a familiar gesture, but he shrugs her off. "Alice, I didn't send them here so you could let them run riot . . ." His words trail out of earshot.

I turn back to Ren. "Alice? Wait, Ren . . ." I watch their backs disappear out the front hall, and there is a look about them that is hard to deny. "Is Mrs. King . . . is Mrs. King Hector's aunt?"

"Shh," she says, looking around feverishly. "He won't like it if word gets out."

"You're serious?"

"We were sworn to secrecy at the very beginning. He doesn't like people knowing."

"Why does it matter?"

"His brother started it," Ren says, and her voice is careful now, like she's worried about betraying Hector's trust. "He insisted that people would say they had an easy ride if they knew, and the teachers would make exceptions for them."

"They kind of do," I counter.

"Now, yes—but they didn't. Not while Santiago was here."

As I stare at Ren, a tight feeling takes hold in my throat. "Do you think Hector's all right? I mean, you saw him earlier. He's okay, isn't he?"

She flinches. "He's . . ."

"Ren?"

"He hasn't really been himself these past few weeks. I've seen him less than usual."

"Why didn't you say something?"

She sighs. "You said you didn't want to talk about him. You've had so much going on, what with the Canters' visit and everything. And he was pretty awful to you—it's not like you owe him anything."

It hits me right then and there, regardless of my feelings, regardless of everything, that I do. I owe Hector a hell of a lot.

I drop my head into my hands and push my hair back from my face. "How bad is it?"

She swallows. "Fred's worried, I can tell."

I push myself up in a swift movement, my mind made up. The chair scrapes against the wooden floor, drawing the attention of the next table.

Ren's eyes widen. "Cara—what are you doing?"

"I have to talk to him."

"Look, he hasn't been very talkative lately—" she starts, but I cut her off.

"I've been so wrapped up in my own head, I've . . . I can't believe I've been so selfish."

"Cara, he's the one who told you he wanted distance."

Even though a part of me is very afraid that he did mean what he said, another part can't help wondering what would have happened if he'd taken me at my word when I told him to back off all those weeks ago. I've been very proud. He looked after me when I needed it, he persevered with me when I pushed back, yet when he pushed me away, I just accepted it.

"You said it yourself, Ren. People say terrible things when they're in pain."

Pain. I know a lot about it. I know how much worse it is when you're left to face it alone.

Fred appears, dusting a fine coating of snow from his coat as he takes the seat next to Ren. "What's going on?" he asks casually as he starts filling his plate.

"Cara wants to talk to Hector," Ren says.

The spoon in Fred's hand freezes in midair. "Good luck with that."

"He'll be in prep, right? I don't know where he sits anymore."

Fred swallows a mouthful of paella and looks at me with a tired expression. "He's been doing his prep in isolation for the last week."

"What? Why?"

Fred rolls his eyes. "You don't want to know."

"So when will you see him next?"

He shrugs. "After his school service, I expect. He's been coming back to the dorm straight after."

"Right," I say, an idea forming. "Well, I'll see you both in a bit."

"Cara . . . ," Fred starts.

"Fred . . ." I emulate his nervous tone and raise my eyebrows at him, anticipating another warning.

"I—"

"You don't need to say it, Fred," I tell him flatly.

"Okay, then, I won't," he says, taking another mouthful. "Just don't be surprised if he's out for blood, Cara. I walked past his father on the way here—"

"I know," I say over him. "We saw him too. I'll see you both in a bit."

I start toward the door, but Ren rushes up behind me before I get to it. "Cara, you won't say anything about Mrs. King, will you? It's just that Fred and I promised Hector—"

"Secret Squirrel," I say without thinking.

"Secret what?"

I feel a twist in my stomach. "Oh, it's nothing. Just this stupid thing we used to say back in California." She looks at me with an expectant expression. "It just means I promise."

"Okay." She gives my arm a parting squeeze. "Secret Squirrel it is."

Mrs. King waits at the front door of the school. Behind her, I glimpse the back of a taxi departing. She turns around at the sound of my feet on the flagstone floor.

"Cara," she says. Her fixed smile makes me wonder what pleasantries she discussed with Hector's father before he left. "Are you on your way to prep?"

I'd just come out with it. "Mrs. King, I'd like you to give me detention."

"We don't do detention, dear," she says with a confused expression. "It's school service here."

"Right," I say. "That then. I'd like you to give me school service."

She stares at me as if to say, *Have you gone mad?* "Cara, we don't just give it out to anybody who asks for it. It's a punishment, not a pastime."

"Ren volunteers to put the younger years to bed. That's school service, isn't it? Well, I volunteer for whatever the people on the list are doing tonight."

"Cara, why would you?" I wait expectantly until a look of understanding crosses her face. "My advice would be to leave him be today. He's not in his, uh, best form."

I haven't been in my best form with him either, I think. That's never stopped him from finding me when I needed it.

"Go to prep, Cara," she says as she heads toward the corridor of her office. "Tomorrow's a new day. There'll be time then."

I watch her disappear before weaving my way back to the dining room, which is thinning out now. The kitchen staff huddle in one corner, sorting knives and forks and scraping dishes. On my approach, Hector's favorite, Mary, regards me with a slightly suspicious expression.

"Dinner's over, Cara. You need to get yourself to prep."

I move closer to her. "I'm going," I say. "I just wondered whether you might do me a favor first."

"Go on," she says impatiently.

"I need you to put me on school service this evening."

She laughs. "*Right.* Cara, that's not how it works. Go to prep."

"I can't," I say, desperate. "I need to see . . . I need . . . It's . . . well, it's Hector."

Her hard exterior softens. "What's he done now?"

"He hasn't done anything. He's just . . . well, his father was here earlier, and I think he was giving him a hard time. I just want to check he's okay and that's where he'll be. So if you wouldn't mind telling me off for something, I'd be so grateful."

"You're a strange girl, Cara."

I give her an imploring look. *"Please?"*

"Madame Monelle has got them waxing skis in the sports hangar in preparation for next term. It's freezing in there," she warns. "I wouldn't opt for that if I were you. Talk to him in prep, or better yet, talk to him tomorrow."

"He won't be at prep," I say impatiently. *"Please.* I owe it to him to find him tonight."

She looks at me for a moment, undecided. "He's had a bad time, that boy."

I nod. "A shit time."

Her eyebrows skyrocket. "Language, Cara! What makes you think you can talk to me like that? Maybe a night of school service will teach you a lesson."

I close my eyes. *Finally.*

"Wait here," she says sternly, her expression unchanged. When she returns, she gives me a sandwich wrapped in brown paper. "Take him this—I noticed he wasn't at dinner."

I take the parcel and mouth "thank you" at her.

"You won't thank me when you enter that shed." She shakes her head and disappears in the direction of the kitchens. She turns back, and in the moment before she shoos me away, I swear I can see the faintest hint of a smile.

47

After prep, Ren gives me directions to the sports hangar. I find it eventually because it's the only building in the area with its lights on. Mary was right about it being a shed—slivers of light seep out onto the snow-covered gravel through gaps in weathered wooden slats that don't quite fit together. A tangle of green shrubbery covers the roof, the vines creeping down toward a few steamed-up windows and curling around the latches. It's like a freezer when I get inside, the temperature almost colder in here than outside. All sorts of winter sports equipment line the walls: wooden sleds, ski poles of every size, skis—hundreds of them—stacked up against the walls. In the center, a handful of shivering students huddle around a wooden bench. Madame Monelle looks on as they brush the long underside of the skis.

"Cara," she says curtly. "You're late."

"Sorry," I mumble. "I got lost. . . ."

"Find a space down at the end. Hector—show her how it's done, please."

Hector looks up as I approach. Just before the hardness returns to his face, there is a flicker of surprise. He sets a ski up on the bench in front of me in silence, but soon his curiosity gets the better of him.

"What did you do?" And even though his tone is low and gray, I feel relieved to hear him speak to me again.

I pull the ski toward me, businesslike. "I swore at Mary."

He almost smiles. "That will do it."

I slide the package toward him. "She made you a sandwich."

"Wondrous woman," he says, but his voice still lacks emotion. He passes me the brush he was using and goes to retrieve another. I watch him for a while in silence, pretending to be memorizing his technique. In fact, I'm looking at his gloved hands, his long arms, imagining the tattoo I know is underneath, trying to formulate what to say to him.

He beats me to it. "So you're talking to me again, then. Is that why you're really here?"

"I told you why I'm here. I swore—"

"Cara, cut the bullshit," he says sharply. "You're far too square to get yourself on school service unintentionally."

I take a deep breath. "Fred warned me you'd be out for blood."

He laughs cruelly. "Ah, isn't that nice? Have you all been sitting coffeehousing about me?"

I stare up at him, and his face is leached of all color. And even though the room is filled with chatter, unhappy, freezing students moaning about the task in front of them, Hector is surrounded by silence. I reach out a hand to touch him, then pull it back at the last minute. *What am I doing?* He's right. We've barely spoken in weeks. I'm still upset with him, aren't I? I search for anger within me, but when I stare at him, I can only find shame.

"They're worried about you." My voice wavers for just a moment before I add, "*I'm* worried—"

"I meant what I said, Cara," he says, looking me straight in the eye. "Distance. That's what I want."

I make myself hold his cold gaze. "Do you? Do you really?"

He looks at me fully, sizing me up. And even though I prepare for the worst, I feel myself flinch when he says, "Yes." Before I can stop myself, I feel my eyes brim with tears.

"Don't cry," he says, and he sounds frustrated now. "Please don't cry."

"Start brushing, both of you!" Madame Monelle shouts down at us. "You're supposed to be working, not lazing around."

I'm grateful for the interruption. I put all my focus into brushing the ski in front of me and try to get my emotions under control.

"I'm sorry," I say. The words are little more than a breath.

He stops brushing and in a voice much more like his own says, "You have nothing to apologize for—"

I start talking over him. "I'm sorry for drawing you into all my drama. I'm sorry you felt you had to prop me up. I'm sorry for all the hurtful things I said to you about your mum, your brother. Hector, I'm just sorry—for everything."

"Cara, I—"

I cut him off again. "You don't have to say anything, okay? I just want you to know that, and I understand if it doesn't mean anything, but I'm here."

He takes a step back, leaning against the bench behind him. "You saw him, then?"

I twist around so I'm leaning against the bench beside him, careful to keep a big-enough gap between us. "What did he want? Everything's okay, isn't it?"

He tries and fails to arrange his face. "Progress report," he eventually says. "He was at some conference in Geneva, so he made the trip here."

"Progress report on what?"

"On me. I . . . well, I haven't been doing so well since half-term. Mrs. King called him."

I clear my throat. "So he came here to see how you're doing?"

He laughs in a callous way that doesn't suit him. "More like to tell me how I should be doing."

"Ah." He watches as I rub my hands together.

He looks at me now, strained, but with one eyebrow raised. I wonder what he means, whether he wants to talk to me about it—whether he wants me here at all.

Above all, I realize, these past few weeks, I've been wondering about him a lot.

I'm conscious that it's been weeks since we've been this close to each other, yet it feels like no time at all. I should never have let him pull away from me—and now it's too late. He didn't let me pull away from him when I wanted to. This was always a two-way game, and I decided to stop playing when it suited me.

I clear my throat. "You're very difficult to read, you know."

"Whereas every tiny feeling you ever have parades itself on your face," he finishes.

"No, it doesn't," I say defensively.

He smiles—tiny but genuine. "It does."

And for a second, all the old easiness between us reinstates itself.

His smile turns into a grimace. "I can't be a friend to you, Cara. I tried. It's just too difficult."

I clutch my hands together to stop them from shaking. He pulls off his gloves and chucks them at me. "Have these."

I clench them into a ball, drop them on the ski in front of me, then force myself to find enough courage to do what I should have done weeks ago: I pull one of Hector's hands away from where it's gripping the bench and squeeze hard.

He exhales loudly and lifts his head to stare at me. With that one look, I try to tell him a thousand things. That I can't be his friend either. That friendship was maybe where it started but isn't where it ended. That the ending part is almost more than I can bear, but I'll do it. For him. Because there aren't words for what he's done for me. And if he was only meant to lift me to here, then that's enough. After all, he's got me to the landing platform from where I can lift myself up—and for that, I can excuse everything else.

So, most of all, I try to tell Hector that I forgive him, like he forgave me.

A minute passes. Then another. And another.

His eyes scan my face and I wonder if he understands, whether he, too, is trying to tell me things. He looks away, swallows nervously, stays silent.

Then, just for a heartbeat, he squeezes back.

48

The day of the ball arrives. All students not in the top two grades are let out at midday. The lower floor of the school is a hive of activity, streams of parents, taxis, and buses arriving. Upstairs, the girls' corridor becomes a crush for mirror space, and a revolting haze of perfume hangs in the air.

"Just to warn you," Ren says as I enter our dorm in pursuit of solace, "I'm going to be wearing a lot of makeup this evening."

"Shocking," I say in mock horror, and head over to my desk, where a FedEx parcel has been sitting since the previous Wednesday. My mother, thrilled by the idea of my actually behaving like a normal teenager and going to a party, made me stay on the phone with her for at least an hour discussing which dress I'd like her to send. In the end, I told her to choose. It wasn't like I was going with a date; it wasn't like a dress would mean anything. But when I open the box, I realize how wrong I was. I should have paid more attention to the conversation, because now I won't be able to go at all. The dress is royal blue, high-necked, and made of a floaty material that bunches in at the waist.

"That's pretty," Ren says, watching me open the parcel in the reflection of our mirror. She fixes the final French plait she was doing around the crown of her head with a pin and stands up to face me.

"I can't wear it," I say, slumping down on my chair. Maybe I'm looking at this wrong—this is the excuse I've needed not to go to the ball. Now that I have an excuse, strangely I feel something close to disappointment.

"Why not? You'll look great in this." She picks up the dress, holding it against her body. "God, you're going to have to ask me to stay with you in the U.S. so we can go shopping. This is fantastic."

"It might be fantastic, but it is also sleeveless." I pull up the sleeve of my school uniform, leaving my scar on full display.

I almost miss her flinch, still shocked by the brutality of it. If she can't contain her reaction, I don't have a hope with the rest of the school. She tries to cover up the movement by quickly—and rather robotically—saying, "It's fine."

"It's not fine," I say. "I might be okay with you seeing it, but I'm definitely not ready for the whole school to."

"No, what I meant was, we'll do a swap. I'll wear this and you can wear mine—it has sleeves." She heads over to the wardrobe and pulls out a simple green dress with sequined shoulder pads. She throws it to me. "You're lucky yours is my color. My mother only allows me to wear clothes from a strict color scheme—the restrictions of being a redhead." She flicks her head in a stupid, girlish way that I know is her way of trying to lighten the mood.

"Oh, Ren, I appreciate the offer, but I can't ask you to swap with me."

"It's done," she says. "I like yours better anyway. Don't argue."

I hang her dress on one of the rungs of the ladder to my bed and start to smile in thanks, then freeze.

Her confusion is visible. "What's wrong? You don't like it?"

"It's not that," I say. "The last time I went to a party I was wearing a green long-sleeved dress, and, well . . ." The long threads of green sequins hanging off me scratched at my skin as I tried to wriggle out of where I was trapped. Then there were the ones that had come off the threads, sprinkled all over the floor and the dashboard, sparkling in a hideous juxtaposition when the lights set out by the emergency services flooded into the car.

She rests a hand on my shoulder. "This isn't the same situation, Cara."

I take a deep breath. "I don't know if I can—"

"What are you going to do with your hair?" Ren asks, purposefully trying to distract me.

"My . . . my hair?" I stutter. How can I talk about hair? How can hair be my biggest concern?

"Don't you think it's time to, er . . ." She mimics snipping the ends of her own hair.

"Well, unless you're secretly a whiz with scissors, I don't think there's much to be done."

"I'm not," she says, grimacing. "I know someone who could probably sort you out. You're not going to like it, though."

—

Hannah, her hair gleaming and perfectly straight, stands behind the chair I'm sitting in, scissors poised. "I don't think we have time to dye it, which is a shame because your natural color is a really dull blond." I get the sense she's enjoying herself—or enjoying my having to rely on her for something.

"Just the ends will be fine," I say, carefully watching the scissors in the mirror. According to Ren, Hannah is the in-house beautician. Anything you want done—waxing, hair, threading, nails, piercings—has to be done by her. I don't care whether Ren says Hannah is the only girl for the job—that she wouldn't mess it up and risk damaging her reputation—I don't trust her farther than I could throw her.

She begins to cut segments of my hair, the dry, yellowed ends falling in clumps onto the towel under my chair. "So, Cara, who are you going with tonight?"

"Ren and I are going together."

Her reaction is priceless. She starts to blink furiously and loses all command of speech. "Like . . . like, as . . ."

I wonder how long I could let this last, then decide it probably won't do Ren any favors. "As friends, yes."

Her mouth tightens. "You didn't want to go with a date?" I don't answer her, so she continues. "Oh . . . you didn't get asked. Oh dear. I'm sorry." She doesn't sound it.

"It was my choice," I say, giving her a withering look via the mirror in front of me.

Her eyes flash. "Why would you *choose* to go dateless?"

I briefly wonder what to tell her, then settle on, "After the year I've had, I want to keep things as uncomplicated as possible."

Her expression shifts. "Yeah . . . I heard about what happened to you."

Before I can show how this surprises me, someone knocks tentatively on the door, then pushes it open. It's Ren, who is now fully made up.

"I'm all done," she declares. "How's it going here?"

"This is quite a big job," Hannah says, her momentary softness hardening again. Ren and I exchange the tiniest of smiles.

As Hannah continues to cut chunks of my hair, she remains a bit of an enigma. Surely if she knew about my accident, she'd have used it as ammunition by now. Before I can ask her how she knows, Joy walks into the room and pulls a bottle of vodka and a stack of shot glasses from under her pillow. She pours two measures and passes one to Hannah. In the mirror, I watch them clink their glasses together, then down them in one. My gaze travels back to the scissors.

"I thought there were going to be drinks at the ball," Ren says.

Joy gives Ren a patronizing look. "The teachers water it down. Everyone knows that. Don't tell me you haven't gotten your own stash too?"

Neither of us says anything.

"Oh, fine," Joy says, refilling the glasses and setting them out in front of Ren and me. She stares for a moment at Ren's braid, thinking. "If you do something similar to my hair, we'll call it payment."

I don't miss Ren's surprise, or the way she looks almost pleased at the inclusion. When they both leave to find another mirror, I realize that Ren is even more on edge than I am about tonight.

Without Ren or Joy, a loaded silence fills the room and I wonder if Hannah is going to resume our conversation. "Are you going to drink that?" She points to the shot on the desk. Before I can respond, she picks it up. Another few moments pass in silence; then she eventually adds, "I noticed your scar when you were changing for PE."

I nod but make no attempt to show it to her.

She puts down the scissors, her expression suddenly vulnerable. "I have one too."

I turn to face her properly and feel myself frowning. "A scar?"

She nods, lifting up her skirt to reveal shriveled, broken skin across the whole of her left thigh. "House fire," she explains, quickly letting go of her skirt to cover it again. "But please don't tell anyone."

"Your secret is safe with me."

She looks at me hard and then busies herself with my hair again. The noise of the hair dryer means that we don't have to say anything else. Just as Hannah finishes, Ren reenters the room without Joy, looking a little flushed. "Ready to get dressed?" she says, not letting go of the open door.

"Ren," Hannah says, the nastiness back in her voice, "I hear you two are going together."

"Oh yes, didn't you know?" Ren replies with a sickly sweet smile. "What about you, Hannah? Who has the great honor of being your date for the evening?"

"Oh, I'm going with Drew," she says proudly. "He's been

harping on at me about it all term, so I relented in the end. Hard not to, really; he's easily the best-looking guy at Hope."

Ren and I exchange a glance. I can tell what she's thinking: now is the perfect time to reveal that our entertainment this week has come from watching Drew ask, and be turned down by, two other girls before trying Hannah. But, for all her unkindness, she has just revealed something significant to me. There could be a million reasons why she has chosen now to show me her scar: to make me feel more comfortable, to express that she herself has been through something frightening, to tell me that I am not alone. Equally, it could be to give herself a platform for sympathy, for something else entirely. Either way, I decide to let her have this one.

"Well, thanks for sorting out my hair, Hannah," I say, standing up and pushing Ren through the doorway before she can say anything.

"At least you look semi-presentable now," she says. "Just make sure you tell everyone who did it."

49

I stay close to Ren in the mass of people making their way down the stairs and being handed two blue poker chips by the teachers in the main hall. The chips are for drinks at the party—we are allowed two alcoholic drinks, and each time we hand in a chip we will be stamped on our wrists so no one doubles up and gets more than their quota.

All the tables in the conservatory are pushed back against the walls. To my left, one is covered right to the edges with baskets of bread rolls, trays of cheese and ham on sticks, mini quiches, and small bowls of French fries. Across the room, another table has been completely dedicated to cupcakes decorated with iced snow-flakes. At the end of the conservatory, people crowd around a bar, and in the center, there's a black-and-white checkered dance floor next to the wall of glass. The hundreds of windowpanes have been polished until they're gleaming, the Christmas tree visible in the center of the courtyard beyond. The room is mainly lit from the outside, where the hundreds of strings of outdoor fairy lights I saw the teachers carrying on School Birthday have been strung around the walls of the courtyard.

The Winter Ball has been completely undersold to me: this setting is far more spectacular than I could have imagined. It's also completely overwhelming.

"Wow, they've really gone all out," I say to Ren as we stand at the edge of the conservatory. "Is it like this every year?"

She nods. "At least, I think so. Last year was pretty similar. Although I spent most of it outside with Fred and Hector."

I search for friendly faces. I spot Fred and Teresa hovering by the bar. Fred places a chip in one of two large glass hurricane vases at the edge of the table, holding out his wrist for a stamp mid-conversation, and it occurs to me why everyone made such a fuss over going with a date. *Everybody* is coupled up.

A group of people brush past us, knocking Ren off center as they go. When I grab her arm to steady her, I notice her eyes are slightly glazed.

"Um, Ren, how much did you and Joy drink in her room?"

"Oh, not that much." She waves her arm in what I think is meant to be a casual gesture, but isn't quite in character for her. "Shall we go to the bar?" She glances over at Fred and Teresa with uneasiness. "The other side, I mean?"

"Maybe we should eat something first."

"Oh, Cara, don't be boring," she says, grabbing my hand and leading me toward it.

I search the room for another option, but before I can change her mind, we're there. I realize I've never seen Ren like this; I wonder if anyone has. The alcohol has amplified her confidence, and, as people crowd in around us, she gets progressively more assertive, clumsily elbowing past them to make her way to the front of the queue. She downs the plastic cup of wine before she has even handed over her token, and all I can do is pray that Joy was telling the truth when she said it was watered down. I step to the side, out of the queue, expecting her to follow, but she gets pulled into conversation before I can signal to her. I wait patiently for her, and she reappears a while later, smiling, her cheeks flushed.

"I don't know why I was so worried about tonight," she says, twirling around on the spot. "This is actually quite fun. I've heard loads of compliments on your dress, by the way."

She stumbles slightly, and I catch her again. "Bread," I say to her. "You need something to soak it all up."

She gives me a bored look, but is smiling when I lead her over to one of the tables. As I am buttering her a roll, she starts to pick up lots of the little cupcakes and reposition them on the wrong plates. I push the roll into her hand and start to tidy up behind her.

"You're behaving like my mother, not my date," Ren declares. I give her a withering look, which makes her laugh. "Come on, we should dance."

I don't know what stops me. Poppy, Lennon, G, and I would always be the first on the dance floor at parties back home. Yet tonight I hang back. The more I look around, the more I see other glazed faces, which tells me Ren isn't the only person here who's hit the secret vodka stash. Ren presses forward anyway, and before I know it, she's dancing in a group. I wave to get her attention and mouth at her that I'm going to the bathroom. There at least I won't be standing around alone.

When I return, Ren's nowhere to be seen. I walk around the tables, letting the minutes add up by feigning too much interest in the snowflake cupcakes. Every so often I lift my eyes to search for a friendly face: for Ren, for Hector—now that we're in some sort of weird truce, I might as well admit I'm looking for him too. Hell, at this stage, Fred would do. But by now the party is in full swing, the dance floor saturated, and even when I paw my way through the crowd and return to the bathroom a few more times to look for Ren, I don't find anyone to hang out with.

After about an hour, I decide to search outside—I can't loiter all night. I push my way out of the conservatory and head down a corridor to the double doors leading to the courtyard outside. The cobbles are cleared of snow, and outdoor heaters have been placed around for students who want to get away from the party. For now, that's just me. Of course it's just me. Gold cushions rest plumply on the benches at the edge of the courtyard, and, making sure that it isn't wet, I sit down on one.

A dark figure emerges from behind the tree, making me jump. "Hi," Hector says. He looks unnecessarily handsome in a midnight-blue velvet jacket as he saunters toward me, flicking the two poker chips between his fingers.

"Hi," I say back.

He stays where he is, his lips pressed into a smile that doesn't reach his eyes. "Not a good party, then?" I shrug, and he continues to stare at me. "Where's Ren?"

"I've been looking for her inside. She's acting a bit strange. I think she's had quite a lot to drink."

"Yeah, well, it's the first time she's done something like this without Fred on her arm in . . . well, I can't remember how long. I imagine she went in for some liquid courage."

He's right, and, since I'm trying to be better, I should never have left her on that dance floor. What if she's been searching for me too? I didn't check the mezzanine levels in the conservatory. Perhaps during our rounds we just missed each other. I start to push myself up to standing. "I should go and try—"

"Not yet," he says in a quiet voice. "Just give me five minutes and then we'll find her. I . . . well, I owe you a proper explanation, Cara."

I let myself drop back onto the bench but shake my head. "Look, Hector, it's—"

He holds out a hand to stop me. "No, let me speak. Just hear me out, okay, and then at least you have all the information before you make any decisions."

"I'm listening," I say, but my words are cautious now. *Decisions?* Decisions about what?

He stares at me, and I find I can't look away. "I've been a bit unhinged these last—"

"Hector, you don't have to—"

"Please, Cara. I need you to understand. London . . . it confused everything for me. My mum, Santi . . . I've never let anyone into my life like I let you in for those few days. And after I went home, I was terrified. Then, well, what I did to you in the lift—I messed up, Cara. I should never have done that. You were struggling that morning—I could see that, and I just wanted to show you how far you'd come. I wanted you to be with me, where I was with you in my head. But I was pushing you too hard. And all for selfish reasons. After that, I couldn't bring myself to be near you."

"Selfish reasons?" I repeat.

"The Kings told me I needed to take a step back, stop trying to force you. They said you needed time on your own, that I was complicating your recovery—I thought they were right. That it was the right thing to do . . . It was selfish of me to keep pressing you—"

I cut him off. "Why are you telling me this now?"

He starts pacing in front of me, sending searching glances around the courtyard, as though the walls will finish our conversation for him. Eventually he just says, "I've been trying to find the right moment to explain everything to you."

I stand up, suddenly annoyed. "You've had hundreds of moments, Hector. You could have told me the other night in the hangar."

"Yeah, well, before then I wasn't even sure if you wanted me to explain. The hangar was the first time you've chosen to come near me for weeks."

"And whose fault is that? It's not like you've made any sort of effort to talk to me either."

He starts to pace more aggressively now, using wild hand gestures as he speaks. "You didn't make it easy for me, you know. It's not like you've given me many openings."

My voice rises. "Since when have you needed an opening?"

He hisses through his teeth. "I thought it was hopeless before. I didn't think you wanted me anywhere near you after what I said to you, after what I did to you. And can you blame me? You just backed off, Cara!"

"You asked me to!" I snap back.

He sits down on the bench and drops his head into his hands in frustration. "Look, this is hopeless," he says, and something in my stomach falls.

It can't be hopeless. Not totally. It's like a bad song on repeat. I can't go through this again.

Hector takes a deep breath. "I'm just going to come out and say it: I lied to you before. I said you were easy to read. It's true and it's not. There's one thing I've never been sure about. Since half-term, I've never been sure if you felt . . . Look, you know me now—you know me better than most here—so you know I'm not very good at apologies. But I didn't want you to go home tomorrow without knowing . . ." He stands up abruptly, but his voice trails off. His green eyes narrow, as he winces. "Listen, I meant what I said the other night. I can't just be your friend."

I blink once. "That's not what you said."

"What?"

"You didn't say you can't *just* be my friend. You said you can't be my friend. Full stop. You said you wanted distance, that being friends with me is too hard."

"It is too hard." His voice is quieter now. "Ren is my friend. Fred is my friend. How I feel about you is . . . well, it's different. Okay? You wouldn't know, because since you've been here I've been better, but I've separated myself from everyone here for a while now. Since . . . since Santi . . ." He rubs the spot on his jacket that covers his tattoo. "You're the first person who's made me feel like I'm part of the real world again. The truth is, it's been terrible not talking to you these past few weeks; I don't know how I managed before you were here."

My heart hammers against my ribs. I am in some twisted dreamland. This can't be real.

"I don't see you as a friend, and I most certainly don't want to be *just* your friend, Cara. You are much more to me than that."

I tilt my head back, closing my eyes and raising my face to the stars. If this were a normal moment, I expect I'd feel the cold on my cheeks, I'd be shivering. Instead, I feel like I'm on fire.

"*Please* say something, Cara."

"I don't know what to say," I just manage to get out.

"Look, it's fine if . . . I mean, I understand if you think I'm too late."

It hits me that this is the moment I can make him absolutely sure of how I feel. I don't think; I don't hesitate. I just kiss him.

The atmosphere around us changes in an instant, all distance reducing to nothing. Everything else becomes surface, irrelevant, and we're contained in this one blazing moment. It is every wonderful feeling I've ever had combined into one. It is the kind of kiss there aren't enough colors for. The kind that flattens the whole world until it's just me and Hector and the night sky.

I wait for the guilt, for the voice inside me to scold, to tell me I don't deserve this feeling of elation. Nothing comes.

When we separate, I can't look away from him. I can't get my head around the fact that something so wonderful can come out of so much devastation.

Something clatters in the courtyard behind us and I spin around. Ren has propped herself up in the open double doors, a terra-cotta pot smashed at her feet, dark soil and a battered plant splayed out in front of her.

"You're here," she says, her body swaying against the door frame.

Everything else seems to tilt upside down except for one certainty: Ren is extremely drunk. Far worse than when I last saw her.

We rush forward. She tries to look up at us but can barely open her eyes. "I think I've had too much to drink," she slurs, her legs bowing underneath her.

Hector catches her just in time. "Jesus, Ren, how much have you had?"

She mumbles something unintelligible.

He picks her up. "I think the party might be over for you. Bed—now."

She nods, her head lolling against his chest as he walks her through the school. He uses his elbow to call the elevator. As the doors open, I falter, just for a moment, and consider taking the stairs. Before my mind is completely made up, I find myself following them inside. I hold my breath as we travel up the six floors, and then it's over and I breathe out, and we're on the sixth-floor landing, where Madame James is waiting, reading in a chair opposite the elevator. Her book falls to the floor when she sees us. "Hector, Cara, Ren! What's going on?"

"Nothing too serious," Hector says smoothly. "She's just had a little too much to drink."

Madame James's nostrils flare. "I told them not to supply you all with alcohol. You don't know your limits."

"Hmm . . . I'm not sure this is from the blue-chip drinks," Hector says, the corners of his mouth twitching. "It would take quite a bit of that to get into this state. I don't see any stamps on her wrists. Do you?"

I open the door to our room, holding it open for them. We must all have the same thought: How do you get someone in Ren's state up a wooden ladder and into bed? I speak up before anyone attempts it. "Do you think, maybe, her sleeping on a bunk bed isn't the smartest idea?"

"You're right," Madame James says. "Here, Cara, will you help me pull the mattress down?"

We position the mattress in the center of the room and Hector lays Ren gently down on it. I grab her duvet and tuck it around her just as the door opens behind us.

Fred stands there, his face sheet-white. "I saw you getting in the elevator. Is she okay?"

"She'll be fine," Hector says. "She just needs to sleep it off."

"And you boys need to let her," Madame James says sternly. "Both of you must leave. This is the girls' corridor, if you'll re-member."

"We know," Hector says.

"Oh, I'm sure you do. Not that you normally pay that rule any attention, mind," she says, her eyebrows sky high. "Go on, both of you. OUT!"

My eyes widen with fear. The last time I was at a party, the situation wasn't so different. I was wearing a green sequined dress. I was sober and supposedly in charge.

Hector places one hand on my arm, the other on the side of my face. "It's going to be all right, you know." And, as I look at him, I do.

Madame James looks like she's ready to explode, pushing both Fred and Hector into the corridor herself. At the last minute, she turns back to me. "I need to go and inform the other staff to shut down the party. Tell me you haven't been drinking too?"

"No," I say sincerely, holding out my stampless wrists to her.

She stares at me, presumably trying to work out whether I've been at the vodka in secret. "Good," she says eventually, patting me on the shoulder. "I'll send up Sister Helen. You're in charge of Ren for the time being. Okay?"

I consider refusing; then I remember the details of tonight. It's mid-December, not New Year's Eve. We're in Switzerland, not San Francisco. That night—the worst night, the unforgettable night. I can't let that night define the rest of my life.

So when I answer Madame James, I do so with purpose. "Absolutely."

50

I don't let my eyes close all night, all my concentration centered on making sure Ren is okay. In the background, I hear the streams of angry students herded prematurely to bed by the teachers. Sister Helen comes in to check on Ren, with a box of confiscated bottles wedged under one of her arms. She leaves, Breathalyzer in her free hand, to test the others.

I spend the next few hours watching Ren from my desk chair. Eventually, stiff from sitting still, the corridor long since quiet with the party officially over, I pull my duvet off my bed and lie down next to her on the floor.

I trace her breaths, in and out, occasionally pulling her back onto her side when she moves in her sleep. I watch her, I'm responsible for her, and she survives.

She wakes up in the early hours. "Oh, God," she says, looking around at her makeshift bed. "Am I alive?"

"Yes," I say, smiling in relief.

"I don't feel alive," she says, pushing her matted hair out of her eyes. Her eyeliner has run down her face, smudged into huge bags that make her look like she hasn't slept in weeks. "What happened?"

"I'm not sure," I say, reaching up to pull my toiletry bag from my desk and handing her a face wipe. "We were together at first, but you were pretty tipsy. Then I lost you and you turned up in the courtyard. . . . Well, at that point, *tipsy* is an understatement. What did you drink?"

Her skin blanches even more. "I had some of Joy's vodka when I was doing her hair. I suppose that could be it."

"How much did you have?"

"Hmm . . . quite a lot. A couple of the other girls came in and they were playing this drinking game. It would have been weird if I hadn't joined in."

"That's probably it, then." In my head all I can think are two words: *she survived.* I was responsible for her and *she survived.*

"Oh, God, was I really embarrassing? I saw Fred and Teresa—they were kissing. Then I couldn't find you and I didn't really know what to do. Most people were coupled up, so I came back upstairs with some of the others and I guess we drank some more." She presses down into the mattress. "How did I get here?"

"Hector carried you."

Her face relaxes. "Oh, thank God. So is that it? Just you and Hector saw the damage?"

"And Fred," I say, watching her reaction. "Fred came to check on you here."

Her face brightens. "He did? Did I say anything to him?"

I try to think of a way to sugarcoat it. "Um, Ren, you were kind of passed out."

She brushes my comment aside with a nonchalant wave of her hand. "Obviously. But I was talking about downstairs at the party. My memory is a bit patchy."

"I don't know. I barely saw you there at all. I went to the bathroom, then I couldn't find you again. The last time I saw you was on the dance floor."

"Hang on. If you weren't with me at the ball, and you weren't with Fred, who did you hang out with?"

I pause. It gives away everything.

She sits up abruptly and grabs her head in pain. "I've got a four-hour car journey ahead of me. I think my world might actually be over."

I laugh, because my world isn't over and seeing her like this is actually sort of funny.

She wags a finger at me in mock horror. "Tell me everything."

And while we pack up our dorm, I do.

Madame James summons Ren to her office to receive her punishment. When she's gone, I look around at the room. It will be four weeks before I'm here again, and there's just one final thing I have to do before I go. From between the pages of an empty notebook I brought with me, I pull a photograph.

There is a hesitant knock on the door. I hastily put the photo facedown on the desk. "Come in," I call behind me.

Fred steps in. "Hi," he says stiffly. "I just came to check on Ren. Is she all right?"

"She's fine. Receiving her punishment as we speak."

"Ah," he says, then shifts uncomfortably. I can tell there's more he wants to say.

"What's up?" I say, frowning.

"Nothing, really," he says, "I just . . . well, I suppose I want you to know that I was wrong about you. I thought you coming here would upset the balance, when in fact you've leveled it out. All of us have things we need to face, and seeing you face yours has made it seem possible for the rest of us."

Is it an apology? I haven't heard the five-letter word, and from his guilty look I realize I'm not going to. But it's an admission all the same—one that I can see has cost him. And he's here, isn't he? If that's not an apology, I don't know what is.

We stare at each other defiantly, waiting for the other to break. After a minute, he laughs and we both admit defeat. I hug him briefly: it's not what you'd call natural, and I know I haven't figured him out properly just yet. But there's time. We separate as quickly as possible; I find myself smiling as we turn away from each other and the awkwardness.

When he's gone, my gaze rests on the pinboard and all the faces there. Seeing them, I recognize a truth that is as wonderful as it is devastating: There is a life after G, and I am living it right now.

I pin her photo up on the board and stare at her for the first time in months. She's all there: her straight, shoulder-length blond hair; her gray eyes; the dimple on the left side of her face. Her smile, which managed to make her look more surprised than happy; the C necklace around her neck in prime position. It takes a long time for me to pull my eyes away from her image, and when I do, they are filled with tears of relief. Because, I realize, I haven't forgotten G at all.

Downstairs, every teacher looks like they're seething. Madame James and Sister Helen seem to have collected enough bottles to fill a shelf of a liquor store; a box full of them sits on a table in the main hall for all to see. Threats are flung far and wide. Parents will be receiving letters. Anyone who is not taking an early flight has to stay and help pack up the party. School service is no longer just a lame threat but a reality that's being liberally doled out.

Then the parents start arriving. In the sea of people in the main hall, I easily spy my mother, her hair bleached to the edge of its life, her outfit immaculate despite her having traveled halfway around the world. Her face lights up when she sees me, and she hugs me without saying a word.

"I've missed you," I say, my voice muffled against her shoulder. And I mean it. It means everything that she is here now to accompany me home.

"Oh, Cara, I've missed you too," she says finally. "Are you okay? I've just been hearing about what happened last night."

Someone next to us clears her throat. I spin around to find Mrs. King. "Madame James has brought me up to speed on last night, Cara." She places her hand on my shoulder. "I've just been telling your mother how brilliant you were."

My mother reaches out her own hand and rests it, almost protectively, between my shoulder blades. She looks around at the chaos; I wonder if she'd ever have sent me here if she knew how different Hope is to the school I left back in the U.S. I am suddenly immensely grateful that none of us knew what I was getting into before I arrived here. We couldn't have known then how much Hope would change me.

"Should Cara be staying to help clear up?" my mother asks.

"No, no," Mrs. King says, smiling. "Cara, you're free to go. We'll see you next term."

My mother collects my bag from the floor. "Are you ready?"

I look around once, checking if the people I most want to see are in my vicinity. In my search for Ren, I spy Joy getting a severe telling-off from a stern-faced woman who could only be her mother. I drag my gaze away to continue looking and finally locate her, deep in conversation with Madame James, Fred waiting patiently at her side. She looks up briefly, as though she can sense I'm staring, and smiles weakly. She mouths something across the space that looks like "I'll call you" and raises a hand in farewell. I look around for Hector, and just as I'm about to turn away in defeat, I see him, weaving through the group of people blocking the stairs.

I hold up a hand to my mother. "Two minutes."

She nods. "I'll wait for you outside. Don't be too long, honey. The taxi's waiting."

Hector's eyes find mine as I cross the hall. He jerks his head in the direction of the mailroom.

"I thought you'd left," he says in a low voice as he guides me through the door.

"Almost."

He pulls his phone out of his pocket, ripping the label from the screen, and holds it out to me. I take more care this time typing in my number.

"It's definitely you?" he asks gently. "I do want to be able to speak to you, you know."

"It's definitely me," I say back, holding his steely green gaze. I don't feel ready to say goodbye to him yet. "So I guess I'll see you next term."

"Ah, yes, about that," he starts ominously. "I have a somewhat horrible truth for you."

I glance at him, worried, but he's smiling. "Go on . . ."

"Do you remember when I told you I had relatives from the U.S.?" I nod. "Well, I've just got off the phone with my mum. She's staying at her rehab center over Christmas, so my sister and I are flying out to stay with my aunt and uncle this year."

"Which aunt and uncle?" I ask, but I already know the answer.

"Mr. and Mrs. King," he says, and he begins to laugh at my expression. "Ren said you worked it out. They have a house—"

"Just outside San Francisco. I know."

"Well?" he asks, the laughter still tangled in with his words. "That's not really a horrible truth, is it?"

Still smiling, he takes a step closer and, just before we say goodbye, he whispers, "I was hoping you'd say that."

Outside, the sky is clear—not a cloud in sight. My mother puts on her celebrity sunglasses as I shield my eyes from the surprising glare of the December sun. She guides me over to the waiting taxi. I slide in next to her without hesitation. As we start down the mountain, I turn back and watch the school disappear.

My mother's phone rings, and when she picks up the call, I pull my own phone out of my pocket. As I turn it on, I click straight to my call log, scrolling past the red notifications of missed calls my mother left when I first arrived here. Underneath is G's name, with an impossibly high number alongside it. I don't have to fight the urge to see whether her parents have made good on their promise to cut the number—I know I won't call her again. And as I reconcile myself to this prospect, I feel something lift.

I open up her contact card and let my finger hover over the screen for a moment. My eyes close and I take a deep breath before deleting her number.

The trees start to blur as we descend, the isolation giving way to the first markers of civilization. It doesn't bother me that I'm going back to California. Maybe I've achieved enough distance; maybe I'm finally ready to face home.

The phone I'm now pressing into the leather seat of the taxi vibrates under my palm. I lift it up into view and a message fills the screen.

Eye mask/no eye mask? H x

I let myself smile before I type back, allowing a moment for the impact to set in.

No eye mask x

EPILOGUE

New Year's Eve, San Francisco

It's almost time—less than an hour until midnight. I am minutes away from a whole year without G.

"Have they arrived yet?" Ren asks, her face slightly fuzzy from the patchy video connection.

"Not yet," I say, replacing the lid on my marker pen, "but we were always late for stuff. There's still time."

"It must be twenty minutes until midnight there, right?" On my phone, I see her looking at her watch. "Where's Hector?"

"He's outside." I see him through the window of G's house—or her parents' house. Is it her house if she's no longer there? Can I still call it that?

Hector and his sister Valeria are hunched over a wooden

outdoor table, pens raised over the casing of one of the sky lanterns G's father handed out earlier, the same as the one I'm flattening between my fingers. I watch as she nestles in close to him, saying something that makes him laugh. I stare for a moment longer than I should—I could watch him endlessly.

"Cara, are you still there?"

I look down at my phone, but Ren's picture is gone now, and I'm left with just her voice. "I'm here. I should probably go, though."

"Call me tomorrow—your tomorrow. Just check the time difference first, yeah?"

I smile, even though she can't see me. "Promise. Speak tomorrow, Ren."

"And, Cara," she says before I hang up. "Happy New Year. I know you're not quite over the marker yet, but I am, so . . ."

"Happy New Year."

"This year will be better, you know. It can only be better."

"Speak tomorrow." I nod before hanging up.

It takes a moment for me to psych myself up to return outside into G's backyard. It's a place filled with so many memories for me—wonderful, terrible, mediocre. I did so much growing up here; to be back now, after all this time, after this year . . .

The yard is full of people, the hedges all around strung with fairy lights. In a corner, G's mom ladles mulled cider into party cups. I spy my own mother deep in conversation with G's dad in the distance, right at the end of the garden where it breaks off into cliffs leading to the sea. The Pacific is black tonight, a moonless abyss.

I head toward Hector, clutching my lantern, ready to pop it out when the time comes. Halfway over to him, someone blocks my path. I look up and am momentarily stunned to find James there.

To say he looks surprised to see me would be an understatement. "Cara! I wasn't expecting— What are you doing here?"

I stare at him, still caught off guard even though I half knew he'd be here. Mrs. Canter did warn me she'd invited most of our old class.

There is a flash of blond and then Poppy appears at his side. "James, we need to write on a lantern," she says, lacing her fingers through his and trying to drag him off toward a pile of spares. When he doesn't budge, she finally looks up and notices me.

"Cara!" she says with something close to amazement in her voice, looking me up and down. "I didn't recognize you. You look so different."

I should say I feel different. I am different. But I don't. My gaze flicks down to her hand in his and I realize I'm not surprised. I'm certainly not in a position to judge.

A moment later, Lennon appears. I never got one without the other then, so why would I now? I feel a tiny, needling pang to think that used to be G and me too.

"Cara!" she exclaims, just as stunned to see me. "What are you doing here? I thought you were in Switzerland."

"It's the holidays there too," I answer. "I fly back in a few days."

She looks at me with wide, fizzy eyes. "How is it over there? Have you got good people?"

"They're not like here," I say, smiling, but don't elaborate. I doubt her idea of "good people" still tallies with mine.

"It's okay there, right?"

I nod once, and there is the longest pause where none of us quite knows what to say. "And how are all of you?" I ask, mostly to break the awkward silence hanging around us.

The kindest explanation would be that Poppy's nervousness causes her to launch into a tirade of everything I've missed. I half listen to the gossip highlights of senior year in San Francisco. I vaguely catch that Lorna Matthews is now dating Scott, who they're all really worried about since he randomly quit the basketball team. I hear words like *shocking* and *can you believe it?* but I barely register them. In the background of the conversation, Hector stands up.

Our eyes meet as he approaches. His contain a question as they flit between Poppy, Lennon, and James, then back to me.

When he's close enough, I see him mouth, "Want help?"

I nod surreptitiously and it takes mere seconds before he's right in front of us.

"Sorry to interrupt, but it's almost midnight, so I hope you won't mind if I steal Cara from you?" he asks, cutting off Poppy midflow and throwing an arm around my shoulders. He doesn't wait for them to answer, pressing me forward and away from them.

I take a few steps before I turn back at the last minute to find them in a stunned silence. "It was really good to see you all," I say over my shoulder. I almost mean it, and that's something.

Hector walks me to the end of the garden, his hand pressed

between my shoulder blades. "How was that?" he asks under his breath as we weave through the group of people starting to converge near the cliff edge.

"Not as horrible as I thought it would be," I reply. He glances sideways at me, searching for the lie. "Really. It was strangely fine. I'm just glad it's one night."

Valeria bounds up as we reach the edge. "I can't make the firelighter stick," she says, pointing at their lantern. "It won't stay."

Hector crouches down and starts attaching the small, square firelighter to the underside of their lantern. I make out the faint markings of a figure eight inscribed on one side, before I do the same with my own.

"We release them at midnight," G's dad calls over the heads of the crowd, holding out long matches to everyone he passes. "Three minutes to go."

I hold on to both lanterns as Hector lights them; then we flip them over, letting the material expand as the heat fills the insides. All around us, people do the same until the black Pacific doesn't seem so dark anymore and the garden is glowing and bright.

"Let the countdown begin!" G's father shouts, and everyone chimes in.

Ten, nine, eight . . .

Clinging to the lantern, which is poised to fly away as soon as I let go, I look left at the crowd behind me, at Poppy, Lennon, and James, the faces from my past.

Seven, six, five . . .

I glance right at Hector, at my present, at everything that lies ahead; he slips his free hand into mine.

Four, three . . .

I look one last time at the lantern, at the words I have written to G, glimpsing only the final line: *I miss you. God, I miss you. And I will never forget you. C x*

Two, one.

I release my lantern into the sky.

"Talking about it helps," she says.
"You've already seen that, haven't you?"
And I suppose in a way I have.

If you have been affected by anything you have read in *The Year After You,* if you are struggling or are worried about someone in your life, or if something just doesn't feel right, there are organizations that offer free advice and support and will listen to you in confidence. Words have power. And if you can't find the words for someone you know, please consider contacting one of the organizations below.

If you or someone you know suffers from depression or mental illness:

National Alliance on Mental Illness (NAMI)
nami.org
1-800-950-6264

Mental Health America
mentalhealthamerica.net
1-800-273-8255 (TALK)

Teen Lifeline

teenlifeline.org

602-248-8336 (TEEN)

Statewide in Arizona 1-800-248-8336 (TEEN)

Teen Mental Health

teenmentalhealth.org

If you or someone you know is suicidal or in crisis:

National Suicide Prevention Lifeline

suicidepreventionlifeline.org

1-800-273-8255

Crisis Text Line

crisistextline.org

Text 741741

IMAlive

imalive.org

If you or someone you know needs grief counseling:

The Dougy Center, The National Center for Grieving Children & Families

dougy.org/grief-resources/help-for-teens/

ACKNOWLEDGMENTS

First, an enormous thank-you must go to my agent, Laura Williams—for your support from the beginning. Thank you, *really,* thank you. I cannot tell you how much it has meant.

A very big thank-you to the wonderful team at Ink Road for lots of things, but especially for first publishing this book in the UK. A special mention must go to Janne Moller, for sending this book out farther into the world. I will never forget the day I found out Delacorte wanted to publish this book in North America, which leads me to Audrey Ingerson. Audrey—I don't know how to thank you for all your hard work, enthusiasm, and joy for this book. I have adored working with you, and I couldn't be more excited that you and the fabulous team at Delacorte are publishing it in the United States and Canada.

Thank you to Araminta Whitley, Philippa Milnes-Smith, and all the other magnificent people I work with at The Soho Agency for your excitement when you found out I had written this book, and for your unending support. I feel very privileged to work with you all.

Thank you to Shelley Weiner and all the friends I made at the Faber Academy. It was a life-changing six months—made by all of you.

Thank you to Thalia Proctor at Little, Brown for reeducating me about English grammar. If you hadn't taken me under your wing, that pesky semicolon would probably still be a thing of myth.

Thank you to Kate Hamilton for kindly filling in all my gaps on how the International Baccalaureate works and to Becky Arkwright for answering my medical questions. You'll both see I have taken a fair bit of creative license with what you told me. Please forgive me.

A big thank-you to Emily Thornton and Rosie Money-Coutts, who read this book before it went anywhere; to Livy Orr-Ewing for living with me when I started writing it; and to Clem and Daisy Francklin for living with me at the end. You all have put up with a lot—I hope one day I'll be able to properly express how grateful I am.

It is no exaggeration to say that the friendships made at the school in this book change lives. So here I thank my own school friends for changing my life all those years ago. Thanks must also go to Clio Eckersley, who isn't technically a school friend, but who is living proof that sometimes life jackets are found a bit later on. This book was written during many evenings, weekends, and birthdays I should have spent with you all. Thank you for understanding, for your support, and for continuing to include me even when I let you down. You have taught me, and continue to teach me, the very best things about love. So much of all of you, and what you've done for me, is in this book.

And finally, thank you to my long-suffering family. To Rose and Jack, for looking after me, always. And to my parents— I wish I could find big-enough words.

ABOUT THE AUTHOR

Nina de Pass started writing *The Year After You,* her first novel, during a creative writing class at the Faber Academy. She has an MA in French and Spanish from the University of Edinburgh and now lives and works in London.

ninadepass.com